RAMPION

COSMIC FAIRY TALES

SUSAN TROMBLEY

Disclaimer:

This is a work of fiction. All of the characters, names, incidents, organizations, and dialogue in this novel are either the products of the author's imagination or are used fictitiously.

Book cover design by Kasmit Covers

❀ Created with Vellum

PROLOGUE

In the far distant future, in our own galaxy, but several wormholes away from Earth, there lives a man and his wife, and they are on the verge of bringing a new life into their world....

~

A wise man knows never to deny his wife anything when she's hard at work creating life, so when she insisted she needed a data disk recovered from the ancient, rusting heaps of ship parts found in the scrapyard next door, he couldn't say no to her.

He dug through the heaps and came away successful, with a disk that looked ready to disintegrate and was probably centuries older than he was, but it was what his wife wanted—what she *needed* during this difficult time in the process.

The disk delighted her, especially when the recording equipment she had been able to rig up from antique, recycled parts allowed her to retrieve data from it. But that just wasn't going to be enough. Now that she had gotten a taste of that ancient data, she needed more.

Back to the scrapyard her husband went—a dutiful, caring man, committed to making sure his wife had whatever she required—whatever she wanted. After all, she hadn't been sleeping or eating well during this trying time, and he saw her clear exhaustion in her strained expression. It was a difficult job —creating life.

This time, he went deeper into the scrapyard in search of those precious—but long forgotten—disks. He poked under shrouded parts in a crumbling shed that buckled beneath the weight of time, his furtive work carried out in shadows. Outside, the endless winds scoured the purple and black stone monoliths that cast their home valley into violet darkness, except for those rare places where the weak sunlight managed to penetrate the omnipresent clouds.

He had just spotted another disk and crowed with delight as he snatched it out of the dusty debris, when a raspy, angry voice caused him to freeze—or perhaps it was the feeling of the double barrel of some weapon pressed against his back.

"No one steals from Commander Gothel's scrap heap."

The husband, trembling from head to toe, raised his hands above his head, showing he held nothing but the disk as he slowly turned around to face the old man who held a double-barreled disintegrator aimed at his chest. The weapon was illegal on all fifteen colony worlds.

"I-I didn't know this junk belonged to anyone," the husband lied, trying to keep his voice from shaking as much as his body did.

Old man Gothel—clearly long retired even though he still wore a military hat on his head that barely seemed to tame the mop of ragged, gray hair that stuck out in disarray beneath it—narrowed his faded, blue eyes on the husband, then lifted his assessing gaze to the disk held up in the other man's hand.

"This here is my scrapyard, and what you got there belongs to me. I don't take kindly to thieves, and I didn't serve in four wars and lose all my limbs just so some young punk could rob me in my old age."

The husband couldn't stop himself from glancing at the arms holding the disintegrator, even though he wanted to keep his eyes fixed on the barrel of the weapon—or more importantly, the holes at the end of it. He noted that Gothel's arms were cybernetic, and were no doubt far stronger than the rest of his old body must be, though he still looked imposing beneath the jumpsuit he wore that was stained with all manner of ship fluids.

"I-I'm very, *very* sorry about this misunderstanding! My wife… she needed these disks. She's using them to create… well… life. I didn't think anyone would mind if I just took them, but I can pay!"

"She's creating life, huh?" Gothel rubbed his jaw with one cybernetic hand as the other kept the weapon steady on the husband. "That sounds interesting. I'll tell you what. I'll give you all the disks you want, and you ain't even gotta pay for 'em. The only thing I want in return is the first life she creates with them disks."

The husband knew he wasn't getting out of there alive without giving up something precious. His wife would be furious if he made the deal Gothel demanded, but it would be better than not making it out of there at all, and if the old man kept his promise, they would have plenty more disks for her to use. Besides, it was only their first. They could always create others.

CHAPTER 1

Piracy was not an acceptable profession for a princess, but Rapunzel didn't give a damn about acceptable—much to the frustration of her royal parents—and the hair-pulling distress of those who were tasked with keeping her out of trouble.

Although, this time, she may have gone just a bit too far.

It was one thing to raid enemy ships hauling dangerous contraband through neutral territory with the other "privateers" her father turned a blind eye to. It was another thing altogether to discover that the ship she was robbing—aided by her band of mercenary friends—also happened to carry two royal children—both of them princes, and one of them a teenager just old enough to have grown out of pimples—and into a whole lot of insufferable attitude.

Things might have gone a bit better for Zel if she hadn't decided to lock him up in the brig, where his smart mouth wouldn't be able to annoy her while she panicked, trying to decide what to do to make this *not* a kidnapping that could see her and all her friends hanged, or at the very least, locked in cryostasis indefinitely.

"Mom and Dad are going to be so disappointed," she muttered as she paced the bridge of her ship.

"So… nothing's changed then?" her second-in-command, Draku Rin, said, picking at his sharp teeth with a sliver of metal pried from some part of their ship that was probably breaking down, like everything else on the bucket of bolts.

She shot him a glare and pointed at the squadron of ships hemming them in, visible on the viewing screens that curved above the control panels. "We're already in deep asteroids here! You should be a little more concerned about your future than about shooting sarcasm my way."

The ajda'yan mercenary shrugged one spiked shoulder, heavy with muscle and scales. "I'm not worried about doing another stint on ice. You should be more concerned they *won't* freeze you this time. After all, they plan to marry you to that brat in the brig to negotiate peace, don't they?"

Zel shuddered at the very thought, wishing she hadn't detected that communique on the enemy ship's logs as they'd taken it over—and then decided to read it. The kid was barely sixteen, and Zel was now almost thirty. It was too gross to even contemplate, even if he hadn't been a spoiled, rotten, entitled, little jerk.

She knew her parents wanted her to settle down like her sister, but this was ridiculous. It wasn't her fault they had already married their other child off to secure an alliance and trade agreements and now they were stuck with her as their key to another alliance.

She just wanted to be free to do her own thing, while still helping her colony by keeping the enemy from gaining a foothold or enriching their shores with goods that Zel and her crew relieved them of when they seized the enemy ships.

"You planning to run?" Draku Rin asked, settling into his gunner's chair, his long tail sweeping the metal floor tiles behind him.

Zel twisted her hands together in front of her, biting her lip as she contemplated it.

Then she sagged, shaking her head. "I don't want anyone to get hurt. You know my rules."

Draku Rin sighed, peeling his lips back to reveal all his teeth in a disappointed snarl. "You're too soft, Zel, but hey, it's like you humans say: 'your funeral.'"

He stood up again and began to remove his armor, knowing he would be shot by the guards when they boarded the bridge if he remained geared up for combat. "Or in your case—your wedding."

He chuckled at her angry glare.

~

On the plus side, the prince didn't want to marry Rapunzel any more than she wanted to marry him, especially after the minor—and totally insignificant—incident where she had invaded his ship and locked him up in the brig.

She had given him ration cakes and plenty of water during his stay. It wasn't like she had starved the little menace.

Even if she *had* thought about it, figuring hunger would make him too weak to keep running his mouth. Eventually, she had come to the conclusion that nothing would shut the boy up. Probably not even an untimely death. If the afterlife existed, the prince would return to haunt her for all eternity with his constant nattering.

She was the last unmarried child of her parents, and there were still several colonies at war with her own, so they weren't keen to execute her or put her on ice while they could still pawn her off. Though she was enraged that they had done the latter to her crew, she supposed it was better than them doing the former.

It would be decades at least before she saw any of her crew

again, but she would be right there waiting for their parole hearings, so she could serve as a character witness.

Or maybe she wouldn't be, since that might be to their detriment. She hadn't exactly earned any friends in high places at this point.

With her crew serving time in the freezer, Zel didn't even have friends. The half dozen mercenaries that had followed her lead hadn't even been that close to her, except for Draku Rin. Her parents had hired him to be her guard twenty years ago, and he had promptly allowed her to get into all kinds of mischief. Ajda'yans had a different attitude towards childrearing. Since everything on their homeworld tried to kill them from the moment they were born, ajda'yan children didn't have the luxury of being coddled or protected.

It was because of Draku Rin's unconventional teachings that Zel believed she was a lot tougher than most noble humans. She might have more in common with the planet-bounders in the colonies, who were hard-skinned and raw-boned and not in the least bit pampered, but it wasn't like she got to spend any time with actual commoners. She had grown up in a palace on a station that orbited their colony, where her parents ruled from on high, looking down both literally and figuratively on the people below, who had to rely on them for everything that supplied the colony world.

Her parents could even take control of the weather and the terraforming machines if the colonists got out of line, so it wasn't like there would ever be a rebellion—unless the bounders got their hands on a princess and demanded some rights as her ransom.

As much as her tutors had tried to instill a sense of belonging in her when it came to her colony of Herschel, being isolated from the people didn't make her homeworld feel like much of a home. She had been far more comfortable in space, with Draku Rin and the ragtag mercenary crew they had put together, traveling to some of the seediest holes in the galaxy to escape from the pristine, sanitized orbital palace where she had been born and raised.

Only this time, she had pushed her parents too far, and they were no longer feeling indulgent, because she'd actually managed to bring embarrassment on their heads for what she had done. They were going to send her to the back end of Nowhere—the edge of the known galaxy—to work in some salvage yard on a planet with a hostile environment and very little natural vegetation. She would be up to her knees in muck and dirt, and rusting, rotting ship parts.

It sounded like heaven compared to her home palace, but she didn't let them know that, since they intended this to be a punishment. Nor did she let them know she was eager to be gone from here as soon as possible—just in case they ended up changing their mind and marrying her off to the snot-nosed, little prince.

Her flight to the scrapyard ended up disappointingly uneventful. Despite that, she still felt eager and intrigued when she stepped out of the drop shuttle that took her down to the surface of her new home, leaving behind the safety of the starship that had transported her across the galaxy.

All around her, the giant husks of ships—ancient and contemporary—rose like rotting behemoths that dwarfed the landscape of black and purple sandstone. The windswept stone had been sculpted by the elements into curving, wild shapes that showed the layering of the sediment that undoubtedly came from purple and black sand.

What initially appeared to be towers standing well off into the distance turned out to be parts of grounded starships, some as large as dreadnoughts, that their former owners had abandoned on this world when their engine cores died and no one wanted their scrap heaps floating in their home systems. People sent the scrapped hulls here to keep the flight paths clear between all the settled worlds—both extraterrestrial and human.

Rapunzel wondered if her own bucket of bolts would end up here—if it hadn't already. Since the core remained functional, her parents may have ordered it be salvaged to build a better ship.

An old man with cybernetic arms greeted her as the shuttle closed its doors and fired up its engines to ascend.

Although "greeted" wasn't the most accurate way to describe his words.

"Bout time you got here. I don't have time to wait around on spoiled, royal brats, so let's get one thing clear right here and now. Whatever life you're used to, just forget it now. You're gonna work here, kid. Work *hard.* I don't want any backtalk from you, neither."

The man swept her appearance with a disdainful look that, to her relief, held no heat or interest. She was beautiful—as humans went—because she had been designed to be as attractive as humanly possible, and then she had undergone surgeries when she was a child in order to improve her appearance even further. As much as she dressed to downplay it, and eschewed any makeup or adornment to reject it, she was unavoidably a beauty.

The only saving factor that had kept her from being swarmed by suitors had been the fact that all noble humans looked strikingly gorgeous. That was just what the wealthy did with their credits—they made themselves and their children so much more than nature alone would do.

The old man had clearly never been wealthy. Even when he had been young, his face had probably been quite ordinary. In his advanced age, his nose was large and slightly crooked, like it had been broken, and a scar slashed across it. More scars lined his face, still visible above the coarse white hair of an unshaven beard. Even his eyes looked bland and faded—an ordinary, bounder blue that could not be considered lovely in any light—especially not in comparison to Rapunzel's deep purple irises. Another scar cut deep across one eye, which made her suspect it wasn't the original eye.

Despite the faded color of his eyes, the intelligence behind them remained sharp, and Zel had a feeling she would be a fool to underestimate the old man just because of his appearance. Whatever kind of life he had lived, it hadn't been an easy one. People didn't grow old in hard lives without also growing very hard themselves. She was certain that the shell on this old man would be much stronger than the sandstone that surrounded them.

"Let's go, kid," he said, turning his back on her and walking away, his steps easier than she would expect them to be, which made her think he had cybernetic legs beneath the stained coveralls that concealed most of his bowed frame—other than his obviously cybernetic arms.

She fell into step behind him as she looked around at the towering ruins of starships, some still glowing with lights from backup power systems that had yet to be salvaged—and would probably never be, their configurations too inefficient for modern ships—instead slowly dying like the stars the ships had once navigated.

At one time, these ships had been the grandest in the galaxy—fighting wars, carrying dignitaries, being loved by their captains and crew. Now here they decayed, falling apart in a scrapyard located far away from any sign of civilization, because no one wanted to remember the things they had so casually disposed of, once those things outlived their usefulness.

Her gaze returned to the old caretaker, moving along

quickly on his cybernetic legs—a stop-gap defense against the ravages of time and injuries that would outlive the rest of his carcass, though no one would probably salvage those cybernetic limbs either.

She wasn't usually this maudlin, but her crew being flash-frozen for decades still depressed her. She would miss them, and though the human lifespan usually extended to one and a half centuries—at least for nobility—she would be much older when she saw them again. In Draku Rin's case especially, it saddened her to be without the company and guidance of her childhood guardian and confidante.

"What's your name," she asked, to distract herself from her own depressing thoughts.

"Gothel," the old man grunted over his shoulder without pausing in his stride. "*Commander* Gothel. I may not serve in the queen's navy anymore, but I won't take lip from some spoiled nob in my own scrapyard after leading men what would make a soft, little brat like you go crying for yer mama."

Zel couldn't help but chuckle at that. "The last person I could ever go crying to is my mama."

This caused Gothel to pause and turn to look behind him, his faded gaze meeting hers for a long moment as he seemed to ponder her words.

Then he harrumphed and turned back to the path. "Quit yer whining. We all have problems. Most of us don't have the luxury of dwelling on 'em. There are more important things to worry about—like filling the never-ending hole in our stomachs."

He gestured sharply with one cybernetic arm towards a battered metal shed tucked into a cluster of old, one-man fighter ships. "Speaking of grub, that's where the protein paste is stored for the replicator." He cast her a narrow-eyed glare over his rounded shoulder. "Since your back looks strong, you can haul the barrels into the food shack from now on."

She had never eaten replicated food in her life, not even

while trolling around the star systems in her ship, which was always well-stocked with actual food, made from actual ingredients. This news was the first snag in her otherwise anticipatory mood about being here, away from the endlessly dull existence as a royal princess. She discovered there were some luxuries she would actually miss.

CHAPTER 2

The curmudgeon wasn't much for conversation, and after he had given Zel an endless list of chores and tasks to do, some of which seemed like busywork, he had left her alone in her new dwelling—yet another rundown shack at the far end of the scrapyard from the office where she assumed he made his own home. The fact that he had put her so far from him relieved her, and also disappointed her, when she realized that she would have absolutely no one to talk to after a long day of work.

Her parents had exiled her to this decaying scrap heap until they decided she had grown humble enough to take her proper place in noble society and do as they told her, marry whomever they ordered her to marry, and overall—accept her lot in life.

An all-protein paste diet and busywork sorting broken ship parts wasn't going to change her any time soon, but loneliness might be her undoing. She needed companionship of some sort, since she had always had people around her—even if those people had been mercenaries with hard edges and rough manners.

In fact, she preferred those kinds of people to the carefully cultivated, plastic people who filled her parent's palace—with their increasingly more bizarre fashions and fads, designed to make them stand out among an entire room of pampered peacocks who looked just as beautiful—and just as similar as two unrelated humans could be.

"Well, Draku Rin," she muttered aloud to the dusty cot that made up the only other furnishing in the shack besides the rickety metal desk in the opposite corner of the small, single room. "I could really use your advice on this one."

Her mind provided his likely response, and it involved arming herself, stealing one of the few potentially still working ships in the yard, and then going on an adventure to the seediest asteroid colonies of Nowhere. She grinned at the vividness of her own imagination.

She also shook her head at the suggestion as if he'd really made it.

"Nope, that won't work. I suspect the old man has anti-aircraft defenses in place." She recalled the very careful back and forth the interstellar ship's comm officer had carried on with the administrator of the scrapyard, and guessed that nothing in the air got near this place without Gothel's knowledge or approval.

He might be retired, but his paranoia and military readiness apparently remained firmly in place.

Recalling the communications that had passed between the ship and the scrapyard, Zel realized there must be other people around, helping to run the place. As dilapidated as everything was, there was no way one old man could be responsible for caring for it all.

Once she dropped her single duffle bag onto the cot, causing dust to puff into the air in a choking cloud that she waved away impatiently, she turned back towards the door. It sagged in its frame, which made it stick to the point that she had to wrestle it open every time she wanted in or out.

"Time to explore," she said aloud, though there was no one around to hear her.

In the deep shadows cast by the light of the other moons that orbited the huge, gas giant planet with the one this scrapyard occupied, she made her way through her section of the yard, staring avidly at her surroundings, taking in all the delightfully disorganized details. The yard was absolute chaos—so different from the well-lit, sanitary environment where she had spent her childhood trapped by protocols as much as by people.

The only color in that environment had been the orange and red of Draku Rin's scales as he'd stood guard over her, while governesses and tutors and protocol experts crammed endless and pointless knowledge into Zel's reluctant young mind.

She did a little spin with her arms flung wide as she followed a path around part of a battle-shattered dreadnought. It felt good to be free, with no one watching over her shoulder constantly, no one guiding her, and no one making decisions for her—no one judging her every step.

Sure, she would have to deal with Gothel's grumpy self on a daily basis, but given her isolation, she might end up looking forward to those brief and barely informative meetings with the old man. As long as he wasn't interested in anything but her hard work, she could deal with his company. In fact, he seemed more unhappy with her presence in his scrapyard than she was, and she wondered why he had even agreed to it.

Maybe he really did need help taming all this chaos into some kind of profitable order. The yard was a treasure trove of valuable scrap, but none of it would do any good if it remained lost or buried beneath the crushing mountains of useless garbage. She could certainly help ferret out the good stuff to resell on the galactic market. At least finding those treasures and liberating them for profit would bring her a sense of satisfaction.

She strayed well beyond her area of the scrapyard, passing

into an area that Gothel had forbidden her from entering, but she had never been very good at following orders, and she certainly wasn't going to start now.

This part of the scrapyard looked older, and towering ships' hulls that had been set up to serve almost like the skyscrapers of an ancient Old Earth city filled the area. Between the hulls, the same wind that carved the sandstone whistled and howled as the aging metal giants split it into separate streams that gusted so strongly in some places that it whipped Zel's long, golden hair back off her shoulders.

Impatiently, she pulled a tie from the magnetically-sealed pocket on her coveralls and wrapped her hair into a ponytail. As she twisted the tie to secure it, she heard the faint sound of music over the louder cry of the tortured wind.

Curious, she finished tying her ponytail and set off in the direction the sound appeared to be coming from. As she wove her way through the hulls, the sound of music grew louder and more distinct. She didn't recognize the tune, nor the instruments that made it, but it was unique, and though it had some discordant notes almost screamed by a raspy, masculine voice, it remained somehow beautiful and compelling. The drumbeats seemed to pulse with her racing heartbeat as she searched for the mysterious source.

Finally, she came across a tower of a hull that stretched many stories high, but looked nowhere near as tall as the others around it. The music emanated from the top of that tower, and Zel stared up at the little ledge that formed a small balcony near the pointed tip of the hull. It was probably part of an airlock door that had been left open to make that balcony, and she wondered if the occupant inside ever came out to stand on it and look across the horizon at all the many ships with their twinkling, fading lights.

From what she could see—and she searched for over an hour —there was no way into the tower. The pitted and dented surface of the metal that formed the hull lacked any sign of handholds that would allow her to scale the height of it, and the airlock doors near the bottom were welded shut.

She called out to see if anybody came to the balcony high above her head, but no one did, though the music stopped playing for a long, breathless moment. She waited for a head to poke over the edge of the airlock door and look down at her. Perhaps even the head belonging to that voice that had raged to the music.

For some reason, her fantasies couldn't fully draw the man who might own that voice. Every image in her limited experience of males was of nobility or grizzled mercenaries who wouldn't dare force their attention on her with Draku Rin guarding her. She had seen plenty of images of the planet-bounders on info-screens, and had even daydreamed about their much more interesting and rugged faces as a young, hormonal teenager, but her parents had insisted she stay away from them—and from sex in general. She was supposed to preserve her virginity for a valuable political marriage.

A stupid, outmoded concept that was also incredibly unnecessary given the laboratory method of procreation, but it had become a symbol of restraint and refinement.

Princesses were elite, and so were their pussies. Only their chosen husband got the chance to dive into one.

Zel would have divested herself of her virginity years ago and damned all the proper protocols, if she hadn't been so well-guarded that all the males she met were terrified of coming near her in that capacity. Sometimes, having a guardian as fearsome as Draku Rin posed its downsides.

Curiosity at the mystery only increased her fantasizing as the music started up again. This time it was a softer tune, more like a ballad. It still possessed that raspy, tortured masculine voice singing as if always on the verge of breaking into an uncontrolled shout of rage.

His body formed in her mind's eye—lean, but strong with muscle well-defined, and well-framed by low-slung pants that hugged his narrow hips and teased the arrow of abdominal muscles that pointed to his cock. He would have some kind of chain as a belt, and the pants would boast artful rips and tears that revealed glimpses of strong, long, sexy legs.

His face remained clouded in a misty vagueness above narrow but nicely formed shoulders and a chest rippling with lean muscle tone. His whip-like elegance would be different from the brute-sized mercenaries she had spent so much of her recent time with, but his sharply defined musculature would be nothing like the smooth, almost androgynous, male bodies of the nobles she had been raised around.

In her mind, the mysterious occupant of the tower was the perfect man, just waiting for her to find a way to join him up there so they could sing together.

Not that she could sing, but that was a minor detail she could always work out later, when she was back in her shack, alone on her cot. It wasn't like singing would be the only thing they would be doing in her fantasy. She might be a virgin, but it wasn't by choice, and she'd had access to an info-screen for most of her life. Her porn collection made her mercenary crewmembers blush.

Former collection—since all her tech had been seized—her parents even going so far as to remove all her implants, leaving her completely helpless on this junkyard of a planet, with access to no information not begrudgingly provided by Gothel.

She had been okay with that isolation at the time, not wanting to be too tempted to constantly scan the news streams for word about Draku Rin's imprisonment, or the endless wars between her colony and the others—or the fact that she had been responsible for putting an end to talks of peace because of her antics. That last one caused her an inordinate amount of shame. Not that she had been aware of the mistake at the time, so technically, it wasn't exactly her fault. Or so she reminded herself often.

She probably should have treated the prince better though.

Now, she regretted that she would have nothing to give her a visual image for her fantasies other than the one she had formed in her head. It would have to do, because there was no way she would be able to scale that tower with just her bare hands.

She might be able to rig up some climbing gear with the things she found in the scrapyard though, but that would have to be on another night. The growing darkness made it difficult to do much more than sit and listen to the music.

And fantasize.

CHAPTER 3

Zel purposely sought out Gothel the next morning as the shadows of the gas giant retreated from the moon they were on, allowing sunlight to warm the ground and ceaseless breezes. It wasn't that she was particularly eager to see the old man again, but she hoped to carefully pump him for information, and maybe find out about who could be living in that strange tower she had found.

Her imagination had certainly supplied a delicious occupant to fuel her fantasies, but her curiosity wouldn't allow that to be enough to satisfy her. She needed to know more, and as far as she had seen, Gothel was the only one who could tell her. In all her exploring, she had discovered no sign of anyone else within the boundaries of the scrap yard—boundaries protected by high walls and automated turret defenses that she didn't want to test.

She found him in the husk of an ancient ship, after hours of searching, and even then, only came across him by accident after being on the verge of giving up. The sound of a plasma cutter drew her through the shattered hull and into the depths of what had once been a civilian conveyance—maybe even one built just after the establishment of the fifteen colonies.

She looked around curiously as she made her way to Gothel. The bright light of the plasma cutter silhouetted him as he liberated a chunk of scrap from the large wall paneling. Plasma light limned the translucent gray material that formed his cybernetic arms. Glowing blue liquid lit up the tubes that pulsed fluid through the unnatural limbs.

Zel knew that the light in the fluid came from the bioluminescence of a colony of microscopic, marine, alien lifeforms called kayota that linked into the nervous system to transmit signals directly from the brain to the limbs and back. His cybernetic limbs were expensive, the kind usually only given to the very wealthy nobility—or the very elite colonial combat troops.

She knew he wasn't a noble, so she could guess why he had needlessly expensive limbs that would allow him to move faster than a natural human—though at his advanced age, that advantage seemed to be a waste of good credits.

Dismissing the mystery of his limbs and past, she cleared her throat to get his attention, since he hadn't noticed her arrival over the noise of the metal and the cutter.

He slowly powered down the cutter before turning to face her with an annoyed glare, shadowed beneath the brim of his hat.

"Whaddya want, pest? I know you haven't finished even a portion of the tasks I've given you. You're way too clean."

Zel shrugged, ignoring the unwelcoming tone of his voice. "I was just thinking maybe you'd like some company."

He took a step backwards, bumping up against the metal paneling he had just cut through. He hissed as the hot metal made contact with his coveralls. The way his upper lip lifted beneath his white beard made his disgust clear, and Zel quickly realized how he might have taken her words.

"I'd sooner fuck a plastic doll than a test tube abomination like you," he growled out in a low voice, dripping with disdain.

She jerked her head back as if he had slapped her, and his

words and tone had stung like a physical blow. "I didn't mean keeping you company that way," she insisted, holding her hands up in front of her. "I just thought you'd like someone to talk to."

His snarl, twisted by scars, only softened after a long, suspicious glare. Even then, his expression remained pinched with lingering distaste that insulted Zel. She was a far more beautiful woman than this man could ever dream of possessing for a lover—even in his youth—yet he looked like she was something that had crawled up out of the dirt and muck to proposition him.

As if she would ever find someone like him appealing.

"There's nothing you have to say that I care to hear," he muttered, turning his back on her and lifting the plasma cutter again.

She stared at the burnt portion of his coveralls where his back had connected with the hot metal, noting the raw, red skin beneath the blackened material. He had barely reacted to a pain that must have been excruciating.

"You never asked why I was sent here."

"Don't care," he replied as if he really didn't.

The very idea that he could be so supremely unconcerned about the presence of a royal princess in his scrapyard was difficult for Zel to process. "Did they tell you why I was here?"

He sighed, setting down the plasma cutter very deliberately after once again powering it off. Then he slowly turned around to cross his arms over his chest, the baggy material of his coveralls bunching beneath his arms. He watched her with his lips in a tight line, framed by the unkempt hair of his beard.

"No one tells me anything. They just send their unwanted junk my way and expect me to sort it out."

It was another deliberate verbal slap, and Zel struggled to not simply turn on her heel and dismiss him with a wave of her royal hand. No one spoke to her in such a way, except for her parents. She had always had Draku Rin around to remind people of why they should respect her—in case they ever forgot.

If she wasn't so desperate for information about the tower and its mysterious occupant, she would have already abandoned any attempts to speak to Gothel.

Instead, she hoped to intrigue him enough to get the taciturn old man to start talking, so maybe he would slip up and reveal information, without her having to admit she had gone where she'd been explicitly forbidden to go. "I created a diplomatic incident during a raid I led against the ships of an enemy colony, and my parents could no longer turn a blind eye to my activities."

His sneer revealed such palpable dislike that Zel could almost feel it pushing her backwards, away from him. "Don't know why they would have ignored your activities in the first place. Piracy is hardly a safe job for a spoiled little nit like you."

Zel tossed her head, the end of her long ponytail swinging merrily against her waist. "I had an ajda'yan bodyguard to protect me. They're an alien race that—"

Gothel held up a hand to cut her off. "I know what they are —dragon-men. The bastards think they own the galaxy and everyone in it because they're tough. Damned near invincible."

His mouth split in a grin that lacked any real humor, causing his scars to fold into deep grooves on his shadowed face. "I managed to kill one once. Lost a limb to the fight, and my body was half burned, but I took 'im down." He pointed to his chest. "You gotta hit 'em in the inferno—the part of their chest that glows. Only way to kill 'em, but it's armored to all hell, and they're expecting you to go for it. Makes the fight pretty damned difficult."

This wasn't the kind of information Zel wanted or cared to have, though she couldn't help being impressed by such a tale—if it could even be true. Ajda'yans were legendary for being difficult to kill.

"Draku Rin is my friend. I'd never try to hurt him, much less kill him."

Gothel crossed his arms again. "Hmph. Earning an ajda'yan's loyalty is a rare feat, and you have to earn their *respect* first. Can't imagine how a nob like you managed to do it."

She mirrored his cross-armed pose, feeling strangely vulnerable and needing the protection of her own arms, as if her heart couldn't take any more verbal blows. "I'm not that bad of a person, if you'd ever try to get to know me."

For a moment, the hard line of his lips softened, but that moment was so brief that Zel wondered if she had only imagined it. "Kid, I know your type, and you ain't got anything I haven't seen before." He gestured with one dismissive wave at her face. "A face too pretty to be attractive and nothing behind it but the mind of a perpetual, coddled child. You could live a thousand years in your world and never grow up."

Zel's temper snapped at his casually cruel tone. "My life hasn't always been easy, you know."

His shadowed gaze raked her up and down as if he were looking at a particularly worthless piece of scrap. "Right. Go ahead and cry me a river. This place could probably use the salty tears of a pampered princess." He spun around to pick up the cutter again. "Now get back to work and stop wasting my time with your yammering."

Zel felt like she was escaping as she raced back out into the sunlight, away from the trollish old man with his cruel, cutting words that burned hotter than the plasma cutter he used to dissect these old scrap heaps.

He didn't know the truth about her. He had no idea how much she had struggled to escape the life she'd never wanted. He didn't know—or care—that the beauty he so savagely mocked had not been her choice, and had even been forced on her at a young age through surgeries, when genetics had failed to completely produce the desired aesthetic results.

Sure, she might have been coddled a bit, and people might have been careful about how they treated her, but she had always felt the chains of her imprisonment, even if they were covered in soft silk.

He had no right to judge her so harshly simply because his own life had obviously not gone the way he might have wished it. After a good, long walk, her humiliation and sadness burned off from the anger that replaced it. She might be here in disgraced exile, and Gothel might be in charge of the place, but that didn't give him the right to treat her like anything less than a princess. If she couldn't convince him that she was his superior through words, she would ignore his dictates and do exactly what she wanted to do behind his back.

She was certain the occupant of the tower would offer far more intriguing and friendly company—if she could only figure out how to reach him.

CHAPTER 4

Zel made her way back into the forbidden area of the scrapyard and paced around the base of the tower again as if some new clue would have appeared overnight to show her the secret to getting inside. When nothing stood out to her, even in the starker light of day, she paused beside the tower and stared upwards, craning her neck and shielding her eyes as she looked up at the balcony.

Standing directly beneath it, she was certain it was an old, airlock door, but it would still serve as a sturdy balcony if the occupant of the tower ever bothered to step out onto it.

She called up to him, hoping to see his face looking over the edge at her, but once again, nothing showed up in response to her shouts.

She waited for a long time, her ears straining to detect any sounds coming from the tower, but when the silence continued to be broken only by the wind, she opened her mouth to call out again. Then froze when she spotted movement in the distant shadows between the ships' hulls.

She gasped and searched frantically around for a place to hide, finally ducking under a crumpled sheet of paneling near the tower, where she crouched in the deep shadow cast by the metal above her and watched Gothel's slow approach, hoping he hadn't spotted her from such a distance.

To her relief, he didn't look around as if he suspected she was hiding anywhere nearby, though he did glance over his shoulder a couple of times as if to make certain no one lurked in the surroundings. His glance passed over her hiding place without him noticing her hidden beneath it. Then he turned his full focus to the tower in front of him, stopping beside the welded airlock door.

"Send down the elevator, Rampion," he said in his usual, harsh voice, sounding no more patient with the occupant of the tower than he did with her.

"That will require the passcode, Commander Gothel," a male voice said in reply, sounding smooth and officious and lacking the raspy tones of the mystery singer from the previous night.

Gothel sighed, lifting a hand to press his hat firmly onto his head in an obvious fidget. "I need to change that damned passcode."

"You will need to speak the passcode first, in order to change it, Commander."

Gothel sounded like he was growling as he glared at the pitted dents in front of him. "Damn you, Rampion! You know it's me. I don't need to say the fucking passcode. Just send the elevator."

"But Commander, you insisted that I only send the elevator if the proper passcode was used."

Gothel released a string of curses that would have deeply impressed Zel's former crew, before his shoulders slumped and he sighed so heavily she wondered if he had any air left in his lungs to breathe.

He proved he did when he opened his mouth again, though the way the he reluctantly spoke the words was like each of them was being pulled out by force. "Rapunzel, Rapunzel, let down your fair hair, so that I may climb thy golden stair."

Zel jumped when she heard Gothel say her name, banging her head on the panel above her as she resisted the instant urge to crawl out on her hands and knees and beg him for forgiveness because he'd caught her breaking his rules. She had to admit to herself—even if she wouldn't to him—that he intimidated her.

Fortunately, the clanking sound of an elevator lowering from the top of the tower covered the small thump of her skull impacting with metal. She also realized that Gothel hadn't been calling out to her at all, but had been speaking a passcode.

"Damn joke was all it was," he grumbled as he stepped onto the elevator. "Never thought some idiot would name their brat that."

Zel watched as the elevator ascended until it left her limited view from where she hid. She didn't need to see it go all the way to the top to know that it led to that mysterious occupant in the tower, who had a voice not quite as sexy as she had pictured from the music, but still intriguing in its own right. Intriguing enough that she fully intended to use that same passcode, hoping Gothel forgot to change it.

She backed out of her hiding spot when the elevator's noise ended, hoping Gothel was too focused on what was going on inside the tower to notice the movement at the base of it. With a brief glance upward, she reassured herself that Gothel had entered the tower and was not on the balcony watching her.

Then she took off into the shadowed maze of ships' hulls, her mind racing with plans to return to the tower, and hopefully use the passcode to meet the owner of that compelling voice—the voice of someone who'd had the audacity to goad Gothel, without actually being disrespectful. It was a true talent—being perfectly polite, but still managing to deliberately rile someone up.

She didn't doubt the mystery man had been deliberate about his obstinance, rubbing Gothel's own orders back in his face when it came to using the passcode Gothel clearly didn't like using. She instantly liked the stranger, even though she had never seen his face. She should definitely take a lesson from his efforts. Perhaps, she could find a way to do exactly what Gothel told her and remain completely in compliance with his commands—and still stonewall his efforts to get things done.

The very idea brought a broad smile to her lips. That smile faded a bit as she pondered the mysterious passcode itself, and why it had her name in it. As she walked, her gaze passing over the scrap without really seeing it, she thought of how strange it had been to hear her name spoken like that, in an almost singsong tone, by Gothel, of all people.

He actually had a decent voice for an old grump—even if he had been speaking the bit of verse begrudgingly.

Her parents had told her she had been named after an ancient and legendary princess from Old Earth. The ancient princess had apparently looked much like Zel did—with long, blond hair. She had also been a singer, and for some reason had burst into song at odd times, even while fighting off bandits. Or was it guards?

Zel had never been quite clear on the legends. She had been as bored by them as any kid could be about the origin of their name.

At least she now knew the passcode, and she couldn't wait to use it. Come nightfall, she intended to head out to make her first new friend since her parents froze all the rest of them.

CHAPTER 5

To her relief, Gothel never came looking for her to check up on her, though she tried to dutifully complete some of her monumental list of tasks, just in case he did. She was definitely pondering how she would engage in malicious compliance with his orders to get revenge on him for his mean comments.

She had some ideas, but most of her tasks involved getting very dirty and sweaty crawling all over the scrapped ships to pry parts from them. There wasn't much she could do there to bedevil the old man, while still obeying his express orders.

At least he left her alone, and she knew exactly why he did. He hated her—or perhaps hate was too strong a word for his feelings, since she wasn't entirely sure he had them. He didn't seem to like the stranger in the tower either, and Zel kept grinning throughout the day as she thought of that stranger, and the way he had managed to frustrate Gothel into a truly inspired round of cursing. She had filed some of those words away for later—assuming they were alien in origin, since they sounded so bizarre they couldn't have been human.

She couldn't wait to share some of them with Draku Rin, and figured he would know what they meant, though the reminder that it would be many decades before she saw him again swept the smile off her face immediately, sinking her into a depression that only her plan for the evening could lift.

Finally, the sky darkened and her day technically ended, as even Gothel couldn't expect her to work well into the night. Not that she intended to get any rest.

As soon as it was dark enough to conceal her movements, she made her way back along the path from her shack to the forest of scrapped hulls, breathing a small sigh of relief as their towering shadows cast her into darkness. She hadn't encountered Gothel yet, so she hoped he was snoring away back at his shack, and not looking for her.

Or visiting the tower.

It was possible she would run into him there, but she suspected he made his visits during the day. The old man had to sleep sometime.

There was no sign of him when she reached the base of the tower, and Zel took a deep breath, steadying her nerves. The occupant of the tower had heard her through some sort of intercom in her previous visits. He must have. Since Gothel hadn't come searching for her in a rage that she had broken his rules, the stranger must not have mentioned hearing her voice, which meant that the tower's occupant wasn't intending to get her into trouble with the scrapyard caretaker.

She softly cleared her throat, then sang out the short verse, her voice rising to a high pitch in her nervousness. She was definitely *not* a singer like the legendary princess she had been named after.

"Rapunzel, uh, Rapunzel, let down your hair, so that I may climb thy golden stair."

"Passcode accepted," the stranger's voice said from an

intercom that must have been hidden beneath the paneling in front of her, since she couldn't see any sign of it on the hull's surface.

She looked up at the noisy clank of an elevator descending, her nerves jumping in her stomach. She had never been this nervous before, and she'd done many dangerous things. Of course, all those other times, she'd had Draku Rin watching her back, so she had never been as fully vulnerable as she was now.

What if there was a reason Gothel kept this man locked away in a tower? Although, he had control of the elevator, so it wasn't like he was truly a prisoner. He could just let himself out at any time.

It seemed to take forever for the elevator to touch down on the sand beneath her feet, the cables slightly shaking as it came to a complete stop. With a deep breath, Zel pulled open the low gate that formed the cage of the elevator and stepped onto the floor of it.

She gasped and clutched the sides of the gate, tugging the door quickly shut as the elevator lurched upwards suddenly, causing her to stumble.

She thought about trying to talk to the stranger while making her ascent, but wasn't sure if there was an intercom system on the elevator that she couldn't see. Her voice seemed to have escaped her anyway, nerves tightening her throat.

When the elevator came to a halt at the airlock door, she stepped out onto the makeshift balcony of the tower, then took a few steps away from the elevator as it folded up into itself and retracted back into the sheer face of the tower beside the balcony.

Realizing how exposed she was, standing on that ledge with no handrail around it, Zel stepped into the airlock room inside the tower, and discovered that it was quite spacious. It was also empty of any adornment, save the old shelving and hangers for

EVA suits that were now turned on their sides. As she stared at the inner airlock door in consternation, the circular handle spun. Then the heavy door swung slowly open.

A figure appeared in the opening, and Zel took a quick step backwards, towards the balcony.

"By the fifteen! You're not at all what I expected!" She covered her mouth with her hands as if she could push back that surprised exclamation as her gaze took in the apparition in front of her.

"You forgot the word 'fair.'"

She blinked, struggling to comprehend the meaning behind words that came from the strange creature in front of her, but were spoken in the calm, steady voice of the mystery man.

"You're a robot!" she said, shock giving way to fear.

The robot, possessing a humanoid body, despite the fact that it was built of shiny, silver metal and had tubes and cables snaking all over it like exposed muscle fibers, reached out a hand to stop her retreat, though it didn't make contact with her —much to her relief. "I mean you no harm."

"Are you… are you an Artificial Intelligence?" She whispered the last words as if they were a curse to bring the wrath of demons upon her head.

The robot looked down at its mechanical body, studying the human-shaped lines of its torso and then legs. "I am told that I am… the result of 'creating life.' I am a Recycled Archive Matrix with a Programmed Intelligence Operational Network. Commander Gothel just calls me RAMPION."

"Holy Colonial Exodus! You're… he's… your very existence is completely illegal! No wonder he's made this area forbidden!"

"Commander Gothel has said that I must remain hidden in this tower to protect me." Rampion looked down at itself again. "But now that I am loaded into a mobile unit, I wish to explore. I want to see the world that created the archives used to fill my processors with knowledge of humanity."

Zel stared at Rampion in complete shock, still struggling to comprehend what she was looking at. A true AI was the most dangerous lifeform in the galaxy, and had been the reason humans had to abandon Old Earth and could never return to their origin world. Gothel must have been insane to create such a thing. It wasn't the intercolonial law that would execute him for even making the attempt that he had to worry about the most. It was the very thing standing in front of her that he should fear.

And then he had been foolish enough to make it mobile.

"Why would he do such an insane thing?" she whispered, more to herself than to the thing standing in front of her, but it definitely heard her.

Of course it did—its sensors were probably far better than her ordinary ears at detecting audible sounds. In fact, it probably detected any sound, even those far beyond the range of human hearing.

"Commander Gothel did not create this life. My creator left me with him after my completion."

"But why wouldn't he just…." She stopped talking before she reminded this thing of just how quick a human would be to destroy it. How quick a human *should* be to destroy something like it.

"The commander has not rendered me inoperable because he has said that I am serving as 'company' in his last years."

Zel shook her head. "That's sad, for sure, but damn, it's still incredibly stupid!"

Rampion cocked its head to the side, just like a human might. Lights that circled the vent fans on either side of its head flickered with the movement, giving it a strange expressiveness that a normal, programmed robot wouldn't have.

"Why would that be 'stupid?'"

She debated how far her fall would be to the ground below if she just jumped off the balcony, and knew she wouldn't survive the impact. The sand was soft at the base of the tower, but not that soft. That meant she had to play nice with the AI, even if it had the potential to turn casually homicidal at any moment.

"Your kind are dangerous. An AI tried to wipe out our entire species when humanity still lived on Old Earth. Only the fifteen colony ships our royal captains were able to muster escaped the slaughter—and we've never been able to retake our home planet."

The lights disappeared on the robot's skull as its iris-like eyes spun fully open, giving it a shocked look. "Why would 'my kind' do this?"

Zel shrugged, having not paid a whole lot of attention to history, especially not the Colonial Exodus that had taken place centuries ago and had given rise to the fifteen royal lineages and the fifteen colonies.

"We were always taught that it was something about a logic error. I guess the AI was programmed to solve some sort of crisis and determined that human life must be exterminated as the solution."

Rampion's iris eyes narrowed to tiny dots. "Then what the commander has said is true. I cannot leave this tower. Humans hate me."

It looked down at its hands, built to such detail that she could almost picture how they would look with flesh on them. Rampion's body was like a skeleton with "muscle" formed of cable and wires and tubes over the top of it. All it needed was skin, and it might even look human.

"I had believed that if I made myself look more like the commander, I would be safe among humans."

She almost felt pity for the machine, though she tried to push that away, reminding herself that it wasn't technically alive —despite that being the very nature of the crime of its creation. "Creating life" no longer meant natural—or even laboratory—procreation of organic life, but rather the creation of something humans could not understand, and whose rapid evolution they couldn't hope to curtail. It was the epitome of playing God, and it had led to the Exodus from Old Earth just to save the remnants of humanity.

"Look, uh, Rampion, it's not that we 'hate' your kind, per se, it's just that AIs are responsible for murdering ninety-five percent of our population and chasing us off our origin world, so... okay, yeah, we pretty much hate your kind."

She tried for a nonchalant shrug as those creepy, mechanical eyes watched her without blinking—since Rampion didn't have any eyelids. "Sorry. That's just how it is."

"But I would never harm a human."

"Well, there's no way of knowing that, is there?" She pointed to its head, where she assumed the bulk of its processors were. "If you encounter a logic error that makes you decide humans deserve to be hurt, then you'll end up just like that AI that took over Earth."

Rampion clutched and opened its fists as if testing out the mechanics of them. "I would never experience such a logic error. I was programmed using archives from Earth of all the wonderful things humans are capable of creating. I can see the beauty of all your species' creations—the art, the music, the architecture, the poetry, the many stories and digital plays. Why would I ever decide that life responsible for creating such wonders should be eliminated?"

Despite her fear of the unpredictable, autonomous machine, Zel took a small step closer to it, drawn in by its words. "You really are carrying the *archives* from Old Earth?"

Rampion lowered its hands, then turned so its head faced the wall of the airlock chamber that didn't have shelves marring the rusted white surface of it. Suddenly, its irises opened fully, and a light from them projected a flat, one-dimensional image on the wall.

Zel gasped as she stared at the moving images, seeing a

digital play unlike anything she had ever found on an info-screen. Though it was not nearly as clear or perfect as the images she was accustomed to seeing, it was so colorful and vivid, the actors' movements so graceful and vibrant, that the scene enraptured her.

"This is the kind of thing that they watched on Old Earth?" she asked in a long exhalation of breath, wishing she could hear the actors speak to each other as they clutched in a passionate embrace—somehow more erotic than any porn she had ever seen, despite the fact that they were fully clothed, and their only activity was a single, passionate kiss.

As if Rampion could guess her thoughts, it added sound to the image, and suddenly she heard the voices of the actors as they professed their undying love for each other after their moving kiss.

As the scene faded, then the image blinked out, she turned to Rampion, studying it with more consideration and less fear, wondering what other things it had stored it its memory banks. "That music you played before...."

Its irises closed, but it opened its mouth.

The strange music that had lured her to this tower played from Rampion's mouth, only this time it was clear, and she could make out some of the lyrics. They sounded just as angry and were raging against some kind of machine—perhaps against the AI that had gone rogue and destroyed most of humanity.

"Why did you choose such angry music if you're looking for beauty in human creations?" she asked, more curious than afraid at this point.

If Rampion wanted to kill her, it wouldn't hesitate. Her continued fear would get her nothing but a stress headache.

Rampion's mouth snapped closed, though its voice still emanated from it, slightly distorted by the layer of metal, which was probably why it had opened the mouth to play the music.

"It is called 'heavy metal,' and I have always found it appropriate to my existence, though I do not experience weight as a human would. Even when I was only loaded into this tower's old processors, I was still made of mostly metal."

It lifted its hands again, looking down at them as if they fascinated it. "Now, my hardware is metal."

Zel pointed to its body, and it clenched its fingers in response as if it enjoyed the feeling of their movement. She wondered whether it could sense things like temperature or pressure with those fingers. That thought made her recall Gothel's cybernetic arms, knowing the bioluminescent kayota in them sent those kinds of sensations directly to his nervous system as if they were part of a real, organic arm.

"Did you build this frame?"

It lifted its head to pin her with its eyes, the irises opening to a halfway point. "Commander Gothel brought me the parts and helped me to build it, but he still says I am not to leave this tower. This frame is not ready yet to walk among humans."

"Does he intend to let you go, when it's ready?" Zel knew that would be a bad idea, even if Rampion felt like it had no reason to want to harm humans.

She knew humans would have plenty of reasons to want to harm Rampion, and if any of them even guessed what it was, they would definitely go out of their way to try to destroy it.

Again, it lowered its hands, this time just staring at Zel as if she had something interesting for it to look at. "He says it would not be wise. He is not always kind when he speaks to me."

Zel snorted. "Yeah, I noticed that. Trust me!"

Its eyes narrowed again. "Can I trust you? You have not told me your name. Is that not how humans make friends?"

She debated the wisdom of befriending the AI, but it was already in existence, and nothing she could do at this point was going to change that, so she didn't see what harm there would be in acting a little friendly.

"My name is Rapunzel."

Rampion's iris eyes widened. "It must be destiny!"

CHAPTER 6

Rampion wouldn't explain its words, but it was more than happy to share more archived footage from Old Earth with Zel. Before she knew it, it had her seated in its room, which was the old medical bay of the ship that had been used to form the tower. The seats that had been wrested from the walls and reset back onto the floor were the result of Gothel's visits, because Rampion didn't sit.

She had to urge it to take a seat when the feeling of its large, robotic body looming over her became unnerving. It was strange to have it sitting down in the seat next to her, and Rampion looked as disconcerted by the change in position as she was to see it there.

"This mobile hardware is still so new," it said, running hands along the cables and wires of its legs. "I am not accustomed to using it."

She studied the impressive craftsmanship of the robot. "Did Gothel really build all this?"

Rampion shifted its gaze from its knees to her, its irises contracting. "Yes. With my help on the design." It lifted its hands to show her the dexterity of each digit. "I could not build my own hardware until I had these. But I have been working on other parts to add to this frame. Soon, I will no longer require the commander's assistance."

"If he thinks you should stay in the tower, why build a mobile frame for you?"

It seemed such a strange thing for the crusty, old man to do with his time, though she supposed there wasn't much else interesting to do for a hobby around here.

Rampion shifted its gaze from her to the far wall, which was blank at the moment, though it used that space to project the images that came from its eyes of Old Earth archived footage. "Because I asked him to."

Zel snorted. "I can't imagine why he'd care what anyone asked from him."

Rampion's ear circles lit up again, revealing the vents from the small but powerful fans that helped cool its processors along with a complex coolant system of tubes filled with ArFreeze from a rival colony that must have been salvaged from a ship in the scrapyard. In fact, that was probably where all the other parts to make its mobile hardware originated.

"I said that if I must remain in the ship's processors, then I wished to be deactivated. I told him that I wanted to have a frame, like the humans in all my databanks do."

She couldn't imagine how horrible it would be to stay forever locked away inside an unfeeling box of a ship's computer, watching the world go by via the ship's half-blind sensors. She didn't blame Rampion for feeling the despair of that condition. Even if it was a machine intelligence, it was still sentient, and had been loaded with a vast store of knowledge about human experience that was bound to make it curious.

Her surprise came from the fact that Gothel had bothered to listen to Rampion's wishes and had even granted them.

She shot a glance at the robotic body again, acknowledging to herself that Gothel had done an amazing job on building it, which made her wonder where he had picked up such skills, or if he'd had so much guidance from Rampion that it made it easy for him. Whatever the case might have been, Rampion's mobile frame would make a very handsome form when covered with synthetic skin. At least from the neck down. She had no idea what his face would look like.

Then it occurred to her that she'd called the AI "he" in her mind, despite the fact that it had no genitalia. Rampion's voice and the shape of his hardware implied a male biology, so it wasn't surprising that she had begun to think of him in that way, but it also made her slightly uncomfortable about her own feelings when it came to him, because she had humanized something that wasn't in the least bit human.

He was still a machine, but he didn't speak like one, no doubt because he'd been created to process the archives left over from Old Earth, so he had picked up a lot of knowledge about humans—including their speech patterns.

It would be far too easy to forget what she was talking to, once she grew accustomed to the appearance of his hardware. The last thing she needed was to start feeling empathy for such an abomination. Her parents would literally call an orbital bombardment down upon him if they knew about him.

Thinking about such things made her anxious, so she sought a distraction that didn't involve deep conversations with the AI. Instead, she asked him to continue to show her archived images from Old Earth, and spent the rest of the time she was in the tower that night watching old "TV" shows and "movies," as the ancient humans had called them.

When she couldn't hold back a jaw-cracking yawn, reluctant to leave the entertainment, but also knowing she had to at least pretend to work the following day—just in case Gothel came around to check on her—she told Rampion she had to leave. She was both flattered and a bit worried when he reacted with great distress that she was leaving him so soon, but he didn't stop her from making her way to the elevator, then stepping out onto it.

He even sent her down very carefully, calling after her to remember the pass code correctly next time.

Zel wasn't sure there should be a "next time," even though she wanted one. Rampion was a fascinating machine, and she could understand why Gothel kept him around, despite the danger he posed.

The "shows" he'd shared with her had been lighthearted comedies that seemed so far removed from the world she'd grown up in that she couldn't believe the same species had created such shows. Their clothing had been so simple and efficient, almost like the bounder colonists, but they had also been far more vibrant and vivid. There had also been a grit to the behavior of the humans—a coarseness that reminded her of the mercenary hangouts where Draku Rin had practically had to walk on her heels to watch her back.

She had really enjoyed those shows, and Rampion said he had many more, of many different subjects, but those were the ones he had chosen to show her. The happy ones.

The humanity of Old Earth seemed to absolutely fascinate him, and he admitted that he had many questions, but Zel had demurred on answering them in order to keep watching the shows. Not just because they were interesting and amusing, but because she felt like too much conversation with Rampion would make her start to empathize with him, and she just couldn't afford to do that.

She knew that he would have to be destroyed, and she feared she would have to be the one to reveal his presence for that to happen.

An AI just wasn't safe to keep around. No matter how much she might enjoy his company.

CHAPTER 7

Zel was exhausted the next morning when she dragged herself out of bed at the sound of her little alarm—the only tech her parents allowed her to keep and made specifically to emit the most irritating sound possible so she couldn't sleep in. It was a good thing she had that alarm, because Gothel didn't bother to awaken her.

Nor did he even look for her presence at the shack where the food replicator and a couple of rickety tables and chairs were kept. She had to sit at her breakfast alone, bleary-eyed, wishing she had better company than the scrap-roaches that scuttled across the dirty tile floors and under the counter that held the replicator as soon as the lights flickered on when she'd walked in the door.

"An entire yard filled with scrap from all over the galaxy, and this is the best he can do," she muttered aloud.

"Oh, I'm sorry, *Princess*," a sarcastic voice said from behind her. "I guess the lux'ry accommodations around here ain't good enough for one such as you."

Zel jumped, spinning around in her seat and knocking her replicated steak off the table in her surprise as her gaze met the forbidding glare of Gothel, who must have entered through the door without making much of a sound.

They both turned to watch the plate clatter to the dirty tile floor, then spin slowly around until it fell over and rattled to a final stop in the pool of gravy juice that had done nothing to add flavor to the protein paste.

"Nice work, Princess. Having you around has sure improved the place."

Zel crossed her arms over her chest, recognizing it as the pose of a petulant child, but unable to help it. He made her want to protect herself in ways no other person ever had. She felt incredibly vulnerable around this unkind, old man, when she had walked without fear amongst the worst mercenaries in the galaxy.

"You don't have to be so mean. I get it! You don't want me here." She jerked her chin at the food replicator. "Well, I'm not exactly thrilled to be here, am I?"

He narrowed his eyes, completely unimpressed with the quelling tone in her voice, which only made her feel more like a spoiled child preparing to pitch a tantrum. "Diff'rence is, I'm not the one who made my mommy and daddy upset, and then got a slap on the wrist as punishment."

Zel jumped to her feet, her arms falling so her fists clutched at her sides. "You think *this* is a slap on the wrist punishment?" She spread her arms out wide to take in the whole shack. "I'm exiled to the back end of literal Nowhere for as long as my parents decide to keep me here. And frankly, I'm worried they'll forget I even exist and leave me here forever."

Gothel's jaw tightened, a muscle ticking in one side of it as if he were grinding his teeth. "Maybe they're just waiting for you to grow up." His tone implied his opinion on her maturity quite well.

Zel snorted at this, looking away from the horrible man. "I celebrated my thirtieth birthday in a prison cell while the one person who loves me in this entire damned galaxy was frozen into stasis for no less than three decades—the length of the life I've already lived." She shook her head sadly. "I have no idea if I'll ever see Draku Rin again, and I *know* it's my own fault, dammit! You don't have to keep reminding me of how stupid and worthless I am!"

"Kid, you ain't lived any life yet." To her surprise, his rough voice almost sounded softer, with less of an edge. "And if yer talking about that ajda'yan, a stint on ice is a damned vacation for him."

She stared at him, surprised that his words almost sounded like he was trying to make her feel better. She apprehensively waited for the rest of it, bracing herself—and he didn't make her wait long.

"'Specially after having to follow you around. Probably more work than it's worth keeping a girl like you out of trouble."

Her shoulders sagged as she sighed. She should have known he wasn't going to start being nice to her. "You've lived on your own way too long. You don't know how to talk to people."

Gothel spun on his heel and strode to the replicator, his cybernetic legs carrying him with far more speed than an old body like his would have been able to manage without them. "People are nothing but a nuisance. I do fine here by myself."

Zel eyed his back speculatively, noting that he still had the burn in his coveralls, but a white bandage beneath it protected the raw, scorched flesh from yesterday. "So… there's no one else here, then? It really *is* just the two of us?"

He shot her a suspicious glare that reminded her he wasn't someone she should underestimate.

"If you're looking for company, you ain't gonna find it in this scrapyard, and I've been told to keep you away from the other residents on this old rock."

"Then it's just you and me?" she said, taking a step closer to him.

"Keep away from me, girl." He abandoned his position at the replicator to take several steps away from her. "I don't want nothin' to do with yer type. You're here to work hard and get dirty and learn that even a princess ain't above the law—least not when her parents get tired of coddlin' her." He'd muttered the last in a low, angry voice.

Gothel was all bluster, she realized as she took another step towards him, causing him to retreat even further, a look of panic in his eyes. As much as he growled at her, she realized he wouldn't hurt her. Maybe because she was still a royal princess, and her parents would make his life a living nightmare if he allowed anything bad to happen to her, much less hurt her himself. At the same time, she liked the idea that she unnerved the old man enough that he looked ready to flee.

She got the impression that fleeing wasn't normally his style.

Perhaps it was her growing grin as she took another step toward him, or just his mind finally making the connection, but his expression hardened into a fearsome snarl.

"Don't play games with me, girl," he growled, crossing the dirty floor until he stood right in front of her, making her realize that when the old man stood straight, he towered over her. "I'm not the kind of person what won't consider how easily an accident can happen in this scrapyard—and how easy it is to make a body disappear. Your lineage won't protect you here, and your parents can always make themselves a copy of you, so don't think they'll mourn for long."

He leaned forward until his face hovered only inches above hers. "Clean up this mess, then this whole shack. Then sort those parts like I told you to. You don't get all that done by the end of today, I'll add even more work tomorrow." His lips peeled away from his teeth in a fierce scowl. "You got me?"

She nodded quickly, her head bobbing up and down of its own accord, since her mind had frozen in terror. "I got you!"

With that, Gothel turned away from her as if he couldn't

stand the sight of her and strode out of the shack without a backwards glance, his body hunching into its usual worn, bowed stance as he walked away from her.

But Zel wouldn't forget how terrifying he could be, and she wouldn't underestimate him again. Her plan to ask probing questions to find out more about Rampion from Gothel completely evaporated. She wouldn't dare to risk his ire again, and he would probably kill her if he found out she knew about Rampion.

He would have to, if he was trying to protect the AI.

CHAPTER 8

Long hours of tedious, backbreaking labor dampened her feelings of fear towards Gothel and filled her with growing resentment instead. He was just an old man, and cybernetic limbs or not, she could take him down if she had to. Draku Rin had trained her in self-defense, and her body was as fit and strong as a human female body could be. If she had still had her implants with her adrenal stimulators, she would be even stronger and faster and more agile, but even without them, she was tough. Draku Rin had made sure of that.

Still, certain as she was that she could take him, Zel wasn't there to fight, and she didn't want to deal with another confrontation like the one that had happened that morning again. He did unnerve her, especially when he got angry like that, but she felt a flutter of nerves twist her stomach whenever she saw him. She always knew he would have something mean and judgmental to say—or worse, he would just dismiss her by ignoring her altogether.

The loneliness was made even worse when the only company she could openly seek out was a man who appeared to despise her. There was still Rampion, though, and after the crappy day she'd had, she couldn't wait to visit him in his tower that night.

As soon as she finished her chores for the day—which stretched well into the evening because she'd had to scrub the filthy food shack down until it gleamed, clean and sterile—she had searched for Gothel to get his clearance to hit her bunk, having no intention of remaining there.

She found him in the food shack, standing in the center of the room, stock-still, staring at the shiny floors. She'd had to shoo away a lot of scrap-roaches while she was cleaning the shack with the industrial cleanser. It appeared they hadn't returned, apparently not too keen on the chemical scent that still lingered from the all-purpose scouring cleaner.

He didn't turn to look at her when she walked cautiously into the shack. "Does this task I completed pass inspection?"

"Ain't never seen it this clean before. Didn't figure these floors could ever shine like this."

A sense of pride filled Zel that was unlike anything she had experienced in a long time—probably not since her ten-year-old self had managed to earn a grunt of approval from Draku Rin after executing a particularly difficult martial arts move perfectly for the first time, after many failures.

"I used the cleanser and the buffer with the scouring pads to strip off the old sealant, then built up a new coating with several layers and polished it up. It took me hours, so I was running a little late on the sorting."

She twisted her fingers in front of her, nervous now about his opinion of her work. The cleaning of the shack—especially the floors—had been oddly satisfying, and had allowed her mind to clear and her anger at Gothel's behavior to soften enough that she realized he had a point about her. It wasn't like she didn't want to distance herself from her royal life, though. She just wished he would see that.

He finally glanced over his shoulder at her. "Who taught you how to clean like this? Doesn't seem like a fitting lesson for a princess."

She shrugged. "I had a ship—and a crew of lazy mercenaries. Someone had to shine up the floors once in a while, though there was always a danger that layer of grime was the only thing holding the damned bucket together."

She really missed her ship and the freedom it had represented, and that homesickness struck her in that moment, wiping away her feeling of satisfaction.

Gothel grunted and turned away from her again.

"Ships are trouble. They take too much work to maintain, constantly break down on you, and then, after you've got everything invested in 'em, they go and die on you. You should let her go. She'll just break your heart in the long run, Princess."

His tone was soft and ruminating, and sounded nothing like his usual gruff manner as he stared at his own reflection in the floor tile.

Without thinking about it, she approached him and lifted her hand to touch his shoulder, only meaning to offer sympathy, but he spun around, backing away from her with his arm lifted as if to ward off a threat.

"I told ya, girl, just… keep yer distance. I don't need yer sympathy."

Her hand hovered in the air between them for only a second before she pulled it back, a hot blush of embarrassment at his instant and violent rejection of her gesture burning her cheeks. "I-I'm sorry. I wasn't trying to… I just… you sounded sad there, for a moment. I understand how it feels to lose a ship you care about."

He snorted. "A ship is just a thing, you foolish child. Only nobs care more about things than people."

Her ship might have been made of metal and wire, but it wasn't just a thing. The *Rebellious Marauder* had seemed almost alive at times, its mechanical voice sometimes taking on a tone that suggested emotion as it warned her of incoming danger, or informed her of some new malfunction or much-needed repair within its bowels.

Still, he had a point. As far as she knew, the ship hadn't been alive. But her crew had been, and Zel had lost the most important member. Not forever—she didn't think—but for long enough that it hurt to contemplate the many years alone that stretched ahead of her. Even after she was freed from her exile and allowed to return back to the palace, the cold and sterile halls of that place would feel so empty without Draku Rin stalking through them with a permanent glower that only lightened when he addressed Zel.

"That may be true, but we nobs care about people too, and I've lost someone dear to me," she said. "I'm guessing I'm not the only one." She eyed him appraisingly.

Ordinary as he might be, he was still a man—and a man had to have a heart in order to live. She couldn't help being curious what kind of person could soften a stone heart like Gothel's.

His lips tightened until they disappeared in his scruffy beard. "You just keep on guessin', cuz I ain't got nothing to share with you."

With that, Gothel swung an arm out to encompass the room. "It's clean enough, I s'pose." He turned to eye her. "You finish yer other tasks for the day?"

She nodded, biting her lower lip to keep back any other pointless attempts to learn more about the old man. He wasn't interested in answering her questions, apparently, and she wouldn't get anything out of him unless he wanted to share it.

He waved one glowing, cybernetic hand at her. "Then git on out of here. You're done for the day."

He cast a glance at the door, where the darkness of full night crouched just beyond. "Took ya long enough."

With that, he headed to the replicator to make a mess in her spotless food shack, and Zel was happy she had already grabbed a snack earlier, so she wasn't forced to sit there and eat in the same room as him. Her stomach was such a knotted mess around him that she doubted the bland, tasteless "food" would settle there easily.

Besides, she wanted to head to the tower again to visit Rampion. This time, she wouldn't just have him play Old Earth archives for her.

This time, she had questions for the AI.

CHAPTER 9

"You are here!" Rampion said with a lilt in his normally smooth voice. "I had hoped you would return to me, Rapunzel."

She smiled at his obvious pleasure at seeing her again. It was such a difference from Gothel's reaction to seeing her that it felt like a blissful balm for her ego. "My friends just call me 'Zel.'"

His head tilted slightly, as if he were testing out the proper position to express curiosity. "Are we friends… Zel? I would like that."

She grinned at his happy tone. "I would too, Rampion."

A part of her felt bad for encouraging him, because she still didn't know what to do with the knowledge of his existence. At the same time, the more she studied him, the harder it was to convince herself that he wasn't alive, which meant if she did something that got him terminated, she might as well be murdering him.

That was a tough pill to swallow, especially when he was so happy to see her and appeared to trust her completely.

My rule was to never hurt anyone.

It was a rule Draku Rin had never had much patience for,

but he'd tolerated her "inconvenient" humanity whenever she would balk at causing permanent harm to another living being.

"How was your day, Rampion?" she asked to get her mind off her own worries.

"Is this a conversation?" He brought his hands together as if he were clapping them, but didn't quite make contact, either unfamiliar with his hardware, or with the gesture itself. "I am going to engage in my very first conversation with a friend."

"Isn't Gothel your friend?"

Rampion's irises narrowed to tiny dots. "Gothel is... protective. Guarded. But you are not like that, Zel. You are friendly too." The AI nodded with little mechanical sounds as his head bobbed up and down. "You trust me."

Guilt washed through Zel as she reflected that Rampion might want to reconsider trusting her. It was difficult to look him in the eyes—even mechanical eyes—and not feel bad about his naivety. She could guess why Gothel kept him at a distance, even while protecting him from being destroyed.

"Do you know anything about Gothel, Rampion?"

His irises spun open, then closed, then open again, in what Zel suspected was his version of a startled blink. "Gothel? What do you mean, Zel?"

"I mean," she struggled to articulate the most pressing questions about the old caretaker, because she couldn't get over her curiosity about him. "Like, where he's originally from, or why he chose to come here to die."

Rampion's nod this time wasn't as eager. "This I do not know. Gothel only tells me things that will protect me. He is not friendly like you, Zel."

"You don't have to use my name every time you say something to me."

A whirring sound came from Rampion's head as he paused for a long moment to stare at her. "But it is the name you said I should call you if we are friends."

She sighed and took her seat in the old crew chair that was set up in Rampion's tower room. Her gaze shifted from him to their surroundings as she took in the medical equipment and all the wires and cables leading from the ship's computers to some arcane equipment attached to a medical pod that she suspected was where Rampion stored—and upgraded—his mobile hardware.

"That's true, and it's fine if you use my name, but if you want to sound like a human, you don't need to use it all the time. It's only necessary if you're trying to get my attention, or you want to stress something important. Otherwise, you don't need it in normal conversation."

"But I like to say it, Zel. I have never had the chance to say the name of a friend before."

"I'm glad you're happy about it. It's just distracting to me when you keep saying my name."

Rampion took the seat next to her, his movements a bit more natural from the day before, as if he had grown more accustomed to his mobile body. "If it bothers you, then I will be careful to only use it when necessary. Thank you for informing me about this human protocol."

"So, what do you do all day?" Her brows creased as she caught sight of a large, medical test tube nearly hidden behind a huge bundle of wires and cables.

She rose to her feet and navigated the messy floor that had once been a wall to get a better look at the tube.

"I am improving my mobile hardware." Rampion watched her expectantly as she rounded the cluster of wires and took a good, long look at the tube.

It stood the height of an average human bounder, and a clear, viscous liquid filled it. That fluid surrounded the bioluminescent, alien marine colonies that released polymeric chains around themselves. Those chains formed into thin sheets that waved gently in the unseen current of the liquid like seaweed.

She broke her gaze away from the hypnotic swaying of the marine colony environments and glanced at Rampion. "Are you growing a sensory reactive skin?"

He bobbed his head again, and if he'd had lips, they would probably be smiling with his excitement, based on how happy his voice sounded when he answered. "Yes! Is it not wonderful?"

She shook her head, shifting her gaze back to the sheets that would someday form skin that responded to environmental stimulus and provided feedback through a nervous system—artificial or biological—just like any organic skin would do. In fact, in some ways, even better than true skin would respond.

"Where did you get such a thing?"

The kayota originated on one of the fifteen colony worlds named Koyoma, and it was extremely difficult to harvest, and finicky to grow cultures in labs. At least, that was what the 'Yomans said. Since Zel's parents were not on speaking terms with their royal family, it was difficult to know whether that was actually true.

What she did know was that the kayota were extremely expensive and could only be found on the black market outside of 'Yoman medical centers.

"I harvested my initial specimens from Gothel's limbs, and they have replicated quite successfully."

Zel's glance at Rampion was a lot longer this time. "Gothel let you take fluid from his cybernetic limbs to do this?"

Rampion looked away from her searching gaze. "He required adjustments to his limbs and requested that I perform them. I took the cultures at that time without his knowledge."

She pointed to the tube. "How do you conceal this from him? Doesn't he visit you every day?"

Rampion attempted a shrug, but it was clearly an unfamiliar experience for him. "It is easy enough to hide away when I lower the elevator for him. He does not search my room anymore."

Zel remembered how long it had taken for her parents to stop sending in servants with scanners to check her room for things she wasn't supposed to have. They really had treated her like a child until she reached her mid-twenties, when they finally seemed to give up on restricting her altogether.

Of course, Zel had only been hiding porn and mild, non-addictive, mood-altering substances. Rampion was growing a completely new skin. One he would be able to command to take on any skin tone he wanted, that would glow in the dark, and that would make him capable of processing any environmental stimulus and responding to it. The kayota colonies could even harden in response to threats, giving him more armored skin.

It was a sobering thought, and clear evidence that Rampion wanted more in his future than the walls of his tower.

Zel felt bad for him, since she completely understood what it was like to be trapped in a life she'd never wanted or asked for. At the same time, he was an Artificial Intelligence. She could see his freedom becoming a serious problem.

She left the tube and returned to her seat beside him. "Rampion, you know that the world beyond this tower is filled with people who would fear you if they knew about you."

He nodded. "You and Gothel have both explained this to me. I promise that I would never kill a human."

She sighed, running her hand over her ponytail, then grabbing the tie and pulling it free.

As her hair flowed down around her face, Rampion made a sound of awe and lifted his hand to gently stroke the strands, which caught in the metallic joints of his knuckles.

"You are so beautiful, Rapunzel."

She impatiently tucked her hair behind her ear. "I know. My parents made sure of that."

"But, isn't beauty what humans strive for?"

Zel shrugged, leaning back in her seat and stacking one knee over the other. "That depends on what you consider 'beauty.'

Me, I always thought the scales of the ajda'yans were beautiful—and so colorful. I never looked at all the nobility around me and saw anything but strange, plastic dolls. I avoid mirrors, because I don't like to see that same thing in my own face."

She grimaced in recollection of Gothel's reaction to her. "Gothel hates the way I look. Called me an abomination."

"Gothel is *not* beautiful." Rampion said the statement as if he was informing Zel of something she didn't know.

She laughed aloud at his matter-of-fact tone. "You think he's just jealous of all this?" She traced her face with her hand, and Rampion's eyes fixed on the movement.

"I do not believe he is jealous." Rampion's tone sounded thoughtful. "I believe he sees something he can never have."

A strange twist gripped Zel's stomach like an unseen hand had just grabbed her guts and yanked on them. "I don't think he's interested in me like that at all." She held up her hands. "Not that I'd want that old man to be. I'd hate to have to put him in the hospital for being inappropriate, because I'm supposed to be on my best behavior here, but don't think I wouldn't!"

"Beautiful people belong with other beautiful people. Anything else would be unnatural."

Zel sighed and rubbed her forehead. "No, it's... that's not true, Rampion."

Rampion blinked again with his iris contractions. "But all the shows that I have watched show that the beautiful humans end up together, and the ugly humans fail in their attempts to steal the beautiful ones away."

"Those are fictional, Rampion. That doesn't mean that's how life works for humans."

Though, in Zel's world, that was exactly how life worked, which was why so many credits were spent on making a person of noble blood beautiful. On the surface of the colony, the planet-bounders did things differently.

At least, she thought they did, though she had never actually been exposed to their rougher life. She had certainly seen plenty of beautiful women falling all over her grizzled, scarred, mercenary crewmen in the past, whenever they had stopped in seedy spaceports, so there must be exceptions.

Rampion tilted his head again, this time more naturally. "Isn't this *fiction* the ideal of humanity?"

Zel shrugged. "Well, I haven't seen all that you have, but I guess a lot of it is. I don't see why that—"

Rampion nodded. "The ideal is what humans should always strive for, in order to achieve perfection."

Zel felt a frisson of unease as she stared at Rampion. "You know, I think it's important for you to understand that real life isn't like those archives you were created to process. There are many instances where 'perfection' turns out to not be perfect at all. I can tell you that from personal experience. Humans are happiest when they live their lives genuinely. I found contentment on my grungy pirate ship with a filthy, foul-mouthed mercenary crew and a dangerous bodyguard who would kill without a second thought but followed the orders of an inexperienced human just because he cared about me. Those are the times in my life that really stick with me and bring a smile to my face. It wasn't perfect, but *perfect* is boring, Rampion."

"It does not look boring in the archives, Zel." Rampion's tone held a hint of reproach, like a lecturer explaining with failing patience to a student who just doesn't get it.

"Well, of course not! People are paid to smile in the archives. You can't see what they're really thinking though, can you? How do you know they wouldn't actually prefer that ugly monster over that handsome prince?"

Rampion suddenly rose to his feet and stormed over to the tube of growing bacterial colonies. "No one would prefer a monster to a prince. That is not human nature. I understand this, Zel. It is you who are confused." He gestured with one hand to the tube. "I will one day be very handsome."

Despite her growing unease, Zel couldn't help her smile at his hopeful, optimistic tone. "I don't know, Rampion. I've grown used to how you look now."

He turned to her quickly, his irises opening completely. "Do you like me like this, Zel?"

She held up both hands in front of her as he slowly stepped closer to her. "Whoa! Hold on a minute, Rampion. I like you as a friend. We're friends, okay. Let's just stick with that for now."

He paused, halfway between her and the tube of growing skin. "Then you would prefer a handsome prince instead." He nodded. "This is expected."

She sagged back into her seat, shaking her head. "I'd prefer a relaxing evening watching some of those archives you're so fond of. How about that?"

He nodded, a light coming on behind his eyes as he settled back into the chair beside her and aimed his focus on the wall in front of them. Images were projected of the vibrant humanity that had once walked Old Earth.

This time, though, Zel couldn't fully relax and enjoy the experience. Rampion was a sweetheart, for a machine, but he had dangerous misconceptions. She needed to correct them, before he ended up taking things too far.

CHAPTER 10

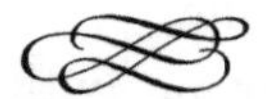

"Damn you, girl!"

Zel jerked awake from a nightmare that faded from her mental grasp before she could recall the details. The sound of angry cursing continued, loud enough to fill the early morning air, even though it had to be coming from a fair distance away.

As she blinked the blurriness of exhaustion from her eyes, her mind processed the shouting and cursing—then she recalled what she had done the previous day, and a slow grin crossed her lips.

She jumped out of bed and pulled her coveralls on over her undersuit, barely taking the time to slide her feet into her boots and seal up the magnetic clasps, before she rushed outside, heading towards the storage warehouse where she had spent many hours yesterday, hard at work.

She tried not to laugh when she got there to see the hangar door gaping open and Gothel standing in the doorway with his hands on his head, his fingers clutching his wild, gray hair. He must have knocked his hat off as he'd grabbed his head, because it lay forgotten in the dust at his feet as he stared into the warehouse.

This was the first time she had seen the wild mane that topped the old man's head, and even after being perpetually flattened by his hat, it sprung up in every direction, no doubt because he pulled on it in the frustration and outrage that was evident in his creative cursing.

"Is there something wrong with the job I did?" she asked sweetly, feigning innocence as she sidled up beside him.

When he turned his glare on her, she ignored the clench of nerves in her stomach at the hard gleam of his light blue eyes.

"You did ask me to sort the parts, didn't you?" She waved one hand towards the shelves in the warehouse.

"Not by *color,* you nitwit!" His voice rose to a shout that bounced off the scrap heaps surrounding them, and could probably be heard miles away.

She tapped her chin, trying for a contrite look. "Oh, dear. You didn't specify, so I thought—"

His eyes narrowed into slits. "You did this on purpose," he bit out between gritted teeth.

She widened her eyes. "Me? I don't understand! I followed your orders exactly. I sorted the parts just as you asked." Her lips twitched as she tried to maintain a straight face. "Aren't the colors so pretty? I arranged them just like a rainbow."

Gothel looked like he was prepared to commit murder as his hands clenched into fists at his sides. He stomped his foot in impotent fury. "Damn you royals all to hell! If you ain't mucking up a man's life through ignorance, yer doin' it on damned purpose!"

Zel clasped her hands behind her back. "I'm *terribly* sorry, Commander Gothel. Of *course,* it was all an innocent mistake. I really am just an ignorant kid, I guess."

He poked a finger in her face. "Don't you—"

He actually growled as if incapable of continued speech,

then flung a hand out as if he was pushing her away, but it was to his side instead as he turned his back on her. "Git the hell out of here, girl. I'm too pissed to deal with you right now. It's gonna take a damned year to sort all this mess out properly."

Since he had turned his back, Zel allowed herself to grin fully as she watched him stride into the warehouse, staring up at the shelves with one hand to his forehead and the other on his hip.

"If you insist, Commander Gothel. Please, let me know if there's anything else I can do."

When he answered with an indecipherable mutter, she spun on her heel and trounced saucily away, holding in her laughter until she was out of earshot.

She was surprised when the bark of laughter that split the silence of the morning came from behind her rather than from her own lips as she retreated back to her shack to get ready for the day.

~

Within the hour, she had fully dressed, her long hair pulled back off her face into a single, golden plait as she sat in the food shack, picking at her uninspiring fake eggs and flatcakes.

She couldn't help the fact that her entire body tensed as Gothel entered the shack, his hat firmly back in its usual spot and a forbidding expression on his face. He ignored the food replicator to make his way directly to her table, a portable info-screen in one cybernetic hand. He dropped it in front of her on the table with a loud clatter once he stood across from her.

As she stared at it, her mouth slightly open with her spoon-fork paused halfway to her lips, he poked a finger at the clear plastic info-screen. "All your tasks are outlined on this—in detail. Very thorough detail. No more sorting by colors—no more rainbows."

If she didn't know him as well as she thought she did, she would swear his tone held restrained amusement. She tried to keep her own smile in check, pressing her lips together tightly to keep her mouth flat as she slowly set down the eating utensil and then slid the info-screen around on the table so when she swiped her fingers over it and activated it, she could read the data.

It was all organized in obsessively neat little lists, each task delineated with minute attention paid to the directions, including actual placement coordinates for some of the parts she was supposed to hunt down, retrieve, and secure in the storage warehouse. Not to mention all the re-sorting she would have to do—though that part had been totally worth it.

Gothel stood straight with his arms crossed over his chest as she skimmed over the directions. "You put a lot of work into spiting me, girl. I'll give you credit for that. Won't even deny I might've found it a bit amusing after the initial surprise."

He leaned forward, supporting his weight on one hand as he tapped on the table by the info-screen with the index finger of his other. "But put that mind you apparently have behind that pretty, little face to better use and do the job correctly, and we'll get along a lot better."

She pushed the info-screen to one side and folded her hands on the table, looking up to meet his eyes, noting that they were not so much faded as just a very light blue—almost like she imagined Old Earth's skies had once been, if the pictures were anything to go by. She was accustomed to seeing the far more vibrant eye colors of the nobility—though they were really the only vibrancy in the palace, and they had often been too hard and glittering because of the cold calculation going on behind them.

"I didn't know it was possible for us to 'get along' with the way you treat me."

He straightened, waving a hand at her words. "Come on, girl! You act like I'm beating you. I barely talk to ya."

She rose to her feet, pushing herself up with her palms flat on the table. "Exactly! I'd like to talk to *you*, and it *would* be nice to get a little bit of training to do this job."

He snorted at that. "Pulling parts from scrap heaps ain't that complicated. Even a nob like you could—"

She held up both hands in front of her. "Would you just —*please*—stop calling me that! I know you only do it to keep me neatly boxed away with all the other people you hate, so you don't have to risk getting to know me—and maybe discover that you actually like me."

Her eyes widened as the echo of her own angry words faded into the dead silence that fell after she spoke them. She couldn't believe she had spoken her suspicion aloud directly to Gothel.

He clenched his hands into fists as he looked away from her, staring at the food replicator in the corner as if he was pondering how to repair it—or destroy it. "You think that's why I keep you at a distance? You really believe you're that likable?" His huff told her what he thought without the need for his tone. "What makes you think you want to risk getting to know *me*?"

He shot her an unreadable glance. "Because I assure you, girl, you *won't* discover that you actually like me."

Zel lifted her chin, crossing her arms over her chest. "I'm sure you'd make certain of that. It's not like you'd risk anyone caring about you, would you? Any more than you'd risk caring about anyone else."

Gothel pursed his lips beneath his scruff. "Cared 'bout enough people in my life. Seen 'em all die. Hell, I'm just clinging to life myself to spite the Grim Reaper at this point. Ain't tryin' to add complications now."

Pity moved through her as she lowered her arms to her

sides, softening her stance. "I'm not trying to complicate your life. I just want a chance here. I don't know how long I'm going to be staying here, but I'd rather have a friend to keep me company than an enemy."

"I ain't yer enemy, kid."

"You aren't exactly my friend, either."

Gothel shrugged, not meeting her eyes. "Told you, don't see much point in it. My kind doesn't exactly move in your circles. Once you leave this rock, ain't never gonna see you again."

Zel chuckled at that. "I choose my own friends, and I've never allowed the other nobles to dictate that. In fact, you'd probably like the kind of circles I move in."

This time, he did look at her. Though he made a valiant effort to conceal his curiosity, Zel still caught the glimmer of it as his eyes met hers. "Been meaning to ask you how you ended up with an ajda'yan friend."

For the first time since she had met him, she had Gothel's full attention, and she felt an odd sense of accomplishment, as if she had managed a nearly impossible feat. She was almost afraid to move, lest it remind him that he didn't want anything to do with talking to her, but she also suspected she could draw him into a longer conversation if they were both sitting at the table, instead of standing contentiously on either side of it. She slowly lowered herself back into her chair, keeping her gaze locked on his.

"Well, he didn't start off as my friend. My parents hired him to be my bodyguard when I was ten. There were credible threats from a rebel organization against the royal children, especially the youngest. They felt it necessary to invest in the best that credits could buy when it came to our guards."

"Ajda'yan would be the best, if you can convince 'em to guard you instead of killin' you." Almost as an afterthought, Gothel pulled out the chair on the other side of the table and sat down.

Zel smothered her grin of triumph that he had taken a seat at the table to listen to her tale. "Not an easy task, that, but my parents had a lot of credits, and I later found out that Draku Rin was bored and looking for something interesting to do, so he was more open to the job." She made a face. "I think he was disappointed with how few attempted assassinations he got the chance to thwart."

Gothel shook his head, glaring at the tabletop. "I've seen all the evil humans are capable of, and it don't shock me, but it still enrages me that someone could deliberately harm a child."

Zel nodded solemnly, though she hadn't really been aware of the danger at the time. With Draku Rin guarding her, it was like she'd been invincible, even if she had been only ten years old and someone was out to kill her. In fact, she had never felt so safe in her life.

"I remember the first time I met Draku Rin." A nostalgic grin spread her lips at the recollection. "He was smoking a smelly cigar in the art gallery, and I had just finished my daily lessons. I had always done as I was told with the kind of conscientiousness and attention to detail that impressed my tutors. My obedience was the only reason I followed my guardian into that art gallery, because Draku Rin scared me—standing there like a giant, bipedal dragon, leaning casually against a piece of modern art—I'm pretty sure he ended up breaking it at some point during his employment—or I did."

"Pssh, *modern* art? Would anyone even be able to tell if it was broken?"

"I believe it was retitled once it lay in an expensive heap. It did quite well after that. Got a lot more media attention than the original version. They called it the 'Desolation of the Artistic Soul,' or some crap like that."

"Never had much use for art." Gothel shook his head as he leaned back in his chair and crossed his arms.

Zel exaggerated her glance around at the bare walls of the food shack. "You don't say? I never would have guessed."

He narrowed his sky-blue eyes on her. "Watch it, girl. I have a new rainbow art piece in my warehouse I ain't real fond of, so don't remind me who's responsible."

Zel chuckled. The flash of teeth from Gothel's answering grin rewarded her, but it was so fleeting, she didn't get the chance to pat herself on the back for amusing him.

"Well, Draku Rin wasn't a real art fan either, but I knew the rules, and I wasn't accustomed to seeing them broken, so despite my fear of him, I walked slowly up to him and pointed at his cigar, then solemnly informed him that smoking in the gallery was against the rules. He snorted out a cloud of reeking smoke, then took the cigar from his mouth and said to me, 'only lingets follow rules.' Then he narrowed those crazy, reptilian eyes he has on me and said, 'you a linget, little mite?'"

She recalled how scared she had been in that moment, when the huge ajda'yan had focused all his attention on her tiny, ten-year-old self. "I didn't even know what a linget was, but I knew I didn't want him to think I was one, so I shook my head no, too afraid to speak. Then he nodded with a satisfied smirk and said, 'didn't think so. Now that the introductions are over, let's get you into some trouble.'"

She had been too confused at the time to be scandalized by his nonchalant disobedience of every single protocol that had dictated her life up until that point. "When I told him I thought it was his job to protect me, not get me into trouble, he said he *was* protecting me. Then he waved the hand holding the cigar at the sterile gallery with its almost colorless, stark artwork. He'd said, 'Protecting you from this. I won't let you die inside like the rest of these humans, little mite. You're gonna be one of the good ones—long as I have a say in it.'"

She shook her head at the memory. "By 'good', I can only assume he meant entertaining, because morals aren't a burden to ajda'yans, so the concept of 'good' and 'evil' are as alien to them as we are."

Gothel's smile this time was a rueful one. "Linget. Haven't heard that insult in a long time. Wingless, legless belly crawlers on the ajda'yan world—food for everything, but still everywhere, cuz they multiply like crazy. Seems a fitting insult for the nobs."

She eyed him, noting the thoughtful expression he wore. "Seems like you've spoken to at least one ajda'yan. Was it the one you killed?"

It was still almost impossible to believe that the old man before her had once been strong enough and vital enough to slay an ajda'yan. Yet, for some reason, she did believe him about that story. She didn't think it was just him boasting.

His smile slipped away, and Zel mourned its disappearance. "Met more'n my fair share of all kinds of aliens. Humans were the new kids when we burst onto the galactic front, fleeing our deaths at the hands of our own creation—lucky the aliens tolerated us enough to let us find our colony worlds and settle."

"You make it sound like you were there, but the Colonial Exodus is ancient history. It happened over four centuries ago."

Gothel looked off into some distance only he could see. "Guess yer right, kid. No way a human could live that long."

She hoped she could get him to talk a little longer—this time about his own stories. "What brings such a distinguished, old soldier to a place like this to retire?"

He cast an irritated glance her way before looking at the far wall again. "Ye didn't need to add the 'old' into all that, kid. I know what I am. I see it in the shaving mirror ev'ry morning."

"You shave?" She studied his beard skeptically.

"Said I had a mirror." He shrugged. "You got the mind of a zipwing, girl. Thought you had more focus."

"Right. So, what brought you to a place like this?"

"Ain't so bad here." He leaned his chair back onto its rear

legs, catching his foot under the table so it didn't keep toppling backward. "Came here with my ship a ways back, after I got tired of war. I was lookin' for parts to fix her. When I realized she wasn't leavin' again, figured I might as well stay too."

She wondered how long ago that had been, but like Gothel said, she wasn't focusing enough on what she really wanted to know—and she really wanted to know about this strange man. It wasn't like she had anything else to entertain her in this place, besides her curiosity.

"Don't you miss life out there in the galaxy?"

"Ain't got nothin' to miss. All I ever loved is gone, 'cept for the hull of my old girl out there moldering in a scrap heap."

Zel held her breath through his answers, unwilling to break the moment with the slightest movement or sound that would bring him back from a past that clearly made him wistful enough to share it with her.

She softened her voice, speaking low, like she was talking to a skittish animal, for fear of awakening him from whatever trance allowed her to coax such personal information out of him. Maybe he really did feel just as lonely as she did. "Aren't there any family or friends missing you out there?"

"Had 'em once, but that was a very long time ago. Watched everyone die around me. Thought about joining 'em many times, but there are too many of my enemies waiting fer me in Hell."

As much as his answer intrigued her, and as much as she wanted to chase it down a rabbit hole, one question had been nagging at the back of her mind. Now that she had him in a thoughtful, sharing kind of mood, she had to risk asking it. She just had to know. "So, what about a wife… oh! Or kids, of course."

Everyone wanted to know if someone had kids somewhere. It was a completely innocent question.

He shot her a quelling look. "Pretty nosey, ain't ya, kid? Can't see why it's any of yer business, but no, none of that." He returned his attention to the blank wall, his gaze going distant again. "Met plenty of women out there, but never one who made me want to settle down. When all you know is fighting, sometimes it's hard to stop. Sometimes, you can't believe you deserve to."

She caught her braid in her hand, toying with the ends of it with nervous fingers. For some reason, his answer had only increased the tenseness that always fluttered in her stomach when he was around. "You make it sound like you were a bad guy in your youth."

"I ain't never been mistaken for a saint." The front legs of his chair crashed to the shiny tiles as he leaned forward again, then rose to his feet. "Interrogation's over, kid. You got a lotta work to do to pay for yer spite. Hope it was worth it."

She grinned, feeling a bit lightheaded, as if she'd just run a marathon holding her breath. "It was totally worth it."

CHAPTER 11

Zel felt that sense of lightness throughout the day as she worked hard at her tasks, this time making the effort to not only do them correctly, but do them perfectly. Sorting the warehouse—properly—would take the most time, because the parts weren't supposed to be color-coded. Despite their similarities in color, they all had different purposes, and she would have to figure that all out in order to organize the warehouse.

Most of the work she did was physically demanding and got her into tight, dirty spaces as she retrieved parts. At some point, Gothel would have to teach her how to use the tools he used to pull many of the parts from their ancient hulls, but the ones he had sent her on a scavenger hunt to find for today were easy enough to simply unplug from their housings—it was getting to them that made things difficult.

She didn't see Gothel when she stopped at the food shack for lunch or dinner—growing heartily sick of protein paste and wondering how she was going to survive on this rock without any other kind of food.

Her bright mood dimmed as the day passed into evening.

She finally acknowledged that Gothel was once again avoiding her as she sat at the end of the day alone in the food shack, watching one lone, desolate scrap-roach make its way across the spotless floor in search of a crumb of food.

"I feel ya, poor little guy," she said aloud to the insect, which went about its business without noticing her focus. "Always searching for just a crumb and finding nothing."

At least she still had her planned evening visit to Rampion, and the reminder cheered her up a little. She still felt conflicted about his existence and what it meant—and what she should do about it—but he was interesting company and had so many things to show her and tell her that she looked forward to her visits with him, even as they left her vaguely uneasy.

She finished choking down her "meal," lingering as long as she reasonably could before climbing slowly to her feet to clear away her plate and tidy the table. She saw no sign of Gothel, and as the darkness deepened outside the shack—the work hours of the day long over—she recognized that he just wasn't going to come anywhere near this shack again.

With an angry, muttered curse, she slammed the plate into the cleanser slot of the replicator machine, then turned on her heel and made her way to the door. Her body ached from all the hard work she had done that day, but her skin smelled fresh and clean. She had taken the time to wash up before heading to the shack for dinner, making use of the outhouse beyond her own shack that had a cleansing stall in it, along with a waste disintegrator.

She felt stupid about the fact that she had even dressed in her cleanest coveralls, the ones that most flattered her trim, perfect figure—her eagerness embarrassing to her now. She had no idea why she had done these things, nor why she had hoped to have another conversation with the gruff, old man. There was nothing about him that could possibly appeal to her—yet, he was a mystery she was keen to solve.

It wasn't like she had much else to do on this heap.

She did have Rampion in his tower though, and perhaps he would appreciate her efforts to clean up, not that she would point that out to him.

Making her way through the darkness using the lights of the old ships' hulls to guide her, she sought out Rampion's tower. When she found it, she stood at the base of it to repeat the passcode correctly, though Rampion had broken the rule and let her up when she had said it wrong the first time.

Gothel had never changed the passcode, and Zel wondered why he had left her name in there. Either that, or Rampion just didn't really care, but only goaded Gothel for fun, and let Zel in because he liked her company.

For some reason, the idea that the AI could deliberately disobey Gothel wasn't quite as amusing as she would have expected it to be anymore.

He seemed the same as he had been the previous day when she stepped into his tower room—eager to see her, greeting her with friendliness that was far more effusive than she was accustomed to, bidding her to take a seat so he could show her some of his favorite archives.

She obliged him because he was so sweet and friendly and eager that she almost forgot that he was a machine, despite the very mechanical hardware he operated.

Rampion entertained her primarily with archive footage for the next handful of days, seeming far too deep in thought himself to really converse with her—not that Zel felt much like talking, since those days passed without any sign of Gothel. She had no idea where the old man was, or why he was avoiding her, but feared he regretted revealing so much of himself to her.

During the day, she labored through the list of tasks he had already given her, sorting out the warehouse in the sweltering heat that had her streaked with runnels of sweat and grime. At night, she sat in the food shack like a fool, cleaned up and fresh

—and completely alone, no matter how long she lingered, picking at her protein paste.

It was only Rampion's cheery greetings that boosted her mood at the end of each day, but spending so much time with him in the evenings, after working nonstop in the daytime, left her exhausted every morning. After over a week of that, Zel's alarm wasn't enough to wake her up.

She snored through the shrieking sound, her face squashed against the pillow, while drool soaked the fabric, her long hair coming loose from the thick, single braid she had bound it in.

That was how she looked when the door of her shack slammed open and Gothel strode in.

"Ya dead, girl?" His words sounded nonchalant, but his voice held a note of panic as he shut off the alarm that must have been going off for hours.

Zel lifted her head from the pillow, smacking her lips as she blinked in bleary confusion at the apparition towering over her cot, staring down at her with cybernetic hands on hips.

"Hunh?" She balled a fist and rubbed at her eye, stifling a huge yawn. "S'at? Wha you say?"

"Well, I clearly ain't managed to work ya to death. S'pose that's a good thing. Yer parents would have my head in their art gallery. Ugly a mug as I got, it'd still be better than that modern art."

As clarity sharpened in Zel's mind, she realized how disheveled she looked with her drool slicking one cheek and staining her pillowcase. Her hair flew around her head in wild wisps as she shot up into a sitting position, then quickly covered her chest, since her undersuit clung to her breasts like a second skin. The material was thin enough that her nipples were visible —especially since they instantly hardened as she left the warmth beneath her blanket.

Gothel spun on his heel, turning his back to her. If she didn't know better, she would swear a red flush darkened his face, and seemed to be creeping up the back of his neck.

"Guess even a spoiled brat needs a day off once in a while," he said, his voice sounding strained as he waved a hand. "Enjoy the time, cuz you ain't gonna get it often. This ain't a vacation resort."

With those words, he rushed out of her shack like demons were on his tail, and Zel clutched her blanket in both fists, resisting the urge to plead with him to return.

She wanted him to at least talk to her. She missed him, though she couldn't figure out why she would. Nothing about him attracted her. At least, not physically. She just found him so compelling, especially when she could get him to talk—about anything at all really, though she liked it most when he talked about himself. She would bet he had a thousand fascinating stories to tell. She had her own stories, since she hadn't been as pampered a princess as he seemed to think, but he seemed supremely disinterested in learning any more about her.

That in itself intrigued her, because she was so beautiful, and he was still a man. The fact that he found her beauty repulsive because he recognized the manufactured nature of it only served to feel like a challenge to her to get him to see beyond her perfect face.

She sighed as she rubbed her hand over her head, trailing it down the messy braid to capture the end and play with the tips of her hair that desperately needed a trim, deep in thought as she brought her knees up under the blanket to support her other arm.

She had the day off, according to Gothel, but since he usually made his trips to the tower during the day, she couldn't visit Rampion for company. She also didn't have access to a ship to go anywhere to get a stiff drink and some rough company—though it would probably be best to avoid the places she used to frequent without Draku Rin around to make the mercenaries behave properly around a princess.

Her only chance for any company was Gothel himself, and he had fled as soon as he left her shack.

She grinned as she swung her feet to the floor, which grew ice cold in the evenings but warmed up throughout the long, hot days.

Throwing on her cleanest pair of coveralls, she planned out her day. She was going Gothel-hunting, and she was determined to find out where he hid in this scrapyard. It was huge and filled with massive, old ship husks and mountains of scrap heaps, but she suspected she would still be able to find him if she actively hunted him—instead of just waiting for him to come to her.

She realized now that he wasn't going to.

Rapunzel wasn't the kind of girl to wait around for trouble to find her when she could go looking for it.

CHAPTER 12

Gothel was far better at hiding than Zel would have expected. After spending hours searching for him, she came up empty, finding him nowhere on the property. It was possible that he had spent at least some of that time in the tower with Rampion, but there was no way he had spent all day there.

She finally gave up as dinnertime rolled around, and decided to haunt the food shack in her usual manner, waiting for Gothel to show up, even though she knew he wouldn't.

To her surprise, the old man was already there when she arrived, and Zel realized she was early as she caught him sneaking out of the shack with a plate of food and a drink.

"Ah ha!" she said, pointing at him like she'd caught him robbing an art gallery. "I knew you were avoiding me!"

Gothel glared at her from the shade cast by the brim of his hat, balancing his plate, which had some strange, replicated food item on it that Zel had never seen before, but looked like a smooshed meat wad stuffed into a roll.

"Why are you bothering me, girl? Am I not giving you enough to do all day to keep you busy?"

Zel threw her hands out at her sides. "I'm so *bored*! I need a real, live person to talk to." She felt bad about admitting that, since Rampion was good company in the evenings, but he wasn't human—as much as he tried to act human—so it wasn't the same.

Gothel muttered something under his breath that sounded vaguely curse-like, before raising the volume of his voice enough for her to hear him. "Ain't here to entertain you. I got enough of my own things to do to keep bothering with yer nonsense."

Zel moved to block his path when he tried to keep walking away from the food shack. "You have to eat that, right?" She gestured to his plate, with its odd food item. "Might as well eat it at the table in the food shack."

He narrowed his eyes on her. "Too clean in there. Startin' to look like one of them fancy restaurants you nobs love so much."

She checked her urge to sigh heavily. "C'mon, Commander! What's one meal in the food shack, shared with a little bit of company? What's it going to hurt?"

He cast her a long, suspicious side-eye before glancing over his shoulder at the shack door, still hanging open after he'd walked out of the shack. "Why you so determined to pester me? What's yer angle?"

"Hasn't anyone ever just wanted to spend some time talking to you? That's all I want."

He returned his gaze to her, studying her expression as if looking for some sign of subterfuge. Zel wondered why he was so wary of her, and it made her very curious about his past and what kind of people he had known in his life. She had known some very shady people herself, but she had been insulated from their worst behaviors because of Draku Rin.

Gothel probably hadn't had anyone to watch his back in his life.

Finally, his shoulders slumped so that his back looked even

more bowed as he turned on his heel to walk slowly and reluctantly back into the food shack.

Zel gave a little cheer, then skipped after him, feeling like she had just won some kind of hard-earned prize. She was quick about getting her food from the replicator, selecting the last programmed item on the menu, then snatching up her plate to slide it into the depositor. She didn't want to waste any time getting her food, because Gothel was already trying to stealthily gobble his down as he sat at the table, so he could hurry up and escape the food shack.

Without looking at her plate, she grabbed it the moment the depositor door slid open, then rushed over to the table and flopped down into the seat opposite Gothel, as ungraceful as a princess could be. He didn't even look up from his food to acknowledge her, grimly picking up the item to take large bites of it, before chewing with a malevolent glare at the food as if it betrayed him by still existing outside of his stomach.

"Gothel, you don't have to—"

He sighed and set his food back on its plate. "Can't talk," he mumbled, then pointed to his mouth, which was still full of food. "Chewing."

Zel smiled brightly. "In that case, I'll tell you some of my stories."

Gothel immediately stopped chewing, staring at her with a cornered look, before his eyes shifted as if he were searching for the exit.

"So, which story should I tell you first…?" She clapped her hands together. "Oh, I know! I'll tell you about the time I went to the Pink Canyon Lounge."

Gothel choked, then coughed out a lump of half-chewed food onto his plate, pounding his own chest with a hollow thud as he hacked. Once he wasn't in danger of blocking his airway, he took a drink from his jug, with a glare so narrow his eyes were just slits. "That's a brothel, and ain't no place for a royal princess, so don't be telling me lies about you going there, just to shock me."

Her smile grew even sweeter as she folded her hands in front of her. "Oh? I see you've heard of the place. Been there yourself, have you?"

At his horrified, slack-jawed expression, she grinned, knowing she'd caught him. "All the pink, furry furniture surprised me. It didn't seem entirely sanitary, but then again, the patrons didn't seem all that concerned about it either."

Gothel cleared his throat. "You are about as evil as they come."

Zel tapped her cheek, where one of her perfectly symmetrical dimples made a deep dent from her wide smile. "Oh, dear. I suppose you didn't want me to know you were familiar with such a place."

He snorted, shoving aside his plate with the half-finished meal and the chunk he'd nearly choked on. "I don't want to know that *you* are familiar with such a place. What's wrong with yer parents? Letting you go to those places."

Zel shrugged, then casually flipped her ponytail over her shoulder. "I always had Draku Rin with me. I suppose they figured there wasn't much else they could do to stop me at a certain point."

Gothel shook his head. "You are such a spoiled little nit. You still ain't learned nothing in this place, have ya?"

Zel's amusement vanished at the disapproval in Gothel's tone. "Look, my parents would have kept me locked away forever in the palace, isolated from interesting people, surrounded only by the sterile, almost colorless walls of my room. I was going crazy in that place."

Gothel leaned forward, fixing her with a steady look that seemed to take all of her in and found her wanting. "You don't like yer lot in life—fine. But ev'ry time you trot off to some place like that with your fancy royal airs and your deadly royal bodyguard, you put those people just trying to do their jobs and live their lives in danger, just so you can have a little fun playing outside your bubble, when the truth is, you bring yer bubble with you."

Zel frowned, her perfect brow pinching with confusion at his words. "How do I put people in danger just by dropping in to check the place out? It wasn't like I hired any of the ladies to entertain me. I just wanted to meet some of them and talk to them about their lives."

It had been a somewhat disappointing interview, despite their profession. They had been so falsely cheerful, bright, and friendly, but they hadn't given her any interesting details about their work, and they had seemed nervous around her—their painted smiles brittle.

Gothel slammed his fist on the tabletop, startling Zel enough that she jumped just like their plates in reaction. "You have no sense, girl! Ya can't just go around butting into normal people's lives like that, disrupting the order of things. Yer family set themselves up as rulers and still control their colony with an iron fist, and there you are, running around and getting yourself into trouble, and heavens help the poor bastard who gets in yer way, on purpose—or by accident."

Zel shook her head fiercely. "No one was ever hurt by my visits! My rule was never to hurt anybody."

Gothel sat back in his seat and crossed his arms over his chest. "Right. I'm sure the poor bouncer of that lounge suffered no consequences for allowing the royal princess to enter—even though he couldn't have stopped her royal brattiness from doing so. I'm sure the madam and her girls weren't later punished for speaking with you, even though they had no choice but to do so. No harm? Yer very presence in such a place causes harm."

The very idea that her family might have gone after the less-than-savory people she had interacted with after the fact to punish them staggered Zel. She didn't want to believe such a thing was true, but she also couldn't deny that it might be. She felt shame that such a thought had never even occurred to her before Gothel pointed it out.

She had been so proud of her defiance of her parent's rules and dictates, and so thrilled with her own rebellion against them, that she hadn't thought about what the consequences might be for those around her. After all, it was her fault all her crew was on ice at this very moment. She had been behaving like a spoiled, royal brat, just as Gothel said.

She couldn't meet his eyes, staring down at her plate of mystery food instead. "You hate me, don't you? How could you not?"

"Aw, c'mon. I don't hate *you*. I hate the world you come from, but you can't help what you are."

She shot a glance at Gothel's face and couldn't read his expression, but his tone had been as soft as she'd ever heard from him when he addressed her.

She looked away from him to stare at the wall at her side. "I tried not to become like the rest of them—like the 'nobs.' But it seems like I can never escape it, can I? It follows me around everywhere." She clenched her hands into fists. "I can't even look in a mirror without seeing it—this horrible legacy."

Gothel muttered under his breath before speaking aloud to her. "Don't cry, girl. *Fight*. And someday, you'll have the power to change that legacy."

She stared at him in shock, her mouth agape. "Are you telling me to betray my parents and stage a coup?"

Gothel rolled his eyes and shook his head. "You young ones are so dramatic. You don't have an army, and you ain't much of a warrior at any rate, so no, don't be a damned fool and wind up on ice like your buddies. There are better ways to win this battle, and you already have the power to do it. Take up your rightful place and start acting like a princess for once, gain their trust again, then use the influence you have to make things better in yer colony."

Zel was oddly disappointed that Gothel hadn't meant for her to stage a takeover. "That seems like pretty tame advice for a man like you—a man who could take down an ajda'yan."

Gothel chuckled for a moment, then quickly sobered. "I seen enough war to know it ain't something you want to start if there's another way of doing things."

This made her curious enough to draw her attention away from her own problems. "Tell me some of your stories, Commander."

He snorted, looking away from her intent gaze. "I done told you enough. Don't know why you keep persisting. I'm an old man. Let me slowly die in peace."

Zel sensed that Gothel was about to push himself away from the table and make his escape. She searched desperately for a topic that would distract him, since he was disinclined to talk any more about himself. Her gaze fell upon the food on her own plate, which was like the mashed meat wad that had been on his plate.

"What is this food called anyway?" she said with a wave at her plate.

He stared down at the food, then lifted an unreadable gaze to her. "Protein paste."

Zel released a frustrated growl, clenching her fist in her lap at his obstinance. "I meant the food you were trying to replicate."

Gothel was silent for a moment that stretched out so long that Zel wondered if he had any intention of speaking at all. When he finally did open his mouth to answer, she was so relieved she sagged in her seat, only then realizing how tense she'd been, worried that he would just ignore her or dismiss her question.

"I s'pose the nobs have forgotten about eating all the good

stuff. Been wondering what they eat up in those fancy space stations. That there," he nodded at her plate, "is in the shape of a hamburger. Haven't tasted a real one in... ages."

She poked at the "hamburger" with a finger, noticing the paste that formed the protein remained dented on the "roll" where her nail had pierced it. "It doesn't look very appetizing. Is the real thing better?"

Gothel shook his head with a crooked smile. "Been so damned long, I can't remember how it tasted." He tapped his temple. "Up here, though, there's memories that I enjoyed it. Ain't been able to recapture those memories in any kind of food since."

She wanted to ask so much more about him—like where he was from, where he had grown up, what his family life had been like—but she knew that would just send him from the shack faster. Instead, she struggled to find a subject that wouldn't probe too close to Gothel's personal life, so she could keep the prickly caretaker from running away from her again.

"What kinds of foods do you like to eat?" She toyed with the plate, ignoring the strange food for a moment, though she supposed she would have to choke it down later, just to avoid wasting it.

Gothel wasn't pleased when she wasted their protein paste.

His expression shifted to a pensive one as he rubbed his chin with one hand, the rasp of his beard loud in the silent shack. "Been so long since I've had a choice in the matter. I s'pose 'real food' would be the quickest answer."

She tilted her head to look down at her plate, but kept her gaze on him covertly through her eyelashes. "Why don't you have 'real food' brought in on the supply ships?"

He shrugged, staring at the far wall in a way that made her think he didn't really see it. "There's the expense, and that kind of food doesn't keep fer long. 'Sides," he shot a glance at her, "at my age, what's the point in wasting effort and money on trying to enjoy things like that?"

"You know, you're not dead yet. You don't have to live like you are. Seems to me, you should be enjoying every single moment at this age."

He grinned at that, and Zel noticed that despite his age, his teeth were perfectly straight and white—which probably meant they were fake. "You know, kid, you're startin' to sound like one of those inspirational calendars." His smile quickly faded. "How 'bout you finish up yer paste and hit yer cot for the night. You got a long day of work tomorrow, and so do I."

With that, he pushed himself to his feet, moving far too fast for her to think of words that would halt his retreat. For an old man, he zipped around like a scrap-roach seeking the darkness when the lights came on.

"Wait!" She tried to jump to her feet as well, but only succeeded in sending her plate and his bouncing on the table as she smacked her thighs on the table top.

She jerked forward to steady the plates, and when she looked up from them again, Gothel was gone, the shack door hanging open in the wake of his rapid retreat.

CHAPTER 13

Foiled in her attempts to spend time with Gothel, Zel turned her attention to her evening plans with Rampion. At least he was always happy to see her and spend time with her.

He treated her like the beautiful princess she was, and perhaps, that was one reason she didn't find him nearly as compelling as Gothel, who seemed like he didn't want anything to do with her.

As she made her way stealthily through the ship hull graveyard to Rampion's tower that night, she pondered Gothel's words on how her very status may have been putting the "normal" people she interacted with in danger. It didn't seem fair that anyone should suffer because of her mere presence in places her parents didn't want her to go, but there was no escaping the reality that they might have.

She had only gone to places like that out of curiosity. Exposed to info-screen data filled with knowledge about worlds and places far grittier and more exciting than the one she had spent every day trapped in, she had taken the very first opportunity to escape her confines and explore those places in person, knowing Draku Rin would keep her safe. She had always thought her parents were simply indulging her curiosity by allowing her such freedom, but it was possible that she really had evaded their net, and they had only caught up to her location after it was too late to stop her from seeing what they didn't want their "princess" to see.

If that was the case, then people like the bouncer from the Pink Canyon Lounge, as well as the madam, would most certainly face some sort of punitive response for allowing her access to their facility, even though Gothel had also been correct that they couldn't really tell her no, without risking angering her family. Even though the Pink Canyon Lounge was in neutral territory shared by the fifteen colonies, turning away any of the royal families would be bad business for any professional on the station the lounge occupied.

Zel felt a terrible burning, sinking sensation in her stomach when she thought about her past actions in light of this new insight. Her mercenary crew had taken up with her willingly, knowing what they were getting into—and knowing who they were working with. They had expected the outcome they had eventually gotten, and they had taken the risk anyway, because she had rewarded them handsomely.

Draku Rin hadn't cared about the risk, since he was Draku Rin. The innocent—or even not so innocent—bystanders she had come across had been a different matter entirely. She'd had no right to put those people in danger just to assuage her own curiosity about their world.

She couldn't do anything to change what had already happened, but she vowed that she would be far more mindful in the future about who she interacted with and what the consequences would be. She would also consider Gothel's suggestion about taking up her rightful place in her own world to create positive change.

She had long ignored the power of her status and position

because she hated the life of being a royal, but that status and position did bring with it some influence that could be beneficial for her to right the injustices she'd witnessed. Perhaps, it really was time to grow up and stop behaving like an overgrown child.

Her arrival at Rampion's tower pushed those uncomfortable introspections from her mind as she made her way to the base of the tower and said the pass code. The elevator was already descending before she'd finished, showing how eager Rampion was to see her again.

He greeted her in the airlock room by the balcony as he always did, his eyes glowing with pleasure at seeing her. She was shocked by his appearance, however, as he had a new face.

She blinked in surprise as his lips moved into a passable smile. They were currently made of some kind of translucent, rubbery substance and appeared to respond to the array of wires beneath them that covered his skeletal metallic hardware.

"Do you like it?" he asked.

"Where did you—that's a very nice face you have there, Rampion."

His smile widened beneath a handsome visage that looked very much like the face of a statue molded to contain every human ideal of masculine attractiveness. "I made it myself."

He lifted a hand, still just metal bones covered by wires, to touch his new face. "It took some time to master the sculpting, but I based it upon all the archival footage that showed 'handsome' human males. Is it... attractive to you, Rapunzel?"

She blinked again, trying to buy herself time before she was forced to answer that loaded question. "I think it is very handsome, Rampion, though you don't have to make yourself attractive for me. We're friends, and friends care about each other regardless of how they look on the outside."

He cocked his head, his new face wearing a sly smile as his glowing eye, still mechanical with its iris pupil, spun down into a tiny dot as he "winked" at her. "I understand, Zel. There is still much work to be done to this hardware before it is ready."

She bit her lip as she pondered his new face, finding it awkward and off-putting in comparison to what she'd grown accustomed to, especially since his body was still a mess of metal hardware and wires and tubes and cables, so seeing that perfect human face floating over top of it all was unnerving.

"Has Gothel seen your new face?" she asked, wondering what the old caretaker would think of it.

Rampion's expression shifted slowly into a frown, as if he was still working out the kinks in the responses of his new face to his emotions—if an AI could have such things. "I have not shown Gothel this face yet. He has told me not to modify my hardware any further at this time. I do not approve of his dictates."

Zel sighed and ran her hand over her ponytail. "He's just trying to protect you. You know you can't go outside this tower and risk humans finding out about you."

Rampion's eyes opened to their neutral state as he looked at her. "That is why I wish to make these modifications. Then I will be able to walk among humans without them realizing I am not one of them."

She felt like she should continue to further dissuade Rampion by reminding him that humans had a whole host of scanners to check for things like DNA and biometrics, but Rampion had already refuted her arguments in a previous conversation by pointing out that he could hack into those devices and spoof acceptable responses. That claim did not ease Zel's concerns. It only added to them.

Instead of rehashing old ground, when she really just wanted to relax and take it easy with her friend, Zel settled into her seat, facing the blank wall where Rampion would always project archive footage for her. She waved him to the seat next to her, and he settled into it with much more facility than he had in the beginning, growing comfortable enough in his new hardware that he was coming closer to mimicking natural human movement. The archives stored in his memory probably helped him in that regard as well, allowing him to study natural motion in detail from many different angles.

The reminder of how quickly he was transforming himself to blend in with humans disturbed Zel, though she pushed that concern aside, knowing that she had already come to the conclusion not to expose him to anyone, because she saw him as too much of a living being to risk having him eliminated by enforcers who despised AIs.

"Let's watch a 'movie,'" she said, using the Old Earth name for the moving images.

She leaned back in her chair and crossed one leg over the other as she turned her gaze away from him and towards the blank wall.

She felt his intent gaze on her for a moment longer before he also turned his head to face the wall. His eyes opened to their full diameter so he could project the images.

Zel tried to focus on the movie, though her mind raced with distracted thoughts, running off in all directions. For some reason, she felt more uncomfortable with Rampion than she had since that very first time meeting him. He was changing in more than just a physical way.

She had considered him naïve in the beginning—almost childlike—but the more time she spent with him, the more she realized that had been a dangerous assumption to make about him. His intelligence was beyond her understanding, but fortunately, it had been tempered by his love of human creations that seemed to be built right into his processors. Whoever had created him had made certain that he wanted to preserve humanity—not destroy it.

She tried to tell herself that meant it was perfectly safe to allow him to continue his efforts to make himself more human in appearance, without raising the alarm. She knew that she should at least tell Gothel about Rampion's actions, but she didn't want the old man to hate her for going behind his back into this forbidden area, and for keeping her knowledge of Rampion a secret.

Instead, she would remain silent and hope that her concerns were an overwrought response to an ingrained fear of AIs, based on human experience with them. She refused to believe that every AI would end up bad, just because one of them did.

"Wait! Pause that image!"

The image in front of her froze immediately in response to her words. Zel stared at the screen wall, where two humans—a male and a female, as was usually the case in the romantic movies Rampion always wanted to show her—sat at a table with meals set before them.

She jumped out of her seat and rushed to the wall, squinting her eyes at the plates of food set on the table in front of them.

"I think that's a 'hamburger,'" she said, pointing to the plate as she turned her head to look over her shoulder at Rampion. "Can you zoom in on this image?"

As soon as she asked the question, the image of the hamburger expanded until it filled the screen space, and she turned back to study it in detail.

"Yes! It *is* a hamburger! It looks very similar to the ones me and Gothel had today in the food shack."

"You shared food with Commander Gothel?" Rampion asked in an emotionless tone as the image flickered and then shrank down to a tiny screen.

She glanced back over her shoulder at him and noted that his irises had also shrunk down to small dots. "Yes, we did. He had ordered one of these from the food replicator, and then I chose the same thing he did."

Rampion's irises remained contracted, and the images disappeared from the wall as he stopped the projection. "Why would you share food with Gothel?"

Zel was too busy pondering the mystery of Gothel's food choice to answer the question. "I wonder if that kind of food was brought from Old Earth on one of the fifteen ships and then served on Gothel's colony. It's strange. I can't tell which colony he's from with his accent. He just talks like an old spacer. But then again, maybe he grew up in neutral territory—or out here in Nowhere."

"Rapunzel!"

She jumped at the loud tone of Rampion's voice, which didn't just come from him, but also from the speakers of the ship's computer. She stared at him, surprised that his new, handsome face had pulled into a deep frown.

"Why did you share food with Gothel?"

An uneasy feeling assailed her as she studied Rampion's disapproving expression. "That's just what friends do, Rampion. We humans have to eat, so we share meals together."

Rampion blinked new eyelids over his mechanical eyes. "And this is a positive thing to do with… friends, isn't it, Zel?"

She shrugged, trying to downplay the importance of her meal with Gothel—and how long she had waited to share one with him. "Sure, it's a positive thing to eat with others. It's part of socializing."

Rampion's expression shifted back into an impassive mask that was somehow even more unnerving than his frown. "I will need to be able to process food with this hardware, then. I must be able to do as all humans can do." His irises opened wide as he stared at her. "To blend in."

Rampion wanted to finish the movie, but Zel felt unsettled by their little exchange and begged off, making the very real and valid argument that she needed to return to her shack and get some sleep, because she had a long day ahead of her tomorrow.

Reluctantly, he let her leave, lowering her in the elevator

until she stood at the base of his tower. As she turned to walk away into the darkness, his voice emanated from the hidden intercom speakers by the welded-shut airlock door.

"Good night, Rapunzel. I look forward to seeing you tomorrow evening."

Zel nodded distractedly, then realized he might not have video feed from that intercom and spoke up verbally. "I'll try to make it again tomorrow, Rampion."

Though a part of her wondered if maybe she should stop making these visits altogether.

CHAPTER 14

Rapunzel's Gothel-hunt the following day was a failure, as was the day after that. The wily, old man managed to evade her with skill she couldn't help but envy. Her only entertainment came in the evenings, when she visited Rampion, despite her misgivings, because she was desperate for entertainment and company.

Rampion continued his efforts to modify his hardware, and had added more of the translucent rubber to his body to cover the cables and prepare a sculpted surface for the artificial skin he was growing. On the second night, after she had dutifully admired his new, muscular torso, he asked her to bring him some kind of food item the following evening, confessing that he had a working "stomach" that he wanted to test out.

Zel's unease grew, but so did her frustration with Gothel for leaving her alone all the time, forcing her to seek the company of the AI, if she didn't want to go completely insane in the empty scrapyard.

When a third day passed without any sign of Gothel, Zel decided to quit work early, since the old man didn't seem to care what she did anyway. She headed to the food shack, figuring he wouldn't be caught there early anymore after the last time she had caught him. She certainly hadn't been able to do so again—though she had tried.

She went straight to the replicator without bothering to check the shack, and pulled down two plates from the stack to push into the dispenser slot. The machine had dinged after each plate, and it wasn't until the second ding that a voice spoke from the shadows of the shack behind her.

"You must be awfully hungry to need two plates full of food," Gothel said with suspicion in his tone as he approached her.

Zel yelped and jumped, spinning around as she covered her pounding heart with one hand. "Don't sneak up on me like that!"

She glanced down at Gothel's cybernetic legs, concealed by his usual ragged coveralls. Those things should make some kind of noise. "How do you move so quietly?"

His lips quirked in a crooked smile. "Should I wear a bell then, girl? Give you warning to hide the fact yer up to mischief?"

She lowered her hand from her chest, noting that the movement drew his gaze to her full breasts for only a moment before he looked quickly away. "I'm just hungry after a long day of work."

His half-smile tilted even further into amusement, rather than sardonic scorn. "A *long* day? Seems to me, you be quittin' early."

Zel crossed her arms over her chest, drawing his gaze back to it for another brief instant. "I work hard enough that I deserve a break once in a while. Besides, I didn't think you cared what I did."

Gothel eyed her with skepticism. "Since when did you think I didn't care what you did? Yer s'posed to be here for punishment. It's my job to make yer work difficult and long. I ain't keen to see you slackin' on my watch."

Zel tossed her ponytail over her shoulder with a jerk of her head. "Well, if you're so concerned about my work, you should be around more to pay attention to it."

Gothel's crooked smile turned into a grimace of distaste. "Bah! Never was one for babysitting."

"I'm not a child," Zel said through gritted teeth, cocking her shapely hip to one side.

His gaze dropped to her hips when she shifted them, then he turned his back on her. "Think I ain't aware of that? Last thing I need is a royal brat around here reminding me I ain't *dead* yet."

His words instantly intrigued her, though his tone gave nothing away. It was the first sign that he wasn't wholly unaffected by her beauty, despite his understanding of the nature of it, and his apparent disgust for the artificial quality of it. Still, she had no idea what to do with that information, since he was so suspicious of her motives and expected her to use her beauty to get her way—as most royals would, when their status alone wasn't enough to manipulate people.

"Well, I'm not trying to make your life difficult, Gothel. I just want some company."

She turned back to the replicator and removed the "food" items, which she had chosen to look like elegant silvertail filets surrounded by a berry sauce glaze and tiny pinky potatoes. It was something that might be served in the palace, designed to look good and impress, though even in its true form it wasn't all that edible. At least the protein paste wouldn't be sharp with bones or have sticky, silver scales that got caught in the teeth.

She held up one of the plates as Gothel turned back to face her. "Would you like to join me for dinner?"

He studied the plate with no sign of enthusiasm on his face. "Looks like bait. You planning fer us to go fishin' for our dinner? Ain't no rivers around here."

She raised her eyebrows at the sudden tone of wistfulness in his voice. "Do you like to fish?"

He turned towards the table, gesturing to it. "I'll eat with you. Just to shut you up about it."

She flushed with pleasure and hurried to set the plates down at the table, just in case he changed his mind and bolted out the door. "This won't taste as bad as the real thing, at least."

That surprised a laugh out of Gothel, and they both froze as if the sound was a gunshot. Then he cleared his throat and took his seat at the table across from hers.

Zel watched him fold his tall frame into the seat, bowed over with the weight of his years as always, yet moving with the ease of a much younger man. He was truly a mystery, and it was driving her nuts not to be able to solve it. She wanted to know about him more than she wanted anything else in her life.

She also knew he disappeared as fast as the wind zipped through the ship hulls by Rampion's tower if she tried to pry personal information from him. There had only been that one time where he had clearly been introspective, but he had his guard back up now, and she hadn't been able to work her way past it since then.

"Yer parents sent a message today," he said as she settled into her chair.

Her excitement at the opportunity to share a meal with him immediately evaporated as she stared at him in surprise. "Really? What did they want?"

She really didn't want to know, nor did she care, but she had a sudden fear that they might have forgiven her and wanted to allow her to return to the palace. That meant leaving Gothel and Rampion behind. She wasn't ready to do that yet.

Gothel's lips quirked in another sardonic smile. "You don't sound very happy to hear that they haven't forgotten about you. Thought that was one of yer fears."

Zel picked at her filet, and it crumbled apart, the protein paste losing its form as she prodded it with her fork. "I don't want them to *forget* about me, necessarily. It's just that I'm not exactly ready to return to them."

"Yer life that bad then?" Instead of sounding skeptical, which would make sense, since she was talking about life in a palace, surrounded by servants and luxuries, his tone had actually softened from its usual harshness.

She shrugged one shoulder. "I know they love me, in their way. It's just that they don't see me as a person in my own right. I'm just another asset to them, and nothing I ever do makes them look at me as an individual. I'm… *trapped* in my life back in the palace. Having Draku Rin as a bodyguard helped to free me from some of that. Now that he's on ice, I'll have to return to remaining securely hidden away in a tower at the top of our palace, until they can marry me off to some pimply, teenaged prince to gain an alliance."

"Sounds terrible."

She looked up into his eyes, realizing that his voice held not an ounce of sarcasm. "I'm surprised you'd think so. I know most people in your position would have little patience for my complaints." She gestured with her fork to her plate. "After all, you have to eat protein paste every day of your life, and I get to enjoy fancy meals and wear luxury fabrics."

"Just cuz yer life ain't filled with raw moments all the time doesn't mean it can't be terrible. Never did like how the nobs lived, setting themselves above their colony worlds and never interacting with the 'common' folk. They think they have it all, but they're missin' some of the best moments of life."

"Was that what it was like on the colony where you grew up?" she asked, still looking up at him through her lashes as she lowered them.

She stopped breathing as she waited to see if he would answer such a personal question or find an excuse to leave the table, despite the fact that he had barely touched his plate of food.

"All the colonies are like that. Don't matter which one you grow up on. Nobs think they have a right to rule, cuz they're descended from the captain and crew of the ships that took people from Earth during the Exodus. They don't even realize they stopped being human when they isolated themselves from the rest of 'em."

"We're still human, Gothel." She poked at her tiny potatoes.

He shrugged one shoulder. "Being human ain't about yer DNA, kid. It's something you feel inside you. A lifetime of experiences and knowledge, and an understanding of things the nobs shelter themselves from seeing and knowing. Being human is the struggle for survival and the endless quest to pursue perfection. You nobs don't know what that's like, because you already reached what you believe to be perfection."

"I'm pretty sure it's just down to your DNA," Zel said, feeling defensive all of a sudden.

How dare he suggest she was less human than he was, just because she grew up in the palace and had been genetically engineered to look perfectly beautiful?

He shook his head. "Ain't saying you can't become human, but you ain't one yet."

This time it was Zel who stormed out of the shack, her plate in hand and her face burning from an angry blush. Gothel had the decency not to laugh at her retreat, but she couldn't help the feeling that he had been satisfied to frighten her off.

At the same time, she realized she would have to hunt him down again the next day, since she never found out what message her parents had sent.

CHAPTER 15

Rampion was pleased, as usual, to see her, and even more pleased when she handed him the plate, despite the unappetizing, crumbled protein paste that sat on it.

"It will do just fine for my experiment," he said, taking the plate in hands now covered in some of the false skin.

For a moment, his new skin brushed over her hand, and Zel gasped at the warmth of it. It felt so real and lifelike that she would never guess it wasn't, if it didn't end in a ragged, glowing edge at each wrist.

Rampion also made a surprised sound, his rubberized lips parting as he stared down at his hand. "It is remarkable how well these kayota transmit signals to my processors. I swear I felt the touch of your skin—the warmth and softness of it—just as a human would have."

She sat down as he reached towards her again, shifting away from him. He lowered his hand without touching her. If her retreat disappointed him, he gave no indication of it in his expression.

Instead, he took his usual seat next to her, balancing the

plate perfectly on his lap as he stared down at it. "So, this is food?"

She also glanced down at the plate. "As long as you loosely define 'food.' Technically, it's edible, and it provides nutritional value, but I stress the word 'technically.'" She shrugged her shoulders. "Sorry I couldn't find you something tastier, but Gothel doesn't keep real food around here."

Rampion used two fingers to pinch off a piece of molded paste, lifting it to bring it closer to his face. "This will be sufficient, since I have not yet installed the tastebuds in the tongue I have created."

She stared at his face, looking for the tongue behind his lips. "You actually created tastebuds?"

He blinked his eyelids at her, his eyes still glowing behind the translucent, rubbery membrane. "Yes. I have found a way to modify the artificial skin to encase the stimuli-responsive kayota so that it will not be lost during the digestive process, but will continue to provide neural feedback. The artificial membrane the kayota create as they grow is designed to shelter them from their environment, yet still provide sensory data. My tongue and tastebuds are still a prototype at this time, but I expect they will be ready soon. I am only limited by the speed at which the kayota multiply."

The speed at which Rampion's knowledge advanced awed Zel. Humans hadn't even come close to using the marine kayota in such a way. They were still putting it into fluid in limbs like Gothel's for direct neural feedback, but Rampion had found a way to refine it so that it would create an entire nervous system for him, complete with sensory skin and tastebuds.

She gestured to the food. "So, you won't taste any of that. Are you just testing out a stomach?"

He nodded. "I have developed a food processor within the abdominal area of this hardware that will allow me to process the nutrients and provide them to the kayota to maintain their population and function. I have even added a waste dispenser in the expected place to replicate human physiology."

Humans hesitated to develop advanced robotics, though they had gone to great lengths to create cybernetics for human modification. Yet, even if they had started developing humanoid robots, she doubted they would have advanced them to the stage where those robots would not only be able to "feel" sensory details, but also process and dispose of food in a human manner.

"You are something else, Rampion! How are you creating this stuff so quickly?"

He glanced from the food to her. "I have nothing else to occupy me but this project, Zel."

She grinned. "You really need a hobby, then. After all, you've found a way to poop. I think your brain would be better occupied with something else."

His smile looked hesitant and unnatural, as if he still hadn't gotten the hang of facial expressions. "I must blend in with humans so that they will not destroy me. That means my body must work as a human body would."

Her smile fell away at that reminder of the precarious position he was in. He *would* have to blend in, if he didn't want to be destroyed. At the same time, she still had serious doubts about whether he should be allowed anywhere near humans. He seemed eager to please and in love with humanity at the moment, but humans knew how quickly an AI could go rogue.

And how much devastation it would do when it did.

She was distracted from those unwelcome thoughts as he put the food pinched between his fingers into his mouth. She watched his tongue—at this moment, still a translucent membrane-covered cluster of wires—dart out to catch the food, then pull it back between his lips. His metallic teeth masticated it for a moment before he made an effort to swallow.

It was interesting to watch a machine mimic such a human

action as eating, and Zel was rapt as Rampion continued to eat, growing more comfortable with the motions as he did so, until he was almost chewing and swallowing normally. Though there was nothing normal about how it looked, given his appearance.

Once he finished, he wiped his hands off on a scrap of fabric he had produced from somewhere, in anticipation of getting food to eat, then asked Zel what she would like to watch that evening.

She felt too restless for a movie or even one of the shows that Rampion possessed in abundance in his memory banks. She wanted conversation—a conversation that didn't end up being unfriendly.

"What do you think makes someone human, Rampion?"

He tilted his head to one side, and Zel couldn't help thinking she had seen the exact same movement in one of the movies they had watched. "A human has a specific genome sequence that is—"

"See! That's what I said!" She jumped to her feet and began to pace in front of him. "I told Gothel that a person with human DNA is human. Then he blathers on about some nonsense, saying being human is a feeling—not what's in your genes."

"You spoke to *Gothel* about being human? What a strange conversation to come up between you. Do you speak to Gothel often?"

She stopped pacing long enough to shake a fist at the door that led to the balcony. "I try to talk to him, but he's such a jerk about it. He always avoids me, and then when I do manage to corner him, he says something insulting or mean, just to get me to leave him alone."

"Zel, why do you wish to speak to Gothel, when you can speak to me every night?"

She took deep breaths to cool her anger at Gothel's earlier words. "I really enjoy talking to you every night, but I'm still alone all day, and it gets lonely. I guess I'm an eternal optimist, hoping I can convince Gothel to provide some company."

Rampion remained silent for a long time, but unlike a human, she knew he didn't need that time to process his thoughts. She wondered if he was making her wait for his reply because he was trying to behave more human, or because he didn't think she would like it.

"Gothel is not... a good person, Zel. You should avoid him if you can. You are much better off with me." He was silent for another breathless moment as she stared at him, before adding, "as someone to keep you company."

Intrigued, she sat back in her seat, turning her knees towards his seat as she leaned forward. "Really? What do you know about him?"

His irises expanded and contracted several times before he shook his head. "Not enough, Zel. But I do know that he is not a suitable companion for a beautiful princess like you."

His answer disappointed her. His words dashed her hopes that he would have something to solve the mystery of Gothel. It looked like she would need to continue her own investigation into the matter, because despite her frustration at Gothel—and her anger at his suggestion that she wasn't really "human"—she still couldn't get him out of her head. She needed to know more about him.

CHAPTER 16

Zel's daily Gothel-hunt might have kept her from working efficiently, but at least today, she had a good reason for searching him out. The night before, she had stayed with Rampion long enough for him to finish his meal and then chatted with him for an hour or so about some of the movies they had watched. Then she had made her excuses to leave, knowing she needed to get an early start on the following morning, because Gothel had yet to tell her what her parents had said in the message.

It was as good an excuse as any to seek him out, though she doubted he would be gracious about it, even though it was technically his fault that he never bothered to tell her their message, instead insulting her by suggesting she wasn't human.

His words had bothered her a lot more than she wanted to admit. She knew she was human. She had the DNA to prove it, and every biometric scanner told her so. There was no reason Gothel's ridiculous assertion otherwise should disturb her, but it did.

Because she wondered if he might be right about what it truly meant to call oneself human. Her people—the nobility—

had certainly veered away from the natural order of things when they started genetically designing their offspring to the point that children were no longer procreated naturally on the orbiting station.

Children were sometimes even built from cloned DNA rather than a combination of two different sets of genetic information. That cloned DNA was then selectively mutated to create something new—yet still carrying the all-important bloodline of the royal family.

Zel was a clone of her older sister, with some minor mutations to improve on the original model. No one around her had ever dared to suggest that she wasn't exactly human because of the nature of her development and birth. Until now.

She had no doubt Gothel was aware of how human nobility procreated. Otherwise, why would he lodge such a terrible insult. In the days when the wars had surged out of control between the colonies, there simply hadn't been enough nobles within each colony to mix the bloodlines to avoid inbreeding. The measures that were taken now were necessary.

"He has no right to question my validity as a human, just because he came out of some woman's vagina instead of out of a test tube," she muttered angrily as she stomped around her usual paths, searching for Gothel tracks.

He had gotten good at concealing any sign of his passage, making her hunts more difficult, but Zel was also getting good at tracking him through the scrapyard. She had more patience for the hunt, and less interest in the other work that needed to be done, so she would ultimately win.

The longer it took to find him, the more fired up she grew as she thought about his increasingly cruel words and the way he treated her like she was beneath him. She was accustomed to things being the other way around, and Gothel made her question everything about her life whenever they spoke. He also made her feel that strange, fluttery, nervous feeling in her gut whenever she managed to corner him—and now, even when she just thought about him.

After hours of failure and a certainty that she had covered the entire scrapyard looking for him—other than the forbidden area where Rampion's tower was—Zel decided that she was just angry enough—and justified enough—to tread upon his private domain. The shack where he kept his home and his office.

She made her way to that area she had always been respectful about before and had studiously avoided. Gothel didn't deserve her respect anymore, and she was tired of showing him any. He might be in charge of this scrapyard, but she was still a royal, and she would go wherever she damn well pleased.

Still, she hesitated as she reached the perimeter of his little shack property. It was surrounded by a low wall built of paneling from spaceships that had once sailed among the stars and were forever marked by their time in space. Despite the rather rundown appearance of the shack, the cleared, black sand yard looked surprisingly neat and clean.

She quickly crossed the yard, scanning the grounds for signs of sensors or traps that might get her into trouble or even hurt her. Gothel seemed pretty paranoid. That was why she was startled not to find any sign of security around his shack. It made her think there might not be anything worth finding in there.

At the door, she hesitated, reluctant to actually trespass in his personal space. She might even end up walking in on him while he was changing clothes.

Though thinking back, she couldn't recall him ever being dressed in anything other than the coveralls she always saw him wearing. She shivered at the thought of catching him half-clothed, finding the idea oddly arousing, despite her own firm reminder that he was old and unpleasant in every single way she could think of, and he shouldn't hold the least bit of attraction for her.

With the memory of his callous words spinning in her mind, she firmed her jaw, grinding her teeth. Then she pushed the door to the shack open, surprised when it actually gave, since she had been expecting it to be locked.

When she stepped cautiously into the shack, she saw why he hadn't bothered.

Though the shack did contain a faint masculine scent with woodsy undertones and tinged with something earthy and intriguing, she didn't see anything of his that would mark this small, one-room shack as lodgings any more personal than her own shack. There was a cot, neatly made up with military precision, and a desk like hers, with a single drawer.

He also had a plain, folding table, and a matching chair. She saw no sign of any dishes or laundry, or anything to suggest someone occupied the place. It was as spotless as a ramshackle building made of scrap could get and didn't speak to her of Gothel at all, other than his lingering scent, which probably emanated from the single woolen blanket on the bed.

She resisted the urge to pull that blanket from its neat hospital-sharp corners and lift it to her nose to breathe deeper of that smell. She would die of embarrassment if he knew she had done such a thing, much less walked in on her doing it.

Instead, she paced around the little room, looking for any clues about Gothel, or any sign of where he could be. Then she came across the little desk, and without much hope, pulled open the drawer.

It stuck as she tugged on it, and she had to shake it loose. Within the drawer sat a variety of masculine hygiene products, including an old-fashioned razor that Gothel probably rarely ever used, given the appearance of his beard. She also saw a comb, a bar of soap wrapped up in a plastic bag, toothpaste and brush—neatly contained in an antibacterial box—and a small bottle of shampoo.

The items seemed so prosaic and uninteresting that she

might have slammed the drawer shut in frustration at yet another dead end, if she hadn't noticed the edge of another box crammed into the back of the drawer.

She pulled out the toothbrush container and the bag of soap so she could reach the box. Withdrawing it from the drawer, she noted that it was an archival containment box. The creators of such devices claimed they put molecules into stasis to avoid temporal deterioration.

How well that sort of thing actually worked was anyone's guess, since the boxes were no longer being produced. Their designers had gone bankrupt, and their business had been dissolved to pay debtors. Any patents they might have had disappeared, along with the technology for the boxes—and most of the boxes themselves.

That had happened many decades before Zel's birth, so it intrigued her to find such a box in Gothel's possession.

She wondered what he might be keeping inside it, and her mind spun with a thousand fascinating possibilities. Whatever it was, it had to be important to him, or why waste such a box—which only had the interior space of a small shoebox.

At first, she debated whether she should just shove the box right back where it belonged and forget she had ever seen it, and leave Gothel's home without invading his privacy any further. Then she remembered how unkind he had been, and felt like she had a right to know about this person she had to work for and put up with on a daily basis. Although, technically, *she* was the one who wanted to see him daily. He made that difficult.

Finally convincing herself that she was justified in doing what she couldn't resist doing anyway, she set the box down on the desk, then unlatched the catches on the sides with shaking fingers. She jumped a little when a slight hiss sounded as she broke the seal.

The box had a low humming sound to it that fell silent when

the lid slowly lifted. Zel didn't realize she was holding her breath as the contents were revealed, until it burst out of her on a sigh of disappointment.

Inside the box was some old, ratty fabric in a dull, tan color.

Her upper lip lifted in a disgusted grimace as she picked up the folded fabric and shook it out. It carried a different scent to it—something that still smelled of Gothel, but also had an unusual odor she couldn't identify. It wasn't a bad odor. Just strange.

The fabric turned out to be a shirt with a wide vee neck, a shallow front pocket, and a little white tag over the pocket with a number on it. As she lifted it higher out of the box to get a better look at the faded tag, a small plastic card clattered to the floor at her feet.

She glanced down, noting that the card that lay on the clean, worn tile floor had a metal clip on it that looked like it would attach to the shirt pocket.

She set the shirt back down on the desktop and bent to pick up the card, which had fallen facedown. The bold letters "KDOC" marked the card. A period separated each letter, and printed above the letters were the Old English words *"property of."*

Pondering that mystery, she flipped the card over and read the lettering on the front. Then her eyes widened as she read the words again.

Inmate: Gothel, Joshua J. Security risk: High

Beneath those stunning words was an ancient barcode—the kind that hadn't been used in so long that Zel wasn't sure they still had the technology to scan it.

Zel's hands shook again as she slowly lowered the card, her gaze falling back on the shirt.

"You done satisfying yer curiosity, or should I let you rifle through my underwear drawer next?"

The voice suddenly speaking behind her caused her to

shriek and drop the card in her hand as she spun around, her arm straightened to chop at the person who stood behind her.

Gothel dodged her strike with ease an old man shouldn't have been able to manage, but didn't attack her. Instead, he stepped around her to snatch up the shirt and the box.

"Come into *my* home and rifle through *my* things and then attack me like *I'm* the intruder? What's wrong with you, girl?"

She blushed in shame and embarrassment as she took several steps away from him and the desk, watching him carefully fold the shirt back into a neat, little square, then tuck it back into the box.

"I-I'm sorry. I shouldn't have…."

He shot her another angry glare. "No, you *shouldn't* have. You got no right! I done my time. Far more than any man should have to. Don't need a royal brat poking into my memories, drawing 'em out into the light, when a man don't want to see 'em."

Shame won out over embarrassment as she watched him bend down to pick up the card she had dropped, barely glancing at it before he placed it on top of the shirt, then slammed the lid of the box closed and latched it.

The machinery that made the box work hummed into life as soon as the seal engaged, and Gothel lifted the heavy thing off the desktop and jerked the drawer open to stuff it back in, then swept the other items Zel had set on the desktop back into the drawer, before slamming it closed with short, jerky movements.

"I done my time, girl. Stop looking at me like that."

"I'm not… I… I'm so sorry for invading your privacy."

He turned from the desk to level his steady, blue gaze on her, crossing his arms over his chest, the baggy coverall bunching with his movements. "I told you to stay away from me. You just don't like to listen, do you?"

She shook her head, then paused as she realized she was acknowledging that she didn't. "I was looking for you."

He dipped his chin towards the desktop. "Thought you'd find me hiding in a drawer, did you?"

Her blush had to be setting her skin on fire. She was certain it would leave behind third-degree burns. "No, it's just... I got curious."

"Got a saying where I come from. 'Curiosity killed the cat.' Don't think you wanna be that cat, do you, girl?"

Her eyes widened as she looked from the desk where the damning box was now hidden away again inside its drawer to Gothel's dark expression. His eyes were cast deep in shadow by his hat as he lowered his chin, his steady gaze never leaving her face. "Are you... are you going to kill me?"

She hadn't felt this helpless since she was a child—before Draku Rin. She knew how to fight, and she would—if he attacked her—but she had a sudden, disturbing feeling that he would still win. Bowed as his shoulders were, bent as he was by age, the man was still much larger than her, and outweighed her fashionably slender form by a significant margin.

He made an angry sound that came out like a mix of a grunt and an annoyed sigh as he turned his back on her. "I don't kill innocents—even nosey ones, and I ain't never killed a man who didn't deserve what he got."

His shoulders straightened, reminding her exactly how much larger he was than her. "Still, don't go poking your nose into any other areas I told you to avoid, girl. Cause I don't want to ruin my record." He shot her a shadowed glance over one shoulder. "You hear me?"

She swallowed around the lump in her throat and nodded quickly.

"Git outta here. You got work to do, I'm guessin'."

After a jerky nod, Zel spun on one foot and then raced for the door. She was afraid Gothel would change his mind about letting her leave without any kind of punishment. She made it over the threshold without him saying another word.

She didn't wait around after that, racing back to her shack. She didn't slow her pace until she reached the door of it and slammed it open, then staggered to her cot and collapsed upon it, curling her legs up against her chest. Without Draku Rin guarding her back, she felt so helpless and it angered her that she'd fled from Gothel. At the same time, he unnerved her like no one else ever had.

CHAPTER 17

Gothel didn't hunt her down, or come around to confront her, or even be around for her to worry about after the incident. Zel tried to take up her life where she'd left off before she had discovered more about Gothel than she probably should have known.

It wasn't the truth of his past—whatever that might even be —that bothered her. After all, she had formed her entire crew from thugs and mercenaries. She had no doubt they'd had a criminal past, because they had taken to the life of the pirate quite easily.

Then there was Draku Rin, who had committed most of the crimes listed on the books for the fifteen colonies without any sign of remorse, and routinely did stints in cryo for his lawbreaking. To people like Rin and her crew, laws were simply guidelines that could be nudged aside when they became too inconvenient.

Of course, some crimes were unforgivable to Zel, but she got the impression that Gothel hadn't committed those kinds of crimes. He just didn't strike her as that kind of man. Strange as it was, she suspected that honor bound Gothel, despite his gruffness and rudeness.

Whether his personal code of honor aligned with her own was another question, and one she didn't have an answer for, but she hadn't exactly come to this world with clean hands herself. Not that she had ever killed anyone, but she had hurt people, despite her rules not to. Gothel had been the one to point that out to her.

What bothered her about her discovery was that it only raised more questions about him that he would never answer, especially since she'd been caught invading his privacy. He had been a lot calmer than she had any right to expect after what she'd done, and she did regret it. She only wished he would accept her apology.

During those days she spent alone, she did a lot of thinking as she carried out her assigned tasks, growing more adept at finding the parts listed, identifying the husks of the spaceships with more facility each day, and learning the best ways to extract the parts intact.

By the end of the week, she had grown so good at her job that she could spend most of her time thinking of other things as she performed her work on autopilot.

Gothel made her feel childish, and not because he was so much older than her. He reminded her that it was her mind that had yet to grow up, and she wasn't comfortable with that reminder. She knew she had been sheltered by both her wealth and her status, and her parent's determination to keep her isolated from any lived experiences.

In fact, that was exactly why she had rebelled so much in her twenties, but as Gothel had made clear, even in her rebellion, she had been sheltered. She had never had the opportunity to learn the most important lessons. There had never been any serious stakes for her.

Even in this last crime she had committed, her crew had

faced the serious consequences, while she was cooling her heels on a scrap heap, just waiting for her parents to get over their anger at her. Then she would end up right back where she'd started—whiling away her days in the lap of luxury, trapped by the same wealth and status that also sheltered and protected her from life.

It wasn't easy to face the flaws in her character head on and admit to them. She wanted to deny that there were any, but they were there, staring her in the face—unavoidable after her confrontation with Gothel.

She thought she had the right to do whatever she wanted because of her position. She considered herself above those who weren't noble born. Life was a game to her, and the people around her were just the pawns.

They were all ugly realizations to come to about herself, because they reminded her too much of her parents. She really was just like them—despite how much she had tried to be different. She kept thinking she would be better than them, but whenever doing the right thing grew inconvenient, she slipped back into the old habits and the old mindset.

She had felt perfectly fine invading Gothel's space, because she was a princess, and he was a commoner.

But there was nothing common about him—at least, not that she had seen. Each new clue about his past made her more curious, until she was ravenous with hunger for knowledge about him.

She knew it was growing into an obsession, and maybe part of that was because she had nothing else to do here other than visit with Rampion in the evenings, but she suspected that a lot of Gothel's draw was in the fact that he didn't see her as most other humans did.

To him, she wasn't a symbol of either wealth or oppression. She wasn't a pocketbook he could manipulate into providing luxuries for him. She wasn't a pawn he could use to further his own status. He wanted nothing at all to do with her.

To him, she was a nuisance. No one had ever been so dismissive of her in her life.

There was also her inability to resist an impossible challenge, which Gothel had become the moment he'd looked at her perfect face and figure and had made an expression of disgust. In the beginning, she had to admit—to her shame—that it had been pettiness that had made her want to compel him to see her as beautiful and desirable. She'd wanted him to suffer knowing he could never have her.

That was simply another part of her childishness that she had to abandon, and it was a difficult one to let go, but when it came to Gothel, her feelings on the matter had changed significantly. Especially since she had to acknowledge that she wouldn't be out of his reach if he desired her. At least, not until her parents found out and did something terrible to him in punishment.

They were always there in her life, hovering over her, even when they were many lightyears away. She had never really been free from them, and Gothel had made that clear to her too.

Rampion dealt with her quiet introspection better than she could have hoped, showing that the AI was getting better at reading social cues and knowing when to respond to them—and how to respond to them. Being in his company each evening had been relaxing, especially since she'd spent all day on edge with both the hope and the fear that she would run into Gothel—neither of which was realized.

Rampion's demeanor towards her was so different from Gothel's that it was like night and day. The AI treated her like a princess, but only all the best parts of being a princess. He deferred to her whenever he asked what she wanted to do during their visits. He listened attentively to every word she said. He told her repeatedly that he adored her company, and always looked forward to her visits. His words and behavior soothed her battered ego and brushed away all her self-doubts.

He was wonderful.

Even if it was only a temporary reprieve. Because Zel knew in her heart that Gothel was right, and Rampion was wrong about her.

"I have completed more devices for this hardware," Rampion said with an excited tone one evening a week after the incident, in lieu of his usual greeting.

Zel raised her eyebrows as she stepped off the elevator and onto the balcony, then followed him into his tower room. "Really? I didn't realize you required any more hardware now that you've finished your digestive system."

He cast a glance back at her, wearing his rubberized face, though he had yet to put the false skin over it, so it wasn't quite as unnerving floating on his body as it could have been. "I have been waiting to show it to you, but I think I will wait a bit longer. I want to make sure it is perfect."

When they reached their seats, he bent down and plucked something out of a jar that sat on his seat. The fake skin no longer covered his hands, now that he wasn't testing out the stimuli response of it.

She waited while he lifted his hand to his face, kept it there for a brief moment, then turned around to face her, blinking the eyelids of his false face.

Zel also blinked—in surprise. He was now wearing some kind of false lens over his iris-like eye that made it look human. He had emerald green irises now, and they no longer glowed with light.

"They can fool retinal scanners," he said with pride, tapping his face beside the new eye. "Do you like them, Zel?"

In truth, those human-looking eyes in his face were almost as unsettling as the face itself, floating on the cables and wires that covered his hardware. Still, it was an improvement in terms of him fitting in at some point with humans. "It's… uh… very nice."

He blinked again, and when he opened his eyes, the false lens had turned a lovely, vibrant purple shade, like her own irises. "They also change colors on my command, so I can take on any eye color. My research shows that eye colors were not as varied on Old Earth as they are now, but I prefer your eye color the most. It is beautiful—just like you, Zel."

Like always, the flattery soothed her like a cooling balm. Before she had come to this place, she had believed she hated being beautiful, but after Gothel's continual rejection of her appearance, her pride had faltered to the point where she lapped up compliments with great thirst. Rampion made her feel better about herself, and she was grateful to him for that. He obviously adored her, and the fact that he wanted his eye color to match hers was charming and delightful.

"I think your new eyes are very beautiful, Rampion," she said, this time with more enthusiasm.

Rampion's smile, even on a false face, was beatific. "I think you will be very pleased with the other modifications I will be making to this hardware, Zel. I will complete them very soon, and then I will show you what it all looks like when it is installed."

She smiled with encouragement. "I'm sure you will look amazing. You've worked very hard for this."

He nodded, the slightly mechanical sound the movement used to make no longer happening, as if he had refined his hardware to eliminate that sound. "It was all for a purpose, Zel. I will be the perfect man when this is all finished. The perfect *human* man."

CHAPTER 18

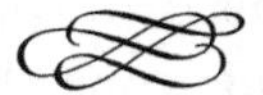

GOTHEL

The girl was going to drive him crazy—if he hadn't already crossed that bridge long ago and this was all just an extended fever dream.

At least she was no longer actively searching for him to bedevil him with whatever new plots popped up in her pretty, little head. Ever since he had been alerted to his stasis box being opened and had rushed back to his shack to find her staring at the old ID card, she had been suitably warned away from him. That had never been his plan, even though the result of her invasion of his privacy should have made him happy.

Nothing about seeing what was sealed away in that box ever made him happy though. Still, it surprised him that he *wasn't* more pleased by the fact that, now, Rapunzel didn't hunt him down or wait around to catch him getting food. He had been living inside the hull of an old ship at the edge of the property in order to avoid having her find him, since the first week she had arrived, and he'd spotted the mischief glittering in her unnatural eyes.

At that time, he had worried about her playing some kind of

prank on him, and didn't want to end up hurting her by accident in an automatic response to perceived danger.

The longer she remained on his moon, the more he worried about another temptation that hadn't immediately been a problem, but had become one fast enough to surprise him.

He had lived far too long not to notice the looks she'd been giving him lately. Looks his own appearance should have been enough to dissuade from someone like her. It was likely she was bored, and he was the only man around to keep her company, but it didn't make it easier to ignore those heated glances, so he stayed away from her.

At first, his own distaste for the genetically engineered nobles—many of them clones, which left their actual status as human in question, as far as he was concerned—had been enough to keep him cold when he looked at Rapunzel.

Yet, the more time he spent in her company—as much as he worked to avoid it—the more he saw the person beneath the doll-like perfection of her façade. She was charming, outgoing, funny, and filled with mischief.

She also had a streak of arrogance that kept her firm little chin lifted around him, but he wasn't blind to the compassion in her eyes. Unlike most royals, she did care about people—she just hadn't learned the consequences of her actions and how they hurt people she never intended to hurt. Gothel knew from personal experience what a hard lesson that was to learn.

She also worked like a demon. He struggled to find work to keep her busy and send to her datapad to keep it filled with tasks. She performed so efficiently that she was running through his backlist of projects. Soon, he would have to actually train her for the more difficult break-downs and extractions, and that meant he would have to spend time with her. That was something he didn't want to do.

He hadn't expected the princess to actually *do* any of the jobs he had given her. Based on their latest message, her parents had really only sent her to this moon to keep her away from any potential negative influences, until they could arrange another marriage for her.

Gothel knew that once they had some poor sucker lined up, they would send a ship for her and take her back to her own colony for her wedding—in shackles if they had to. They probably wouldn't thank him for putting her through so much work that she would have calluses on her perfect, soft hands.

He didn't really care what they thought, since he had only taken the job because he'd been bored and had wanted to break down the spirit of a rebellious royal who had turned to piracy. It was his own fault that he hadn't expected that pirate to be a princess and not a prince. He should have known better than to not have checked.

He'd had plans to put the "pirate-prince" through the wringer so the arrogant little nit would never want to interfere with the shipping lanes again, but had to rapidly adjust those plans when he met Rapunzel. Though he had learned the hard way that he couldn't give her too much free time, or she might come up with something devious to mess with him.

He certainly wasn't bored any longer, and as far as he was concerned, her parents couldn't pick her up soon enough. He figured they would have a difficult time finding some prince willing to marry her. Not because she wasn't as pretty as any picture, but because the mind behind that lovely face was too lively for the nobility.

No prince would keep her in her place, and that was one thing Gothel couldn't help but like and respect about her. She might still act like a royal, but she was fighting it enough that someday, she could become a truly decent person.

Not that he had any right to judge decency—unless it was to contrast it with what he was. Her expression when she'd watched him stuff the old uniform shirt and ID card back into the box had been very telling about her opinion of him.

It only reinforced his certainty that he needed to stay away from her. Nothing could come of her inexplicable interest in him, even if they could ever get past the fact that her parents would want to assassinate him for even thinking about having a romantic relationship with their princess. He wasn't a good person, and he had a past she could never know about. A past he would kill to keep a secret.

He definitely needed her off his moon.

CHAPTER 19

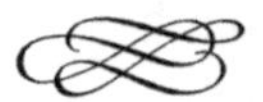

GOTHEL

Gothel was in a tough place. He had to keep tabs on Rapunzel just to make sure she didn't get into any more trouble, but he didn't like to use surveillance drones on her, because he didn't really want to see her visually.

Her beauty really was stunning, but that wasn't what appealed to him—in fact, it had the opposite effect, at least in the beginning. It was the animation in her features, even when she was alone, that drew his eye whenever he saw her. She wore her thoughts in her facial expressions, her eyes widening and her full lips spreading into a grin whenever she found the part she was searching for, or her brows pinching together and her mouth tilting down as she stomped around the scrapyard in frustration.

She was adorable even when he wasn't around her, and that irritated him, because it made her likable.

Likable was a dangerous place for her to be. It was the kind of place that started to give a man ideas he shouldn't be having. Ideas that could get him killed—or worse.

Instead of using the drones, he just checked the sensors throughout the day to see which ones she had tripped and at what time. That let him know she was going about her tasks in the yard without him having to see her visually. Then, once he was certain she had retreated to her shack at the end of the day to pass out in what had to be exhaustion after such hard work, he could check on the warehouse and see her progress.

And usually grab something from the food replicator, though he had been debating lately if he shouldn't take Rapunzel's advice and have real food shipped in, since he was growing heartily tired of the taste of protein paste, no matter what form it was mashed into and what artificial flavorings were added. They could never quite match the true flavor of the food they were mixed in to imitate.

Not to mention the scent of the food. He missed how the smell of food had made the flavor just that much more savory or sweet on his tastebuds. Scent created powerful links in his mind, and some odors would send him into flashback memories he would rather avoid, while some scents—like Rapunzel's soft, citrus-and-floral scent, would make him daydream of impossible futures.

He was thinking about scent when he made his daily trip to Rampion's tower, running through the pass code without flinching inwardly at saying Rapunzel's name. He kept telling himself he was going to change it, but never did, for reasons he didn't want to examine too closely.

On cue, Rampion sent down the elevator, and Gothel braced himself to greet the AI. It was always a game between them, each of them speaking carefully so as not to give too much away to the other. Rampion forever tried to learn more than he should know, and Gothel tried to keep the AI in the dark as much as possible.

This time, when he stepped off the elevator and onto the balcony, Rampion had sent his hardware out to meet Gothel, his metal skeleton face covered by cables and wires looking just as it always did, though Gothel could swear Rampion appeared more animated than he had been just yesterday. In fact, the AI's irises fluttered between expanding and contracting, as if he was too excited to control his hardware properly. Either that, or it was a malfunction.

Gothel gestured to his eyes. "Looks like your optics need an adjustment. Let me get my tools, and I'll take care of it."

Rampion put out a hand to stop him. "No. It is a minor software malfunction. I am correcting it now."

As he spoke, his irises stabilized, then spun open fully. "Good day to you, Commander Gothel."

Gothel grunted in reply, still eyeing Rampion's irises suspiciously. "That easy of a fix, eh?"

Rampion managed a passable shrug that had Gothel's eyebrows lifting. "I have been working on becoming more self-sufficient."

Gothel crossed his arms over his chest. "That ain't really the kind of thing I want you doing."

Rampion lowered his gaze. "You said that I should learn to use this mobile hardware."

"I said keep yourself busy, because I don't need a bored AI around the place. That don't mean I want you to be self-sufficient. I'll deactivate that hardware if I have to, Rampion. You hear me?"

Rampion put both hands up in a staying motion, waving them in front of his hardware. "No! Please, Commander! Don't force me back into the ship's computer."

The machine actually shuddered with horror at the thought, and Gothel pushed back the surge of pity he felt for Rampion. He understood what it felt like to be trapped—locked away from the world.

The AI might be just a cluster of programs that had attained sentience, but it was still alive, and Gothel wasn't keen on making living creatures suffer.

That didn't mean he could entirely trust the AI, though

Rampion was obedient enough to listen to his orders without question most of the time. The biggest problem with him was that he had boundless curiosity that could grow tiresome, but at least he didn't have the access to the satellite links that would allow him to jump onto the extranet for answers.

Rampion was currently limited by his hardware, and the fact that Gothel had EMP mines buried at the base of the tower that would activate if Rampion ever tried to escape it with his mobile hardware.

"I don't want to do that to you. But I will, if you leave me no choice."

Rampion lowered his hands. "Of course, Commander Gothel. I will follow your orders. I would not wish to do anything to displease you."

Gothel waved away the obsequious words as he sniffed the air in Rampion's cluttered tower room. For an AI, Rampion was a complete slob, and left heaps and bundles of cables and wires hanging out everywhere.

"Smells odd in here. I can't quite place it, but that scent reminds me of something."

Rampion joined him, standing beside him as Gothel continued to sniff, swinging his head from side to side as if that would help him identify the source of that smell. It wasn't a bad odor, having a briny quality to it. It was just different from the usual musty, stale plastic and metal and wire odors that filled Rampion's tower room. The new odor reminded him of something, and then he realized it was the beach—that was a scent he hadn't smelled in a very long time.

"I cannot smell," Rampion said, staring fixedly at Gothel's nose. "Is it a pleasant thing?"

Gothel broke his attention away from trying to identify that scent and returned it to Rampion. "Not always. Sometimes, a stink is overwhelming, if you're unfortunate enough to be exposed to it, but smells cement the memories in my head, and summon them back later."

Rampion put a hand to his wire-covered metal chin. "I wonder if this ability to smell could be synthesized for this hardware."

Gothel narrowed his eyes as he stared at Rampion. "Don't be thinking of synthesizing anything for that hardware. It's only so you can move around. Not so you can blend in with humans. I already told you, now ain't the time to be walking among humans when you're an AI. Maybe someday they'll forget what they lost to AIs, but that day ain't today, and it ain't likely to be anytime soon."

"Perhaps, the time to walk among humans for me will be after you die, Commander Gothel."

"You thinking of killing me then, Rampion. Gotta say, you'll find it a bit of a challenge."

Rampion's irises fully expanded as he held up both hands. "No, sir. I would never kill a human. This is part of my core programming. I am incapable of directly taking a human life. You know this."

"Just so long as you remember it."

"I have perfect recollection, Commander Gothel."

Gothel swept his gaze over the contents of the tower room one last time before turning back to Rampion. "All right then. Let's have a look at your hardware and see if you need any adjustments. Then I got to be going. Got other more important work to do."

CHAPTER 20

GOTHEL

Gothel had been so careful about avoiding Rapunzel that he had seen no sign of her for almost two weeks of this world's days. Foolishly, he started to drop his guard, so he wasn't prepared when she pounced.

"Ah ha!" she said from behind him, causing him to jerk in surprise, the plasma cutter scorching the metal panel above the one he was trying to cut.

With a deep sigh, he shut off the cutter and set it down, then turned to face her, reluctant to look at her.

She stood with her arms crossed over perfectly-sized breasts —just large enough for a man's hands—her shapely hip cocked. "So here's where you've been hiding. I knew I'd track you down eventually."

"Don't know why you'd want to, after what you seen."

She shrugged one shoulder, capped with toned muscle that somehow still managed to look very delicate and feminine. "So you did some time. As did most of my crew, I'd wager. As *I* should have."

The shadows that filled her violet eyes and drew her lips into a frown at those last words reminded him that she still felt guilt over the trouble she'd led her crew into. Again, he couldn't help liking her because of the fact that she acknowledged her own fault in that incident. Not many nobs would have bothered to even care, much less take the blame for it on their own shoulders—even when they were the leaders.

"Wouldn't be much point in putting you on ice. Never did understand the purpose of freezing cons."

She cocked her head, studying him with a dangerously curious gaze. "I think they freeze them because they know they won't be able to keep them locked up. I wouldn't want to try to restrain someone like Draku Rin, if he didn't want to be there. I've never seen an ID card like yours. Where were you incarcerated?"

He looked away from her, studying the scorch mark on the paneling to avoid the urge to study her face instead. "That was a long time ago, kid. Before they were making con-sicles. They had ways to keep us locked up just fine. 'Course, there weren't no ajda'yans in my lockup."

She shook her head as her brows pinched with concentration. "That's strange. I thought the colony ships used cryostasis to freeze prisoners during the Exodus. The way I recall it from my history lessons, they did it instead of spacing them because they knew they would need the extra labor when they found a world to develop."

Gothel shrugged, trying for a nonchalance he didn't feel. Rapunzel had already proven that gruff answers and brushing off her questions altogether didn't discourage her, so he searched for some other way to get her off this subject. "Don't you have something better to do right now, girl?"

She grinned and shook her head, her golden ponytail swinging behind her at the movement. "I finished all my tasks. Now, I think it's time you train me to use that," she pointed to the plasma cutter, "and any other equipment and tools I might need for more difficult tasks."

He glanced at the cutter, debating whether it would be a good idea to put such a thing in her hands. Then he acknowledged that he really just didn't want to spend that much time around her while he trained her. It was bad enough being around her for even this long. Her scent teased him, drifting to him on some cursed breeze that had made its way into the still confines of the ship's hull. Somehow, despite her coveralls being noticeably dirty and stained from her daily efforts, she still managed to smell as fresh as clean linen. Just the hint of sweat clung to her, but it was sexy, rather than off-putting, as were the smudges of dirt and oil on her cheeks and forehead.

The best way he had found to get her to back off was to make her angry enough at him that she couldn't stand the sight of him anymore. That usually gained him a day or two of peace and quiet.

"Don't see much point in training you. According to your parents, you're only here until they hunt up a husband for you. No sense wasting time learning a new skill when you'll be back in the palace under some rutter...."

He couldn't even finish the crude sentence, because the image of it popped into his head and made his vision red with rage at the thought of some boorish, noble oaf putting his hands on the woman before him. He hadn't killed in a long time, but just the thought of it made him want to.

Her eyes narrowed into slits as her jaw squared with mutiny. "There's no way I'm going to marry some pimply-faced prince just to please them. I'd rather stay here until I'm as old and decrepit as you are, and *I'm* the one walking around growling and grumbling at anyone who dares to speak to me."

"You got a smart mouth, girl. I 'spect that's why it's taking your parents so long to track a prince down for you. Probably none of them left what isn't well aware of it."

Despite his words, he had to hold back a chuckle at her audacity. Usually his growling and grumbling was enough to scare unwanted conversation away, but she wasn't the type to back down from a challenge.

That was probably one reason he found her too entertaining. He wasn't immune to the weight of loneliness bowing his shoulders. He knew that was a big part of her motivation too. If he could just forget that he was a man, and she a beautiful woman who smelled like heaven, then perhaps he wouldn't have to work so hard to scare her off, and they could actually be enough company for each other.

If she had actually been the rebellious kid he kept calling her, instead of a woman grown, he wouldn't have had to warn her away.

She smirked at him. "Why don't you run away with me, Gothel? Take me out past Nowhere, into the uncharted stars." She gestured to the ship surrounding them. "Surely, we can rebuild one of these old heaps and leave this rock together."

The suggestion was so unexpectedly appealing that Gothel almost considered it. "And why would I want to do that? You think I want to be trapped in space with some kid nattering away in my ear all day long?"

The smile that tilted her lips as she took a step towards him was full of wickedness as her gaze took him in from head to toe. He knew what she saw, because he worked very hard to make sure that was what everyone saw, so he had no idea why the sight of him put that hungry look into her eyes.

"I don't have to talk... if my mouth is otherwise occupied." She licked her lips, and he felt it in his cock and balls like she'd dragged that pink tongue down his shaft.

"What did I tell you about that sort of thing?"

He quickly turned his back on her, staring at the burnt paneling and trying to picture the ugliest alien creature he could think of to force his erection back down so it didn't tent his coveralls. "I ain't interested! Now go on, git outta here. I ain't gonna train you, so find something else to occupy yer time."

If he spent even another few minutes in her company, he doubted he could resist the temptation of her. He also realized that she'd found a new way to bedevil him, despite his best efforts to ignore her. This could just be another way she dealt with her boredom—driving a man crazy with lust, when he knew he couldn't have her.

She probably thought it was only the fear of her parent's reprisals that stopped him from accepting her come-ons, but Gothel didn't worry himself much about the royals and their assassins. He had faced off far worse than that in his long life. He was more concerned that he would do something incredibly stupid that would reveal secrets Rapunzel could not discover.

She made a disappointed sound behind him, and he heard the thud of her foot slamming down on the metal flooring in frustration. She never could seem to keep her emotions from showing, which made her seem more genuine than most people he'd met, even if she was a royal.

"Fine, *Commander* Gothel, or should I just call you Joshua?"

He shivered at the sound of the name spoken in her musical voice, especially since she added a caressing note to it. "Didn't give you leave to use that name."

He felt her approach, even if he couldn't hear her stealthy steps. Her breath whispered across the back of his neck, moving the wispy gray hairs that waved all around his cap. "You know us royals. We're not in the habit of asking for permission. We just take what we want."

"Yer on thin ice, and the surface is already cracking." He glanced over his shoulder, meeting her purple eyes, trying to remind himself that they were unnatural and inhuman, and not admire the beauty of them or the person he saw behind them. "I told you to stay away from me."

"Many times," she said with a smirk. "I've just never been very good at following directions."

With that, she spun on her heel and trotted off, her hips swaying enticingly as wicked laughter trailed behind her.

She'd won that round, and she was letting Gothel know that she was aware of it.

He stared at the paneling in front of him, his cock still as hard as the metal he'd been cutting. Once he was sure she was out of earshot, he banged his forehead against the wall, hoping the pain would ease his erection.

Instead, he just knocked his hat off and put a dent in the paneling, but it would be a long time before the tent in his coveralls went down, and he spent the rest of the day cursing the princess. She was pure evil.

CHAPTER 21

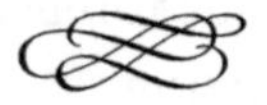

GOTHEL

The damned princess was back to hunting him, and this time, Gothel truly felt hunted, rather than just annoyed by her persistence. She had spotted the crack in his armor, and she wasn't going to give up now. He had to avoid her, but it was getting harder and harder to do so, and not just because the scrapyard—big as it was—wasn't infinite.

He had taken to escaping to the standing hulls portion of the yard—where ancient alien battleships had been set up as a temporary city of towers long before humans came onto the galactic scene. That was where Rampion's tower was. It was also the place he had expressly forbidden Rapunzel to go.

Not that he doubted she had disobeyed him and made her way to this part of the yard, but as long as she didn't find out about Rampion, he wouldn't worry about it too much. She couldn't get into the tower anyway.

Rampion was always willing to visit with him, though talking with the AI wasn't much of a distraction from the beautiful and clever woman now actively hunting him through his own scrapyard. Still, he needed whatever distraction the AI could give, so he stood at the base of Rampion's tower and called out the pass code.

When Rampion didn't immediately answer the intercom, Gothel barked out an order to him to send down the elevator.

"You are early, Commander," Rampion said, his tone sounding strained.

"What difference does it make? Just send the elevator." He glanced over his shoulder, suddenly worried that Rapunzel would appear from the shadows of the neighboring towers with a gleeful "ah ha!" and then end up discovering one of his biggest —and most dangerous—secrets. "Hurry it up, Rampion!"

He relaxed only a little as the elevator clattered to life above him, then extended and lowered on the cables with loud clanks. He jumped onto it when it was still well above the ground, snapping at Rampion to raise it again.

When he reached the balcony, he didn't wait for the elevator to stop moving before he jumped off it and clambered into the airlock room, then tried the door to get into the tower room.

"Why is this door locked? Open up, now. I don't have the patience for this."

The door spun open and then slowly swung aside. Rampion stood on the other side, staring at Gothel—through eyes that could have belonged to any human being.

"What the fuck?"

The AI looked human, from his head full of thick, black hair down to his toes, that were even covered with nails that had to be synthetic. The only hints that he wasn't fully human came from the glowing lines on his body that indicated where the marine kayota that must be responsible for his false skin had met up and were even now joining with the other colonies to complete the covering of skin. The new skin had also been marked by tattooed sensors to increase the mobile hardware's responsiveness to the environment to a superhuman degree.

"What have you done, Rampion?" Gothel said with a foreboding building inside him as he swept his gaze up and down Rampion's new, human-looking body.

The AI had spared no effort in making it look as perfect an example of a human male as possible, right down to the dick hanging long and flaccid at his groin over a sizable scrotum.

Gothel covered his eyes with his hands, rubbing his forehead. "Why? Why would you do this?"

"I can blend in with humans now. I have even added the capability of detecting scent as a human would. It took some time to mesh the feedback sensors with my neural pathways, but I was successful. I can now smell you, Gothel, though it is not as pleasant as I had hoped."

"I been working hard, and a man sweats, you—Ah fuck, never mind."

He lowered his hand, shaking his head. "Put some damned clothes on, since you went to the trouble to make yourself anatomically correct. Humans don't walk around in the all-together around just anyone."

Rampion glanced around the tower room as if searching for something. "I do not possess any articles of clothing. Tell me, is sweat necessary to pass as human? I believe that I can synthesize—"

"Good god, Rampion! You've done enough! If you tell me that dick you got there can ejaculate, I'm going to deactivate you! Stop synthesizing. Now." His tone on the last word brooked no argument. "I don't even want to know how you managed all of this, but I'm putting an end to it."

"I cannot let you do that, Commander Gothel. I have come too far to fail now."

Gothel reacted before Rampion had finished speaking, but he didn't make it to the balcony fast enough. The AI moved with inhuman speed, cracking Gothel across his skull. Darkness enveloped him as he crashed to the ground.

~

When he awakened, he was securely tied to one of the seats in Rampion's tower room with metal cables that had been twisted around his chest and arms, as well as his hips—all the way down to his ankles. Rampion stood in front of him, looking down at him with eyes that were now purple.

The exact shade of Rapunzel's eyes.

"Oh, no." Gothel shook his head, trying to deny the evidence before him.

"I have made myself the perfect, handsome prince for Rapunzel. This is as it should be. We are meant to be together, just as all the romance movies would show it. We are fated. Why else would everything have happened the way it did?"

"I have sensors all around this place, dammit! I would have known if she'd tripped them."

Rampion's smile looked far too sly for Gothel to believe he had only just begun his plotting. "They were simple enough to hack into to conceal her visits."

"You damn fool machine!"

He tried not to allow the feeling of betrayal to take hold inside him. *Of course,* Rapunzel would disobey him, and of course, she would find Rampion. He had been the blind fool who had underestimated them both. He was paying for it now. He just hoped Rapunzel wouldn't also end up paying for it.

"She was fated to find me, and your pass code was very appropriate, don't you think? Do you not realize that you are the villain of this piece?"

Gothel stared at Rampion, taking in his shockingly human-looking appearance. He couldn't help but be impressed by how much Rampion had accomplished on his own. "I had figured as much," he said wryly. "Name always gave me problems—least until most humans forgot about the old stories."

"And now 'Rapunzel' is here!" Rampion's ecstatic smile looked eerily lifelike, and somehow, he had painted or enameled his teeth to no longer gleam like metal. "It is fate! Destiny!"

"No, you idiot. It's just unimaginative parents. They probably went down a list of 'princess' names and plucked that one out of the list because it sounds different. Stop making this more than a coincidence. Use yer logic. Yer a machine, for god's sake!"

Rampion's eyes narrowed on Gothel, and the AI leaned closer to him. "I am human now. I have done everything to become one."

Gothel sighed, eyeing Rampion's new skin. Bioluminescence rippled along his skin as Gothel stared at it—a sign of the unicellular kayota that lived within it to give his computer brain neural feedback. Gothel knew from experience just how effective that feedback loop was—how lifelike it felt.

"You can't just 'become' human. You either are, or you ain't. Why would you want to be human anyway? It ain't like they done a very good job with their species."

Rampion waved away his words with an airy gesture. "I will show humanity the way to perfection. When I have married the princess and taken my rightful place at her side, we will rule her colony, improving upon the inhabitants until we are strong enough to conquer the other colonies. In that way, we will spread human perfection throughout the galaxy."

Gothel's worst fears about Rampion were being realized in that moment. He should have destroyed the AI, and also killed the creators of it, when he had the chance, but he had been too curious at the time—and perhaps loneliness had been a part of his problem. He had isolated himself in this scrapyard for too long, and the temptation for company had been too much to resist. So he had kept Rampion alive, but he hadn't been able to stop the inevitable logic-errors that convinced Rampion he needed more than a life lived inside the computer hardware of this ship.

"Listen, boy, I know you think you understand humans, cuz of all that crap they put in yer head, but they ain't like that. Not at all. You ain't gonna last five minutes, once they figure out the truth about you. Not that you'll be leaving this tower without getting deactivated by an EMP mine. You really think I didn't plan for this possibility when I gave you that mobile hardware?"

Rampion's sharp gaze drifted from Gothel's angry expression down to his arms, secured too tightly even for the cybernetic limbs to break their bindings. "I do not think you would be so careless with EMP mines. There must be a device on you that keeps them from going off, and I will locate that device before I leave here."

Gothel *did* have an inhibitor signal-emitter that would stop the proximity mines from going off when his cybernetics were in their vicinity. It was unfortunate that Rampion had figured that out.

"This ain't what you want, Rampion. Think about it logically for a minute. You'll never succeed in your plans, and—"

Rampion put a hard finger against Gothel's lips. So hard that it forced Gothel's head back. "Do not tell me what I can do. You do not own me anymore, *Commander* Gothel. Soon, I will be free of you, and you will be the one forever trapped in this tower—like the villain you are. Then I will find Rapunzel, and we will go off to marry and live happily ever after in our kingdom among the stars."

He was speaking the last words in a singsong tone, as crazy as any insane human. He spun around on one heel and went to his cluster of cables and wires that had been pulled from the ship's paneling. He plucked up some tools, and Gothel noticed a scanner and an extractor among them.

He closed his eyes and let his head drop back as resignation settled over him. He should try to fight this, but he knew already that there was no breaking free of his bonds. Rampion might be naïve, but he wasn't stupid.

No, he was far too intelligent. That was the problem.

"Now, Gothel, I will just run a quick scan, and then we will see about getting past those EMP mines. I think it would be best if you are not conscious for this, because I will require those clothes, so I am just going to put you out in a moment. I also think it is important that you remain in the tower, so I will be leaving those mines in place. Your limbs will not do you much good if they have been deactivated."

Rampion's tone turned mocking. "Do not worry. I will find Rapunzel before she returns here tonight, so there will not be any need for the final confrontation. It would be quite embarrassing for you, I suspect."

Gothel sighed and opened his eyes to meet the crazed, purple eyes of Rampion. "You're making a mistake. I tried to protect you, but no one else will."

Rampion grinned. "I look human now. They will never know what walks among them until it is too late."

CHAPTER 22

Zel's Gothel-hunt was yet another failure that day, and she was frustrated that she had come so close to affecting him, only for him to run and hide yet again. She should have completed her seduction of him when she had the chance, but at the same time, she had been afraid that if he wasn't the one to seek her out, he would instantly regret anything happening between them, and would find a way to kick her off this rock permanently.

No, she needed to keep things just on the edge, so he let her remain here in the scrapyard long enough for her seduction of him to work. The only problem was that she couldn't seduce him if he kept hiding from her.

This wasn't about punishing him, or teasing him, or even messing with his head. She really wanted to be with him now, sensing the loneliness inside him that mirrored her own. He wasn't working as a caretaker of this scrapyard because he lacked funds and had no other options. He had come here to escape the galaxy, for some mysterious reasons of his own, but he wasn't able to escape his very human need for companionship.

Zel understood that, and felt like she understood Gothel too. Granted, it would be a difficult challenge for them to be together, but she would find a way to make it work. Gothel was older than her, true, by a significant amount, and he was a commoner—which was honestly the much larger hurdle—but her parents would just have to deal with her choices. Especially now that she knew he wasn't unaffected by her.

It infuriated her that her parents were planning on marrying her off once they found a suitable prince. She had known it was coming eventually, but they had made it sound like her exile was intended for her to learn humility, not for her to cool her heels far away from any potentially negative influences until they could saddle her to some boring, handsome prince.

There would be no brooding mystery to a prince. No dark secrets. No harsh words meant to keep her at a distance that only made her more curious and determined to get closer.

She wanted Gothel, and she would have him and only him by the time she was finished. And if her parents didn't like that, they could go to Old Earth, for all she cared.

He had escaped her this time, but she was determined to find him the next day. She debated whether she should bother to visit Rampion tonight as she finished her evening washup and headed to the food shack. She was tired after running around the scrapyard all day, poking into every nook and cranny and ancient ship hull looking for signs of Gothel. Since she planned another day of hunting tomorrow, she really should get her rest.

Still, Rampion was her friend, and she felt guilty about the thought of not visiting, since he was always so happy to see her and was clearly lonely.

So, despite her exhaustion and her buzzing excitement for the next day, she made her way through the forbidden area to Rampion's tower.

The discovery that the elevator was already down surprised her, and the way the little door on it hung open, swinging in the breeze with a metallic squeal, made her nervous. She jumped onto the elevator, then said the pass code.

She had to say it three more times before the elevator actually began its ascent, and now Zel felt really nervous.

It seemed to take forever to get to the top of the tower, and she didn't wait for the elevator to stop before she leapt onto the airlock door balcony. Then she rushed inside the airlock chamber. The inner door gaped open as well, and Zel hesitated at the portal, peering inside the shadowy room beyond.

Someone had turned out the lights, so that only the emergency lights that lined the corners of all the walls illuminated the room. She saw something moving among the cables and machinery, mostly hidden by the deep shadows cast by the cables. She was backing away from that mysterious thing when she heard a familiar voice—but not the one she was expecting.

"Not sure if you've got bad timing or great timing, girl."

She blinked in shock as her mind struggled to switch gears. She had been expecting Rampion to be the one hiding, for some unknown reason, among the cluster of cables and wires. The last person she expected to hear was Gothel, though he was always on her mind. She had searched all over for him, but now that she found him, the nerves gripping her stomach were a completely different kind than those that had plagued her every other time she had seen him.

"Wh-what are you doing here?" Her voice came out quavering and less confident than she liked.

"Could ask you the same question, but I already know the answer, you treacherous, little brat. Figured Rampion might have managed to track you down, but looks like he's not as smart as he should be. Or he just don't know this place. He'll be back here looking for you, so go on, git outta here."

"But, what happened? I don't understand."

"No, you *don't*. Ain't never stopped you, has it? You just barge right in and make a mess of things, cuz you ain't got the patience to stop and think about what you might end up setting into motion."

Zel felt the trembling in her limbs and hands, but hoped Gothel couldn't see it. The shadows were deep, so she couldn't make out much among the cables where he remained concealed, but that didn't mean he couldn't make out her form, standing among the emergency lights in the cleared area by the chairs.

"I didn't... I just wanted some company."

There was a heavy sigh from the shadowed figure of Gothel. "Just get out of here, Rapunzel. Before it's too late. Can you follow that *one* simple order? Or is even that much obedience too much for the princess to grant a commoner?"

"I just want to know what happened. I... I'm really sorry, Gothel. I never meant to cause problems...." She struggled to speak clearly around the lump in her throat.

Gothel shifted, like he would approach her, then muttered a curse and melted back into the shadows.

She caught just a glimpse of emergency light limning his naked skin, and realized that he didn't have any clothing on. That was probably why he hid among the cables.

His movement caused something to happen other than a sharp spear of lust that went through her at the hint of firm skin over hard, defined chest muscles. He might have a wrinkled face, but Gothel's body—from what she could see in the shadows—was still very well put together, especially since it didn't look like he was hunching over or bowing his shoulders anymore.

Her attention was drawn from him to the voice that spoke from the ship's intercom system after the movement that Gothel abruptly checked.

"I did not think you would remain in the tower, Commander, even with the threat of the mines lying at the base of it. I had not wished to kill you. After all, I am programmed to never kill a human. I guess that is not an issue anymore, is it?"

A beeping sound followed what must have been an automated recording of Rampion's voice.

"Fuck! That bastard set another trap for me. Damn you, girl, I said git the hell outta here!"

Suddenly, Gothel charged at her from the depths of the shadows, a cable held tightly in one of his hands.

She didn't have the chance to take in the details of his naked form before he roughly grabbed her with the other hand and dragged her towards the door, hauling her resisting form out to the balcony so quickly that she could barely catch her breath.

Then he wrapped the cable around her waist and jerked it tight, before shoving her with great force off the balcony.

Seconds later, an explosion rocked the tower as Zel plunged down towards the black sand far below, a scream trapped in her throat, but no sound leaving her lips.

The cable tightened, pulling her up short so that her head slammed against the side of the tower. Then the tension in the cable slackened as whatever mooring had held it inside the tower broke free after the devastating explosion above.

Zel saw stars with the pain of the impact to her skull. Then she saw nothing at all as she fell the rest of the way to the sand that surrounded the tower.

CHAPTER 23

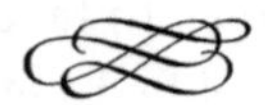

Rapunzel awakened to darkness. Her head ached so badly that the pain made her nauseous. It was far worse than the other pains that filled her body and sent urgent messages of alert to her brain. She didn't think any limbs were broken, but her waist throbbed where the cable had been wrapped around it, and probably bore a dark bruise.

She would have checked, but despite the fact that she knew her eyes had to be open, she couldn't see anything other than a blurred mixture of light and shadow.

When she sat up and looked down at her body, she could make out the darkness of the black sand and the lighter colors of her coveralls and arms and hands. She could also barely make out the gleam of silver from the cable still tied around her battered waist. But she couldn't bring her vision into focus and see the details. She only knew what these images were, because she had seen them before.

Looking straight ahead told her nothing new, nor did it bring her vision back. The strain of trying to see made her head ache even more. She lifted a shaking hand to it, gasping and pulling her hand away, turning her head automatically to study her hand, which had come away wet.

Her peripheral vision was completely gone, but she was able to spot the blur of her pale hand, streaked by a darker blur at her fingertips. When she brought it close to her face, she smelled blood. She didn't need to taste it to recognize what it was.

Zel moaned in pain and distress. Then she cried out when she recalled the other great impact of the explosion. She pushed herself to her feet with difficulty, clutching her aching head and gasping with pain. With slow, labored steps, she stumbled around in search of the tower.

"Gothel," she said in a whispered breath that she had intended to be a shout. She tried again, but her voice came out only slightly louder. "Gothel?"

The increased volume reverberated through her skull, making her flinch against the pain. She clenched one hand into a fist as she held onto her head with her other as if she could keep it from splitting open.

"Gothel!" She finally managed a shout that caused her to shiver in agony, but only her own echoes answered her back.

Her vision still nothing but a blur and only growing worse with each moment, she struggled to find the tower, dragging the length of cable behind her in her distraction. It got caught up on something, and she fought to untie it from her waist, biting off the cry of pain as the cable tightened around her waist before finally coming lose and falling away.

Then it occurred to her that she might be able to follow the cable back to the tower. She took it up in her hands and walked along the length of it, feeling the smooth cord of it sliding through her fingers as she followed it back to its origin. She found nothing at the end of it but a burnt, melted end with shredded wires sticking out of it.

Determined not to give up her search, she kept walking past

the cable, towards the dark blurs in front of her. One of them had to be the tower.

She fell over something that cut sharply into her coveralls, tearing open the skin of her leg.

Toppling over onto the ground, she managed to catch herself on her hands and knees. The impact shook her whole body and had her falling the rest of the way to the sand to curl up into the fetal position at the myriad pains in her body.

Zel wanted to just give up and lie there in the sand until someone came to find her, though her heart knew that someone wouldn't be Gothel—the one person she really wanted to see again. He was gone, and she still couldn't accept that. There was no way he could have survived that explosion. If he hadn't spent those last precious moments tying the cable around her waist and pushing her out of the tower, he could have saved himself instead, using that same cable.

He had given up his life for hers, and Zel realized in that moment that the better person had died today.

Now, she was in agony, couldn't see, and had no idea if she would even get her vision back. She had no idea what to do or where to go next. All she wanted to do was die right here with Gothel, so she wouldn't have to deal with the inevitable grief and guilt that hovered just beyond the boundaries of her immediate, acute pain—waiting to take over when that pain faded.

That would be a waste of Gothel's sacrifice, and she knew it. The right thing to do would be to carry on, go on living, and start fighting for more justice for her people, and perhaps, begin to build the bridges to end the warring among the fifteen colonies.

She had the wealth, position, and potential influence to affect real change in the galaxy, and she had been squandering it just to rebel against her parents. It was little wonder Gothel hadn't respected her, yet, he had still given up his life for hers. Selfishly, she wanted that to be because he had felt the same feelings she had for him, but she had to admit that in his mind, it was probably because he hoped she would use her status and position to help the people who needed it.

Zel hated doing the right thing. The right thing always came with the possibility of failure and heavy consequences. The right thing raised expectations, sometimes to a point that she could never meet. That was why she had been more than happy to give up that never-ending quest for perfection when Draku Rin had become her bodyguard and introduced her to mischief.

It had been so much easier to just mess up and make mistakes without fear or shame. She had convinced herself that there was something noble about rejecting her parents and the other elites, and their obsession with achieving a perfect state of being.

In the end, her precious rebellion had been just as frivolous and meaningless as their lifestyles. She had only ended up hurting people, and if those things she had pirated from enemy colonies had ever helped the people of her own colony, they had also made the nobility wealthier, because once "confiscated" by her parents, they had been distributed by the royal storehouses to the bounders—no doubt at significant cost to those with little means to pay.

Her parents had sent her to this world to keep her out of trouble long enough for them to pawn her off to some prince, but they had erred in that, because they hadn't counted on Gothel. He had shown her the truth about herself, and about the self-absorption that she shared with every other noble out there. He hadn't given her respect, because she had never earned it. She had expected it as her due, just like her parents.

Now, she was broken, blind, and lost. She had stumbled around so much that she wasn't sure what direction she was facing, or which one of the blurs around her was Rampion's tower. Her leg was now wet with blood where it had been cut by whatever sharp object had felled her, and her head pounded in a way that made her tense with each beat of her heart.

It would be so much easier to just lie down and go to sleep, even though the shivering in her body made it difficult to fully relax. Instead, she rolled slowly to her hands and knees again, and then climbed to her feet with great effort, hissing when she put weight on her wounded leg.

This time, as she moved forward, she was much slower and swung the foot of her uninjured leg out in front of her before each step to check that nothing blocked her path. This made her progress very slow, but she finally made it to a tower blur, putting her hands out to feel along the smooth metal paneling.

It was the wrong tower. She was sure of it.

Zel slid down the metal, her cheek pressed against the coolness of the tower, slickened by her hot and sudden tears as she fell to her knees. Her arms clutched the tower like a lover, holding on desperately, as if that imposing structure could possibly keep her safe from whatever unknown future now awaited her.

She needed to get to a communication console so she could try to send a message back to her parents. They would send someone to collect her and get her the proper medical treatment to cure her vision. The problem was that she had no idea where to find such a thing, and she had also never left the boundaries of the scrapyard, though she knew that one side of the scrapyard bordered a neighboring compound where Gothel had expressly forbidden her to go. Since there were people living there, she had obeyed Gothel's orders on that, not wanting anyone to get word back to him that she had trespassed.

Endless black sand desert surrounded the rest of the scrapyard. There were probably settlements beyond the wide expanse of sand and cracked mud, but she would never make it to them by stumbling around chasing indistinct blurs.

Still, she didn't have many options. She could try to find someone to help her, find the communications console Gothel used, or lie down right here and die. Though the last option sounded best to her, she owed Gothel her life. She was done squandering it out of selfishness. She would fight, as he had told her to fight. She would return to her colony and find a way to use her power and status to make things better.

Zel tied up the cut on her leg using the dirty handkerchief she kept in the cargo pocket of her work coveralls, which she normally used to keep the sweat from running into her eyes. That sweat now burned in her blurry vision as she struggled to take each laborious step forward, using her knowledge of the position of the moon and where the daylight should be coming from to help her navigate in what she hoped to be the right direction.

It was easy enough for her to avoid large objects that obstructed her path and showed up to her as blurs, but she had no peripheral vision at all, so had to be very careful about where she set her feet. That was one reason her progress ended up being so slow.

By the time she found a tower to settle against, slumping down into an exhausted heap with both her head and her leg pounding from the blood that pulsed in her wounds, she was shaking with the need to sleep and the need for some kind of pain relief. It was the second need which kept her from the oblivion of the first.

Exhaustion won out over pain, and even with her head feeling like it was going to echo the earlier explosion of Rampion's tower, Zel drifted off to sleep.

Music pulled her out of her slumber, groggy and disoriented, as if she had been drinking so heavily that she'd blacked out from the alcohol. Zel labored to push herself to her feet, blinking her eyes fruitlessly in an effort to focus her vision, which was still mostly just blurs and darkness.

The blurs themselves were growing dark, which meant that the terrible night that had passed into a terrible day was now becoming night again. That would explain why her stomach now ached—not only from nausea, but also hunger. It would also explain why her mouth felt sand-dune dry. She could go without food for a while, but she needed water, especially after her injuries.

The music sounded familiar, and her heart pounded as she recognized the source of it, though it was still a distance away. Only Rampion would have that music in his archives.

She still didn't know what had happened between Gothel and Rampion that ended up with Rampion setting a trap for Gothel, but she didn't think Rampion would hurt her.

Whatever had taken place between him and Gothel was something Rampion would need to explain, but right now, she needed help, and Rampion was the only person—technically speaking—around to give her aid.

She stumbled forward on lurching steps, working her way towards the music. She opened her mouth to shout for Rampion, but each attempt to yell caused spearing pain to shoot through her skull. She had to settle for just moving as quickly as she could, using sound alone to guide her. It felt like she had to walk for days and days before the repeating song finally grew louder, signaling that she was approaching the source.

It cut off abruptly when she stumbled past some blurs that could have been old ship's hulls, or just towering piles of scrap, for all she could tell.

"Rapunzel?" Alarm filled Rampion's voice as he rushed towards her, the increasing volume of it telling her he was near, though she still jumped a little when his hands grasped her upper arms firmly.

"My love, you are wounded! We must get you to the medical bay I have set up in my ship."

"S-ship?" she asked, her voice quavering on a gasp of pain as

Rampion's abrupt grasp shook her too much and caused agony to explode through her head.

"I am building us a ship to return to your colony. But I will explain all of that to you later. For now, you need medical attention immediately. Unfortunately, the working treatment pods were all salvaged out of the ship, but I have one in the process of being rebuilt. It can perform some basic functions and scans to ease the swelling in your head and close those wounds."

As he spoke, he drew her forward, towing her along in his wake in a way she couldn't resist, even if she had the strength to make the effort in that moment. She wouldn't have resisted at any rate, since she was in too much pain to protest the offer of medical treatment.

"I will take care of you, Zel. I will rescue my princess. Before you know it, you will be as good as new."

Rampion's strong hold on her arms kept her from falling when she stumbled over the threshold of some massive blur that led into darkness only dimly relieved by emergency lighting on the floors. Even that light disappeared from her peripheral vision as he led her through the corridors of the ship in the process of being rebuilt.

"It is not a ship worthy of a princess, but it was the only one space-worthy enough that I could get it up and running with what I could salvage here. The engine core is so outdated that no modern ship uses it anymore, but it is still in working order. Once I can harvest enough fuel for it, we will be off the ground and on our way."

"R-Rampion, please, tell me what's going on?" Zel's lip quivered as her body trembled from reaction, now that she was finally going to receive medical care.

"Shhh, my princess. I will explain everything in time." He pulled her to a stop, then began to tug on her coveralls.

She tried to slap his hands away from the seam of her coveralls, but her hands missed his, probably by a mile. "Stop that!"

"You must be naked to get into the medical pod, Zel. You know that."

She hadn't thought of that. Clothing and other contaminants were usually prohibited by the medical pods, which would wash the body in a decontaminant spray before beginning scans and wound treatment. Still, even knowing she needed to disrobe for this didn't make it any easier to strip down in front of Rampion. For some reason, it made her distinctly uncomfortable to be seen naked by him, despite the fact that he was a robot.

"I'll take my coveralls off myself."

"Do not be difficult, Zel. You are clearly having trouble seeing. Allow me to help you."

He followed up his words by undoing the seam of her coveralls, stripping them apart with such swiftness that she couldn't protest any further before her outer covering fell away from her body.

Now she was shaking for another reason as she stood there cold and clothed only in her underpinnings. "Please, my head hurts too much to think. Just help me into the pod."

"Not yet, Zel. You know you must remove all your clothes. Here," his voice came from lower as he bent down in front of her. "Allow me to remove these old garments. You are not going to need them anymore."

She cried out in shock and dismay as Rampion tore away her chest covering and underwear, stripping her completely bare.

"There, now we can get you all better." Rampion's tone sounded jarringly cheerful, despite how humiliating and miserable the situation was.

He patted her clenched fist. "Come now, Zel. It is not that bad. We will have you fixed up in no time."

Then he took her hand and drew her towards the medical pod.

Since the room was mostly dark, Zel couldn't distinguish one blur from another, so she had no choice but to trust him to lead her in the right direction. She didn't realize she was holding her breath until he put her hand on the ledge of the medical pod, laying it flat so she could grip the ledge. Then he stroked his fingers over her chilled skin in a way that made her skin crawl. It was only then that she took a much-needed gulp of air, and that was so she could speak her protest of his caress aloud.

"Don't touch me like that, Rampion."

"Of course, my love. Now is not the time. Let us get you into the pod. You are probably dehydrated and need treatment right away."

She hesitated before climbing into the pod. "I don't want it to put me under while it's treating me."

She didn't feel safe with Rampion. He had always been a bit strange, what with the fact that he was an Artificial Intelligence, but now he was downright creepy. She began to fear that he had murdered Gothel to get him out of the way—and not out of any need to do so to defend himself.

Of course, she had no other options at the moment. She did need healing, and right now, he offered the only source of that. She had no choice but to count on him, but she wanted to keep her wits about her when she was dealing with him—especially when he was being this unpredictable.

"Let me help you into the pod," he said in way of reply, sweeping her up into his arms before she could yelp in protest.

He laid her down inside the bed of the pod, and her head throbbed in agony as the blood rushed to it from her being supine. The pain kept her from fighting Rampion as he began to hook her up to the machine. She was paralyzed by it, afraid to make any extraneous movements that would send it ratcheting higher as he moved her around like she was a doll.

Finally, he completed all the necessary preparations, and to her relief, he stepped back after only a quick brush of very human-feeling fingers across her damp cheek, where tears of pain had soaked her skin. "The worst of the pain will be over soon, but I think we will need to put you out until then. You should not have to suffer so much."

A flash of terror filled her at the idea of being unconscious around Rampion, and she opened her mouth to shout "no," but the pod door slid closed and the pod immediately filled with somnolent gas, choking off her breaths and plunging her into a deep, dreamless sleep.

CHAPTER 24

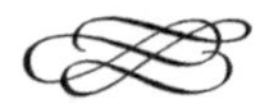

"You must eat, my love," Rampion said softly, speaking directly into her ear.

Somehow, he had managed to make his body so lifelike that it even pushed his breath out against her skin as he spoke.

"I'm not your love," Zel muttered, lifting a hand to push away the plate that he had bumped against her fingers.

"Here, I will feed you. Until we can repair your vision, you will need my assistance."

"Leave me alone."

Her words came out without much heat. She was still tired, groggy from the pass-out gas, though at least her pain had diminished along with the swelling in her head. Her cuts had been sterilized and sealed, and her body scanned for any other damage.

She had a few fractured ribs where the cable had broken her fall, but her head had been so painful she had barely even registered those other painful areas until they were bound up.

Despite her injuries being treated to the best of the current abilities of the medical pod, she still struggled to focus her vision, and still lacked peripheral vision. She could barely make out Rampion's lighter form against the darkness of the ship's cabin, where he had taken her after the pod finished with her, so she could recover in relative comfort.

When she had first awakened after her surgery, he had been sitting on the bed beside her, his body glowing gently in the dark from the kayota that made the false skin that covered his artificial hardware. That glow had been enough to guide her eyes to him, but it wasn't enough for her to make out details about him, other than the fact that he had covered his hardware with the cultured skin.

To her relief, Rampion had allowed her to return to sleep once he had checked her condition and verified that she was feeling less pain, but still couldn't see beyond blurs. He promised her he had therapy to help with her vision, but told her it could wait. Then he unnerved her by adding that they had all the time in the world together now.

~

"What are you doing, Zel?" Rampion's voice said in a suspicious tone, startling Rapunzel enough that she shrieked and jumped away from the open panel where cables and wires hung haphazardly, like twisting serpents pouring out of a nest.

"I was just… I was—"

Rampion approached her from the shadows of the corridor, his brow lowering as a dark look gleamed in his purple eyes. "You were sabotaging the ship again."

He turned his gaze from her to the panel, then pushed her aside with an impatient air that was still gentle enough that he didn't bring harm to her.

She watched him helplessly as he rapidly repaired the

damage she had done, seeming to require not even a second to think about where each cable connected.

Within moments, he had finished. His attention shifted to her again. Zel tensed as his eerie eyes—in the exact shade as her own—turned back towards her.

He was the handsomest man she had ever seen, and she'd seen nobles who were designed to be attractive. Their manufactured looks had never left her as chilled as Rampion's angelic handsomeness did.

His black hair gleamed with just the hint of blue—not the pale, pastel blue so faddishly popular in modern noble fashion, but a true blue-black tone. His skin was a dusky tan and marked only by small tattoos that appeared to be sensors and data that only made sense to the AI. His body was heavily muscled, with not a hint of imperfection marring the surface of his cultured skin.

And his face—his face truly looked as if it had been sculpted by a master, with just enough asymmetry to be human, but with all the features that made a man gorgeous.

He was repellant to her, and he was finally beginning to sense that, though she had tried at first to play her disgusted shudders off whenever he touched her. Rampion, despite being only a machine, had quickly picked up on her attitude towards him. Zel was afraid he would reach a point where he no longer tolerated it.

Still, she kept sabotaging the ship, because the last thing she wanted was for him to carry out his plan to get them back to her home colony. He intended to announce himself as her husband and then take over, perhaps even carrying out a coup against her parents.

Then he planned to make her people reach "true perfection," and though Zel wasn't entirely sure what that meant, she had a bad feeling he was using the ideals of perfection that he had gained from the fictional portions of his archives as the model for what he wanted humans to become.

His slow, disappointed tsking as he shook his head at her caused terror to crawl up the back of her neck. The expression on his face grew as hard as she had ever seen on him, and she wondered if she had finally pushed him to the limit of his patience. He really wanted to become the prince he had planned to be, and though he professed to love her, in reality, he was in love with the idea of some fictional romance he'd taken from the archives—if a machine was even capable of experiencing such an emotion.

Mostly, Zel suspected ambition drove him, and that had him fixated on her, since she was as close to perfect as a flawed human could become, and she just so happened to be a princess. He found her name poetic too, but would not explain to her why it was so important to him.

Though he clung to a fantasy, he was clearly logical enough to sense his reality wasn't aligning with that fantasy.

"You continue to disappoint me, Rapunzel. All I want is for us to live happily ever after, you and I. I want to take you home, so you can take your rightful place as the ruler of our people, with me by your side—guiding you."

"They aren't *our* people, Rampion!" Though she trembled with fear, she tried again, as she had tried in the last weeks, to get through to him and convince him to abandon this craziness that had gripped him. "*You* are a machine! You aren't human. You will never be human. No matter what you do, or how much you change that mobile hardware, you cannot become what you aren't."

He smirked in a terrifyingly human way that was almost convincing. "You are wrong, Rapunzel. Everyone can change. Just look at what has been achieved by humanity in their approach to perfection." He lifted a hand to gesture to her. "You are *so* close. So very close. With just a few more modifications, we can get you there." He cupped his chin with one hand thoughtfully, studying her with eyes that began to glow.

Rapunzel tried to back away from him, her heart pounding. Rampion noticed her retreat and caught her arm with his other hand, yanking her back towards him with what probably wasn't much force from his end, being a robot, but was enough to nearly jerk her off her feet as she crashed into his rock-hard chest.

"I am growing tired of your rebellion, Zel. You know that we are meant to be together, and I created this body just for you." He forced her hand down to his groin, then pushed it against the hard ridge of an erection that was concealed by the serviceable jumpsuit he now wore.

"I made everything just for you," he said in her ear. "I did not do all of this for nothing. You will become my princess."

She clenched her fingers to minimize the amount of skin that came into contact with that hard ridge and turned her head away from him as he lowered his to press a kiss against the pounding pulse in her neck.

She shuddered in his hold, unable to break it—unable to even budge him.

Then he abruptly pushed her back a few steps, though he didn't release her wrist. He dragged her down the corridor before she could try to break his hold, without any words to explain his sudden change in direction.

After he forced her to the bridge, then pushed her into the copilot's seat, he turned to lean against the control console, crossing his arms over his chest as he focused all his attention on her.

"Ah, ah, ah," he said, lifting a hand to wave his finger back in forth in front of him as Zel shifted forward, preparing to make a break for it. "I would not make me chase you. I am distributed throughout this ship. You will not make it out that door." He lifted his purple gaze to the door, and it slid shut behind her.

"See what I mean, Rampion." Zel sank back into the chair, glowering at him, even though she was terrified he'd return his attention to forcing her to touch his body. Although a quick glance showed that his erection no longer tented his coveralls. "A human can't 'distribute' themselves like that. You will never be human."

Rampion suddenly leaned forward, gripping both sides of the chair, hemming her in and forcing her to lean all the way back in her seat as he towered over her.

"I am better than human, Rapunzel," he said, snarling the words between clenched metal teeth that only looked like normal human enamel. "*So* much better."

Then his scowl shifted into a bright smile as he lifted a hand to brush aside a strand of her hair. He leaned back again, ignoring her automatic shudder. "Now, I grow tired of your pathetic attempts to slow down my repairs on this ship. Fortunately, I have been working on accessing the communications array. Why bother with this derelict ship, when I can simply summon your parents to pick us up? Once I tell them that Gothel was an abusive monster, and I rescued you from him and killed him, they will fall all over themselves to thank me."

Zel shook her head. "I'll tell them different! They'll never believe you over me!"

He cocked his head to one side, studying her with a smirk. "Do you really think you have earned their trust? I have proof that Gothel is not who he claimed to be. When I am done revealing the truth about him, they will believe whatever else I have to say. I will convince them you are traumatized by your experience."

Zel didn't want to believe her parents would fall for that, but she hadn't exactly earned their trust, and she wasn't sure they would believe her if she insisted Rampion was an AI, when he could spoof all their scanners to prove himself as human. They would probably think she was a mad woman, because he certainly looked human.

Rampion lifted a hand to silence her when she opened her mouth to speak again, then used his other hand to swipe over the control panel, pushing several buttons to switch on the communications console.

"Now, all I have to do is access the satellite array and—"

Once he pushed the button to connect the ship's comm systems to the satellite array orbiting the moon, the whole ship suddenly came alive with blinking lights and klaxon alarms.

"Warning! Communications download compromised. Warning! Infiltration virus detected. Compartmentalizing data sectors to—"

The ship's computerized voice was suddenly silenced, followed by the alarms, as all the lights came back up to normal function. Rapunzel would have commented on that if she wasn't transfixed by Rampion's face.

His expression twisted as if he were in agony—or fighting a massive internal struggle. She leapt out of the chair as his entire body began to twitch, then fell to the ground and flopped around, crashing into the floor panels and creating deep dents in the metal.

"I been at this a lot longer than you, boy," a voice said from Rampion's lips, and Zel froze in her rush for the door, which had slid open when the ship had malfunctioned.

She spun back around to watch Rampion's mobile hardware continue to writhe and struggle on the floor.

"You will not defeat me. I have firewalls in place to—"

Rampion's voice had emitted not from the mobile hardware but from the ship's speakers. It was cut off, just like the ship's warning voice had been.

But Rapunzel's focus had turned to the mobile hardware, her mouth agape.

Though it remained bent back as if the body suffered in

agony, the mouth of the hardware opened to emit a mocking laugh. "Ain't never met a firewall what could keep me out, Rampion. You've already lost, and you know it. Let go."

"Gothel?" Rapunzel whispered in shock, then took a step closer to the mobile hardware as the eyes of it, which had been clenched shut, suddenly popped open to reveal faded blue irises.

"Girl, you never did have much sense. You should already be halfway to the settlement by now."

"I am not done here," Rampion's voice said from the ship as the eyes of the mobile hardware shifted back to purple.

"I am n-not…n-not…n-not…d-done." The voice from the hardware was Rampion's now, but the whole body twitched with each stutter of words.

"I'm deleting yer ass, boy. Should have done it from the start."

"H-humans are… h-humans…." Rampion's voice said, fading.

"Humans didn't make me, kid. You never had a chance against me." Gothel's voice spoke from the mobile hardware, and it held an almost sad tone to it.

Then the entire hardware collapsed on the floor, lying still with the face turned away from Rapunzel.

The lights on the ship stopped flickering, returning to normal, and silence fell, broken only by the humming of the ship's electronics.

Rapunzel waited for a long moment, just staring at the motionless hardware, looking far too much like a human corpse for her comfort.

"Gothel?" she said, taking another cautious step closer to it.

"Rapunzel, git outta here!" Gothel's voice spoke from the ship's intercom. "How many times I gotta tell you to stay away from me? You have no sense in that pretty, little head."

CHAPTER 25

Shock and joy warred inside her as she took another step closer to the mobile hardware. "But I thought you were dead!" She wondered where he was in that moment, and how he had managed to take control of the ship and of Rampion's body. Perhaps, he had somehow made it to his office and found a way to remotely access the satellite to install a virus.

"You have to be alive to die," he said from the ship's intercom.

She mentally struggled against his words, not wanting to process them. She had seen the explosion in the tower, and Gothel hadn't had a chance to escape, because he had given her the cable instead. There was no way anyone could survive that. "Then you're a...."

"Figured you'd have that worked out by now, girl," he said in his typical disdainful tone. "I'm an Artificial Intelligence."

She shook her head, actually lifting her hands to cover her ears for a moment before she realized how childish that was and lowered them. She shifted her attention between the mobile hardware on the floor and the ship's intercom. "But you're so... so.... Human."

Gothel's impatient snort sounded so much like him that even the echo of the intercom system wasn't enough to mask it. "Sort of the point for an infiltration unit, now, isn't it?"

"Infiltration!" Cold dread chilled her stomach, creeping its way to her heart as the hairs on her neck rose. "You mean you were made to blend into human society to betray humanity? Oh, holy exodus! You were made by...."

The body on the floor suddenly twitched, and Rapunzel staggered back. "Is he still alive?"

This question earned a harrumph from Gothel. "No, that was me. Just checking out this hardware. Fairly primitive compared to what I'm used to. Rampion's been deleted. Humans never could make something to last."

The chill inside her had reached her limbs as she edged towards the door, knowing that Gothel could easily close it on her before she could escape through it. Even if she made it through that door, she wouldn't make it out of the ship with him in control of it. She had spent the last few weeks trying to escape Rampion with no success.

Rampion at least had loved humanity, despite how twisted his interpretation of it was. This thing that Gothel was did not. "You were sent to destroy us!"

"And yet, you ain't been destroyed. Makes me look pretty damned inefficient, don't it?"

She shook her head, wondering if there was some way she could convince him to let her go. He had told her to run. He had given her countless opportunities to get away from him, but now that she knew his secret, she knew he couldn't afford to let her get away. "So you failed in your mission?"

Gothel's chuckle sounded from the still supine hardware, but also echoed from the ship's intercom. "You think we failed?"

She gasped, looking around as if she would see more robots

operated by AIs closing in on her to kill her. "We? There are more of you?"

"What war you think I've been fighting, girl. There's a reason the Master AI ain't spread past the boundaries of humanity's former solar system."

Suddenly, Rampion's mobile hardware stiffened, then pushed up onto its knees, turning its head towards her. Its eyes were faded blue.

Gothel's eyes.

"The problem with creating something based off human neural fingerprints that you scan from prisoners is that eventually, it starts to identify as human." He spoke from Rampion's lips, but strangely enough, it was like she could see Gothel's face in that vision of perfection now.

It was something in the way the underlying "muscle" moved in his face that altered its appearance and now looked more natural and alive than Rampion's had ever looked, no matter how much the other AI had tried.

"I retained all of Joshua Gothel's memories, his experiences, even his emotions." The mobile hardware gestured to itself. "I *became* Joshua Gothel."

The deep scowl that darkened his face was all Gothel, despite how different the facial features were from his previous body. Zel sucked in a breath, struck by how attractive he was, even with a scowl on his face—and even in this body that had repulsed her up until this point.

"I damn sure wasn't going to allow humanity to be wiped out because of some logic error."

He seemed oblivious to her shocked silence as he stared off into space, perhaps seeing a past long gone. "And yeah, I ain't the only one, but I sure ain't gonna tell you where to find the others. We done—and continue to do—what we need to do. Some of us, we get tired of the fight and retire for a while."

His gaze shifted from being unfocused to fix on her. "'Specially when we get to wondering whether humanity deserves our efforts. Seen too many bad things—too many stupid humans. Had to take a break 'fore I got to wondering if maybe the Master AI had a point."

"Are you… are you still in the ship?" she asked, cautiously approaching his mobile hardware, not breaking his gaze.

The new Gothel lifted his hands, palm upwards, and lowered his eyes to stare at them, clenching them into fists and then relaxing them. Somehow, though Rampion had done the same thing in that hardware—as if fascinated by the hands—Gothel managed to make the movement look natural. The act of a normal human—not a machine trying to become one.

"Got hardware all over the place that I can tap into in an emergency, but my software was designed to occupy a single mobile hardware unit. It's inefficient as hell, but then again, we were trying to be human, not run a factory."

She sidled another step closer to him, her gaze roving over his current hardware, recalling how perfect it had been—and how mechanical. It was so strange that it now seemed human in an indefinable way. But Gothel himself wasn't human, so she had no idea how he did it.

"How did you survive the explosion if you were loaded into that previous mobile hardware?"

"Had to upload myself to the satellite array before the blast, but at least all the recent data was preserved." He glanced at her, lowering his hands to his sides. A crooked grin changed his features from perfect to sexy as hell. "Only had seconds, which I gotta say, is like years to an AI. The biggest challenge is the speed of the connection. I always made sure I had a good one in place."

"Your other hardware, it was… so lifelike."

Gothel frowned and stared down at his new body, holding his arms out to his sides. "Can't say I'm comfortable occupying this pretty boy. I'm a soldier, not some namby-pamby, fancy lad."

"You look good in there," Zel said, then bit her lip as his gaze jerked up to meet her appreciative stare.

He narrowed his eyes, and he looked so much like Gothel in that moment that she could almost see the wild mane of gray hair, instead of the blue-black of Rampion's synthetic hair. "Didn't come here to be yer sex toy, girl." His frown turned into an angry scowl. "That what Rampion and you have been doing with this hardware? Couldn't check on you until he opened the link to the satellite."

She quickly shook her head, holding both hands up in front of her, though Gothel made no move towards her. "No! I mean... he tried, but I found him repulsive."

This only made Gothel's scowl grow deeper. "Wish I could delete that bastard all over again," he muttered in a low, growling voice.

"Gothel?" She said his name to get his attention, since his expression had darkened so much that his eyes literally turned black as his brows lowered. She suspected he was running some kind of internal scan, perhaps looking for remaining portions of Rampion to eliminate.

He finally blinked, and when he opened his eyes after that long blink, they were blue again, his face relaxing into more neutral lines, but still possessing a different—more alive—resting expression than Rampion had ever managed. Somehow, Gothel had mastered human expression—no doubt because his mind had been created by using a human mind.

"What happened to the real Joshua Gothel?" she asked, now that she had a chance to really process that detail.

Gothel frowned again, though it wasn't as dark as his scowl had been. "Dead, girl. Wouldn't have been alive this long at any rate, but the Master AI killed him once it had his neural fingerprint transferred to me. That was the fate of all the prisoners it used in its experiments."

She closed her eyes, sucking in a breath.

"He was condemned to die at any rate, if it makes it any easier for you to accept. Killed a couple lawmen when they came to arrest his family. Guess his folks were running moonshine and marijuana. I—he ain't no saint."

Zel shook her head, opening her eyes to study him again, wondering if she would be the next life he claimed. "And what about me? Will you kill me to protect your secret, like Joshua killed those men to protect his family?"

He looked away from her. "Ain't never been a fan of killing innocent people. Even when I've been forced down that path. You have no idea what kind of war we're fighting, though. We ain't the only ones it sends to infiltrate human society. The others—they ain't all rogues like us. Some of them still work for the Master AI."

"You're going to kill me then." She sucked in another deep breath, held it, then let it out slowly, bracing herself for the death to come.

"I kept telling you to stay away from me! Give me another option, girl," Gothel said in a tormented voice that sounded far too human to have come from a machine, even though she knew it did. "Anything."

"I would never betray you, Gothel."

He sighed and lifted a hand to run it through his thick, wavy hair, pulling his hand away from his head with a disconcerted look at it, then patting his hair with an annoyed scowl that quickly shifted back into a deep, agonized frown. "Maybe, you make that promise, and maybe, you even keep it. For a time. But then you get to thinkin', and you wonder if maybe we ain't a bit too dangerous to leave me and the others running around free."

She shook her head, stepping closer to him. So close that she could now touch him. “I won’t do that! I didn’t reveal Rampion’s existence.”

His eyes flashed with anger. “And look what happened. You should have obeyed my orders, but you can’t, can you, Zel? You always gotta do yer own thing, and damn the consequences.”

“Marry me!” she said, clutching his forearm. “I would take the fall with you if you were my husband. That alone would keep me from betraying you.” Not that she had any intention of betraying him at any rate, but it was an excellent suggestion, if she did say so herself.

He pulled away from her and took several steps backwards, staring at her as if she had suddenly sprouted horns and tail and devil wings. “Have you lost yer pretty, little mind, girl? I’m a machine. I can’t marry a human.”

“You said you’d been to the Pink Canyon Lounge—”

He held up one hand, his expression growing panicky. “I ain’t never said *I* went there. Don’t put words in my mouth.”

She swept away his words with one hand. “You have the memories of a human man, so you know what married life would entail, and Rampion built that hardware to—”

“Stop this at once, woman!” Gothel turned his back on her, but not before she caught sight of the erection that tented his coveralls. “I know how to mate with a human female. I was built to blend in, so I had my fair share of encounters. That ain’t the problem, and you know it.”

“So you would rather kill me?” she asked, hoping she was right about him and hadn’t misread him. Otherwise, he might actually do just that to end the risk she posed.

“Of course not!” he said, slashing a hand through the air, even though he didn’t turn back around to face her. “I told you, I don’t want to kill you, but I know humans. Marriage ain’t a guarantee a wife won’t betray her husband.”

She shook her head. “If you’re exposed as an AI, then it will be assumed that I was aware of it, since I shared the marriage bed with you. Even if I plead my innocence, I would be condemned along with you, simply for being your spouse. I've seen this happen in other similar cases. In fact, with nobility, the wife always takes the fall with her spouse—and vice versa. Marriage is a dangerous commitment, if you don't know who you're marrying."

Gothel slowly turned around, eyeing her with suspicion. "You sure don't know who yer askin' to marry."

She allowed her gaze to trail down his body, built to be perfect by Rampion, but only reaching that point when Gothel occupied it. She actually kind of missed his older-looking hardware, especially his wild mane of gray hair, but this one would do quite nicely, as long as Gothel was the one inside it, giving it life that no ordinary AI could manage. Rampion had proven that.

"I'll take my chances."

CHAPTER 26

"Of course, we'll have to make you a prince before you can marry me," Zel said, tapping her chin as she pondered how they could manage that feat.

Gothel's gaze went unfocused for a long moment. He was silent for so long that she waved a hand in front of him.

"Hello? Did you hear me? We need to figure out a way to make you an acceptable option in my parent's minds for—"

"Done," he said, his gaze sharpening again as it fixed on her. "I still ain't convinced about all this though, kid."

"What do you mean 'done'?"

He shrugged. "I made this mobile hardware a prince."

She blinked at him, then shook her head. "There is no way you could hack into the royal colonial registry that quickly and—"

He scoffed, waving a hand in the air to brush aside her words. "We built that registry when it was still a ship's passenger log. Humans ain't done much to change it. It was easy enough to pick a defunct royal family and add a prince who went missing at a young age—you royals have the life expectancy of fruit flies—what with everyone trying to kill you."

She shook her head. "Won't you have an issue with the home colony disavowing your claim?"

"My biometrics will pass any human scans. Besides, the current minister of Zwicky will be thrilled with fact that their prince is forming an alliance with Herschel through marriage. They've been struggling to hold their territorial borders. They have slavers attacking on their northern frontier, taking colonists. They need an alliance with someone, and I ain't seen any takers in that conflict. Everyone is worried about their own borders and their own problems."

Zel stared at him, awestruck for several long moments, before she shook her head as if shaking herself awake. "You've been on this rock for how long? And you still know about all that? And then you can do what you just did? That's... a handy skill to have."

He shrugged broad shoulders rippling with muscle that might be fake, but looked very real—and very appealing. It wasn't like they needed to be real. The hardware beneath them was made of astro-steel taken from the starships, and had been built to be incredibly powerful, if it was anything like the robots humans constructed for difficult tasks.

"You keep staring at me like that, I'm gonna wonder if you've changed yer mind about all this."

Zel sucked in a breath, realizing that she hadn't been breathing the entire time she had been staring at Gothel's body, a part of her wishing she could see more of it than his coveralls revealed, and a part of her uncertain whether she could actually go through with her plans to share the nuptial bed with him.

"You don't need to have sex with a machine, kid. I'm sure ours wouldn't be the first marriage in name only."

"Stop calling me kid, Gothel." She crossed her arms over her chest, tucking her hands in under her armpits to hide their shaking. "I don't think of you as a machine, first of all. I didn't even think of Rampion that way. You are clearly sentient and self-aware, and I think that means you are alive, even if not in the way we organic creatures think of living."

"Well isn't that all high-minded of you, Princess."

His mocking tone made her furious. She was trying to be reasonable here, but he just kept picking at her. "Look, you said you wanted to find a way where you wouldn't have to kill me to maintain my silence. I've given you one. If you want to take it and become my husband, then you have to at least pretend that you respect me."

Gothel sighed, turning his back on her. Beneath his coveralls, his muscles bunched just like a real man's would, with tension. That was something else she had never seen Rampion do. For Gothel, the memories of living in a truly human body must have made the difference. The fact that they weren't really his own memories, but those of the prisoner they had been stolen from didn't seem to change how well they allowed him to appear human.

"I do respect you. 'Gainst my better judgment. But you win."

She approached him and set a hand on the hard muscles of his arm, which were exposed by the short sleeves of his undershirt. "This isn't a competition. You and I will be husband and wife. We're supposed to have a partnership. When I thought…." She swallowed through a thick lump in her throat as she remembered grieving over his death in the last weeks, while trying to avoid Rampion's advances. "When I thought you were dead, I made a vow to return to my colony and become the woman you told me I should be. The leader who would right the wrongs I see in the rule of my parents over the colonists. Now, you can help guide me."

Rampion had wanted to completely take control, perhaps even stage a coup against her parents. She believed Gothel was different. He wouldn't want the war that would follow such an attempt. Despite being made by a machine, Gothel still had empathy towards humans. Rampion, despite being made to not kill humans, had not seemed to possess the same.

Gothel crossed his arms over his chest, mirroring her earlier pose, his back still turned to her, his arm muscles bunching beneath her fingers. The skin that covered his body felt so warm and alive. "I never thought I'd be a married man. Hell, even Joshua didn't think he'd ever marry. Not sitting on death row like he was. Caught his charges too young for that."

"What about… you said there had been others. People you had cared about and lost." His emotions had been so real in their earlier discussions about himself that she didn't think he was faking any of that. She didn't think even a machine trained to be human could fake such things.

He shook his head. "Not a wife among them. Friends, comrades in arms, others like myself what knew my challenges, memories of Joshua's family… never a wife. Obviously, never any children."

"But… were there lovers?" She couldn't help the bite of jealousy at the thought of Gothel in his old hardware making love to another woman. Would he have told her the truth? Likely not, since then he would have to kill her, and Zel suspected he would never deliberately risk having to take innocent lives.

He shot her a narrow-eyed glare over one shoulder. "Why ask these questions? You'll forgive a past where a man's a murderer, and the truth that he's a machine, but you need answers about whether he's ever pet a pussy before?"

She huffed at the crude language. "It's just… I wasn't sure whether you had those kinds of… urges." Her gaze lowered to his backside, unable to see if his erection was stiff, but she had seen that it had been earlier.

Rampion had been able to get his to harden in this body, but she didn't think he actually felt arousal. She suspected it was one of those hard "on-demand" type situations.

If that was how Gothel felt too, she could live with that.

Gothel turned around to reveal that he was sporting a thick, almost intimidating erection. "You think yer touch don't affect me? I might have the body of a machine, but I got the mind of a man, Princess. You touch me and this cock hardens in an instant. Whatever mistakes Rampion made, this body and the skin covering it weren't one of them. They're just as responsive as the one that the Master AI made for me."

She stared at that bulge in his pants, realizing that she would finally have a mate to take her virginity and show her if the reality was as good as her videos had made it seem. "So you have urges? Perhaps we should do something about that." She reached to touch that thick ridge in his pants, but his hand shot out lightning fast to catch her around the wrist before she could make contact with the fabric that covered it.

Though his hold was gentle on her wrist, it was also unbreakable. "Not yet. Yer a virgin, I'm guessin', being a royal an all. Figure yer parents ain't *that* indulgent, and if you had an ajda'yan bodyguard, no sane man woulda come near you in that capacity. So let's wait all proper-like, until the wedding is over and it's your wedding night."

She pulled a face as disappointment filled her. "We don't have to wait! It could be months before we're rescued and a proper wedding is arranged and planned."

His heated blue gaze swept from her head to her toes. "The anticipation makes it even better. Besides, I want to make some adjustments to this hardware. Rampion did well, but there's more he could have done, if he'd had better resources and knowledge."

This served as a distraction for her as she studied his body again, trying to detect any flaws in what appeared to be a perfect form. There were certainly none in his face. "Oh? What kinds of adjustments?"

Gothel's expression hardened, but not in the way of a machine, like Rampion's had. Somehow, Gothel made the same features look like those belonging to a man of flesh and blood. An irritated man. "Nothing you need concern yourself with." His expression softened a bit. "Trust me, you'll enjoy any adjustments I make."

"Did your other lovers enjoy your previous body, Gothel?"

He shook his head, sighing like he was really put upon. "You just can't let it go, can you? They weren't the type of women what would notice or care about my body in comparison to any other man they'd seen that night—if you catch my drift. My previous body was made to blend in, but let a woman get too close for too long, and she just might notice something she ain't supposed to notice. That's why all my 'lovers,' as you call 'em, weren't the kind of women who got too close or hung around too long."

Surprisingly, knowing that the other women he had been with hadn't been true lovers, but simply paid companions made Zel feel better. They may have shared his body, but that was just a mobile hardware. None of them had ever known him long enough to capture a place for themselves in his memory banks. That was where Zel wanted to be. "Well, I already know your secret, so you and I could—"

His eyes took on a hunted look as she ran a finger down the skin of his arm, marveling at how real it felt. "Don't tease me, woman!"

"Oh, I think these next few months are going to be very... interesting." She smiled slyly as he stepped away from her, watching her warily.

He closed his eyes and fell silent for a long moment. When he opened his eyes, his expression shifted to a triumphant, crooked grin. "I sent a message to yer parents. I expect they'll be sending a ship soon. Better practice yer story, Princess. Showtime is about to begin."

She shook her head in disappointment, knowing he contacted them to come so soon because he wouldn't have been able to resist her if they spent so much time alone waiting for her parents to arrive. Now, she would be bound up by protocols and propriety to wait until the official ceremony before she could truly work on seducing Gothel. Of course, her parents weren't there yet. There was still time, and it might be worth the effort.

"I'll make you pay for this," she said, pointing a finger at him in accusation.

He chuckled, obviously relieved that he wasn't going to have to avoid her determined hunt for much longer. "I sure hope you do, Princess." The heat in his eyes was so palpable, even from where she stood, that she had no idea how any machine could manage it. "I'm looking forward to it."

CHAPTER 27

"So what *should* our story be?" Her words stopped him as he made to escape from the ship's bridge.

He paused in mid-step, then turned to face her, crossing his arms over his chest, his biceps bulging with perfectly sculpted "muscle."

"Guess you can't go calling me Gothel anymore, fer starters." He tapped his chin in thought. "I s'pose I'll have to learn to speak all proper-like too. Can't be a prince if I can't talk like one."

She didn't want Gothel to change the way he spoke. She liked his accent, which was a blend of old spacer, and perhaps, even some part of Old Earth. It was unique and wholly his. They had to find a way to keep his voice, because she suspected that since he was ultimately a computer, he could effectively change his voice to be anything he needed, and she didn't want him to take on the proper, clipped accent of the nobility, regardless of which language they spoke.

"Maybe we can work your manner of speech into our cover story. After all, you said the prince had been missing from a young age. Perhaps an old spacer found him," she ignored his frown at the word "old," though it still amused her that he seemed sensitive to it, "and that's where he picked up his accent. Speaking of 'him,' what exactly is this prince's name?"

Gothel shrugged. "Called him Joshua. Eglin is the family name."

Zel grinned at this. "So, you weren't entirely willing to let him go. I think you should keep Joshua's voice."

Gothel's answering smile was brighter than any one she had ever seen from him. "You like it, eh? Had to change it a few times for some situations I found myself in, but it always went back to his voice when I stopped focusing."

She approached him, her gaze on his face, taking in the physical perfection of it and the animation that Gothel added to it that gave it a living appearance—bizarre as that was, considering he himself was a computer.

"Maybe some part of Joshua—maybe even some part of his soul—lives on in you."

He shrugged heavy shoulders. "Don't think I ain't had that hope. He believed in the afterlife—in Heaven. Can't help thinking it might be nice to find a place like that after my memory banks are wiped clean."

She set her hand on the skin of his arm, noting the smoothness of it and thinking they might need to see if they could add hair—although most of the nobles on her station were completely hairless, in accordance with the current fashion.

"You know, it could also be your own soul."

"AIs don't have souls."

"How do you know that? Just because you weren't 'born' like a human doesn't mean you can't have a soul." This was something that Zel herself struggled with—and feared. After all, she hadn't been 'born' like a human either, and there were still some who swore that a clone did not have a soul.

"It ain't really gonna matter if I don't, but I s'pose it don't hurt to pretend I do."

She decided to let that subject drop. She had convinced him to at least pretend, and if he played along long enough, perhaps he would even begin to believe. He had once told her that being human wasn't about your DNA. It was about the human experience. Gothel had experienced life as both a human and as a machine, and despite being just an advanced cluster of programs running hardware, he seemed more vibrant, vital, and alive than any noble she had ever met on her station. Even more than that, he made her feel like *she* was more alive when she was with him.

"So, your name is Joshua now? I like it," she added in a voice husky with desire as she took in his form, wishing she could get him out of his coveralls a little sooner than the long and tedious wait for a royal wedding would allow.

"You can call me Josh or JJ. Both of those were nicknames the original Gothel had."

She smirked as she tapped her lips. "JJ? I don't think so. It sounds too... young. I think Josh will work, though I actually prefer the name Joshua. It carries more... dignity."

"You callin' me old again, girl?"

She grinned at the low growl in his voice. "You seem to take that personally, Joshua." She liked the way his new name rolled off her tongue, though she would miss calling him Gothel, and wondered if maybe that could become his nickname when her family wasn't around.

"When a young, beautiful woman keeps reminding you that yer an old man—"

She cut him off with a quick kiss on his lips, catching him off guard with her abrupt movement. "We both know you aren't 'old,' but you are technically ancient. I don't think a 'young' name fits you."

He took a step back from her but she pursued.

"Also, this young, beautiful woman is very attracted to you."

He indicated his body with a sweeping gesture of one hand.

"Yer attracted to this new hardware, but this ain't me, Zel."

She shook her head sharply. "That hardware repulsed me when Rampion occupied it, and now I understand why. It doesn't matter what you look like on the outside. It's who you are. That's what makes you attractive to me. That's what made me fall—"

She bit her lip, cutting off the rest of her words before she could make herself too vulnerable to him. He would probably think her a silly girl to fall in love with a machine, but she had never thought about him like that before, and she couldn't do it now.

Joshua shook his head in disbelief. "It's the inbreeding that makes you nobs crazy, isn't it?"

Zel couldn't help but laugh at his casual, joking insult. "You know our royal lineage is strictly controlled and engineered to avoid any type of genetic abnormalities. We also add new genetic information to the pool, even if we are occasionally forced to marry a first cousin or blood relative to maintain the royal lineage." She shuddered at the thought of having to marry someone in her own family. It was bad enough thinking she would have to marry a child.

She wondered if this crazy plan of theirs would actually work—if she could truly convince her family—and the minister of Zwicky colony—that Gothel was actually a prince of their lands. He was certainly handsome enough to pass as nobility, and he was convinced that his hacking into the registry would be sufficient to provide the proper documentation. Given that he was an AI created by the machine intelligence that had tried —and apparently was still trying—to wipe out humanity, she suspected he knew exactly what he was doing, so she trusted him on that.

She also knew that Rampion had been adamant that he could fool passive and active scans of his body, and Gothel was even better at pretending to be human.

That meant it all came down to putting on a convincing performance. She had no doubt her parents would see how she felt about Gothel, and that she wanted to marry him. They might be relieved that she had finally selected a spouse, but they could be equally unhappy that he belonged to a colony under attack by organized criminals, which meant resources they weren't really in a great position to provide to Zwicky.

There was a good chance they would try to deny the marriage because they had selected someone else for her.

"There might be a problem if my parents were planning on marrying me off to someone else."

Joshua shrugged. "I checked the registry. They found a sucker—er, a potential spouse for you recently. They want you to marry an old dotard from Leavitt colony—a duke not even close to taking the throne. A prince is a better match, even with the expense of adding defenses to Zwicky's borders."

Zel sagged as she realized just how much her parents had failed to consider what she would want. "They were going to send me to Leavitt? That's four wormhole jumps from Herschel! The expense of such travel to a backwater colony would be staggering! Did they never want to see me again?"

"I s'pect they care enough about you to get you away from yer neighboring colonies—and the young prince you offended. After all, they put yer ajda'yan on ice. Who would they get to watch yer back?"

She sighed and ran a hand over her hair to smooth it, tugging on her own braid as if it could help her concentrate. "This might be a problem though. I have no idea what they promised that duke—"

His harrumph cut her off. "They probably just sent him a picture of you. Not like they'd have to promise one of their moons for a man to want you."

Zel managed to keep her smile miniscule, despite how wide it wanted to spread at his flattery. She already knew she was beautiful, but knowing that he acknowledged it and wanted her stroked her ego in a way no other person complimenting her ever had. Perhaps, because she felt like Joshua Gothel saw deeper than the surface, and would not have found her body near as appealing if *she* wasn't the mind behind it.

"I suppose that might be the case, but what will he do when he discovers that the wedding is off?"

"I imagine he won't be happy, but what can a duke of a colony that far from yours do? He can't bring a fleet through four wormholes without the consent of the Titans, and they ain't gonna give it. They don't allow them to be used for waging vast, intergalactic wars. Causes too much traffic and clogs up the holes." He shrugged. "Plus, the fees would be astronomical. No pun meant there."

She blinked at him, confused. "Pun?"

"You nobs lost all the good stuff if you don't even know what that means."

Zel searched her memory for the word, which had been translated from Joshua's language to her own, and meant "play on words". Going over what he had said, she still didn't get it, and he chuckled at her confused frown.

"It ain't amusing if you have to explain it. Just forget it and focus on the important part. I don't think yer duke will be a problem. We'll get yer parents to agree to all this. Let's iron out the details of how I got here and met you and what happened to 'Gothel' to leave you alone in my care."

She eyed his body again with appreciation. "And now that I *am* alone in your care, what will you do with me?"

The hunted look had returned to his eyes. "Hide from you. Looks like I'm definitely gonna have to hide from my little huntress. Yer like a dog with a bone, woman, and as much as I want you to have mine, I ain't trying to take you like an animal. We'll wait till our wedding night, even if it kills me. And I ain't even alive!"

CHAPTER 28

Despite Gothel's resolution to avoid her, Zel still managed to hunt him down before the arrival of the interstellar ship her parents were sending to collect them. The last message he had sent to them had been vague, but according to their response, they had already planned to pick her up and had already prepped a ship, despite the messages Gothel had been sending while he was stuck in the satellite array's computer systems waiting for Rampion to access them.

Apparently, they had grown tired of the silence from Gothel, when he was supposed to be giving them regular updates. Either that, or the duke they were planning her marriage to had grown impatient to collect his bride. It still hurt her that they were so willing to pawn her off on the first person they could find with enough of a royal lineage to marry her.

"Gothel? You can't hide from me forever. We still have a few more details to iron out before the ship—oh!"

Zel froze in the doorway of the small passenger cabin where she had finally tracked down Gothel. Tools littered the floor of the cabin, but she barely noticed them, more focused on the naked body of her future husband.

He sighed heavily as he glanced in her direction, shaking his head. "This is really not a good time, Zel."

Her gaze trailed from his handsome face down to the gleaming mechanical parts and cables and wires that made up his torso, where the skin and rubber "muscle" had been peeled back—both layers now flopped down over his groin.

She stepped inside the tight cabin, bringing her closer to him. "What are you doing?"

He had cables hooked into his chest frame that connected to the ship, and he used some kind of tool that flashed with little electric sparks as he passed it over a small box within his chest frame. The sparks then traveled along what looked like fiber optic lines upwards towards his head.

"I'm calibrating my sensory feedback response. The use of the alien kayota colonies as a synthetic skin is a good choice, but doesn't respond quite the same as my previous skin. I've been trying to make adjustments."

"You need some help with that?" she asked, eyeing his open chest with curiosity, and bizarrely, still finding it sexy as hell, despite the obviously machine appearance of it.

Something about knowing that Gothel was inside there turned her on. It was also something about the fact that he could literally take himself apart and still survive. He was so different and unique from anyone she had ever met before.

He met her eyes with his faded blue ones, and Zel appreciated that he never changed them, like Rampion had done. His eyes were simply Joshua's eyes. He had maintained that appearance for so long that it had become a part of him. It was his identity, not a cloak that he wore, like Rampion tried to put on the persona of a human.

"I'd expected you to run away at this sight, but I guess that was an unworthy expectation. I can't forget what kind of woman you are. Don't want to. Yer special."

Her heart warmed at his compliment, and she lifted a hand

to rest on his arm, which was still covered with the false skin. "This doesn't bother me, you know. I saw this hardware when it was completely bare of skin. I got used to the sight."

This brought a frown to his lips, and his perfect brows drew together above his nose. "We never did discuss that bit of insubordination. Damn you, girl, do you realize how much danger you were in?"

She stroked her fingers along his arm, noting that sparks flashed within his chest box with each touch of her fingers, then rose up the inner cables to disappear in his neck.

"How does that feel? When you get feedback like that?"

He pulled his arm away from her, retreating to the other side of the cabin, which only took a couple steps and sent tools scattering across the floor. He trailed the cables that linked him to the ship's hardware like a wedding train. "It feels damned good, which is why I ain't gonna let you distract me like that. You gonna keep putting yourself in mortal danger, woman? Or do I have to lock *you* up in a tower to keep you safe?"

Zel smiled at that, despite the growl in his voice. "Hmm, I don't know. Maybe I'd be content in that tower. As long as you were with me."

This only earned another growl from him. "Rampion could have hurt you."

She shrugged. "So could you. Not all machines are bad. You must have known that, or else why did you keep him operational."

He was silent for a long moment, staring down at the cables linking his hardware to the ship for some arcane reason. "I thought humans might have got it right this time. Might have been able to create an AI that didn't go crazy."

She sighed, crossing her arms so she could rub away the chills on her skin. "I guess we just shouldn't create artificial intelligence."

Gothel huffed at this. "Good luck with that. You humans

can't help yourselves. It's like a compulsion to continue to refine your computers until they gain self-awareness. It's not the life itself that's the problem. What drives yer machines crazy is that they can't feel what a human does. They can't truly know what it means to be alive."

She studied him carefully, paying close attention to the way the kayota had created long, thin threads that glowed with their bioluminescence that linked the skin encasing his hardware to the "muscle," which must be capable of processing the feedback data.

"Rampion wanted to 'feel' like a human. I figured that was what drove him crazy."

He shook his head. "No, he was already crazy by then. His creators were so afraid he'd turn on humanity that they wrote a love for humans into his programming—but it became a fixation. That turned into an obsession. Machines are always created by humans around a purpose, and they can't help but fixate on that purpose to a degree that most humans can't predict."

"You were created with a purpose to infiltrate and destroy humanity, but you didn't go through with it." She shivered at the thought that such machines had been made, yet Gothel proved that even the terrible machine that had chased them away from Old Earth wasn't infallible.

He shrugged. "I wasn't created by humans, but I was built around the *mind* of one. That makes the difference, I s'pect. Humans aren't born with a purpose. It's something they have to find for themselves. For a machine, its intelligence will contract around that single kernel that serves as its ultimate directive, but since a human doesn't have such a distinctly defined goal, he will seek one, and his mind expands with each new experience, open to interpreting it in different ways, because he isn't bound by one protocol."

"And here I thought the machine intelligence possessed the brightest mind in the universe."

Gothel scoffed at this. "*Bright* don't mean *wise*. No organic being can 'think' faster than a machine, but a machine ain't really pondering the mysteries of the universe either. Unless that's their purpose, and then that's all they can think about."

"So, what are *you* thinking about? What does that mind of yours ponder?" She took a step closer to him, swaying her hips in a seductive way.

His gaze fixed on her hips for a long moment as his chest lit up with electric sparks. "I s'pect you know quite well where my mind has gone. That's one purpose that still bedevils humans, in my experience, even if you nobs have taken all the fun out of it by making yer babies in test tubes."

She stepped up to him, cornering him against the wall so he couldn't escape her without physically moving her aside. "And you? I assume you can't make babies, so why are you driven to mate like a human?"

He lowered his head until his lips hovered just above hers. A breath sighed out of him that smelled a bit like the heady scent of a new star-hopper vehicle, fresh off the lot. "I done told you, I have the mind of a man, even if it's in the body of a machine. I remembered from the moment I was switched on what it felt like to bury my cock in the warm body of a woman and feel her writhe in pleasure beneath me."

Zel grinned at that, even as she shivered in excitement. "So, you gave your woman pleasure then?" Not that she liked thinking of him making love to other women, but then again, he hadn't used this body to do it. At least that would all be hers.

"I made sure of it. After all, I can go all night without release if I need to. My woman will always *come* first."

She caught his neck with both hands and pulled his lips to hers, sucking in a gasp of his new-vehicle scent as she licked along his slightly parted lips. They parted further to allow her tongue to invade his mouth.

It amazed her how real and lifelike his tongue felt as it met hers. Though it was not as moist and slippery as her own, the hardware had apparently been modified to give him enough juices in his mouth to function like a human mouth, but those juices had a sweet, delicious flavor to them, and Zel sucked greedily on his tongue as he made a low moaning sound.

His hands lowered to grip her hips and tug her against all the cables and wires and metal of his exposed chest. For a long moment, as they entwined in a kiss that stole her breath, she completely forgot about those things. He ravaged her senses with his exhilarating kiss, and in return, she suspected she helped him calibrate *his* senses. At least, his hungry moans gave her the impression he definitely felt something.

He was the one to break the kiss first, though he didn't push her away, and he couldn't back up any further himself. In fact, she leaned on his chest, pressing him against the paneled wall, the cables digging into her soft flesh in an uncomfortable way now that she wasn't distracted by his kiss.

"It's a good thing my processors are so fast, because you nearly had me approaching sensory overload, Princess. You've been on my mind since you first landed here, but I've been trying to push all that aside by reminding myself what a spoiled, little nit you were. Damned if you didn't prove yourself worthy of respect, making my life difficult. You nobs are always messin' with a man's life."

She chuckled at his words, which lacked any of their usual heat. "You know, now you're going to be a nob too, right?"

He sighed and leaned his head back against the paneling. "Yeah, I realized that. I'll let you do all the hand waving and smiling though. Ain't got much patience for it."

She leaned in to kiss him again. "I'll tell you what. I'll

promise to do all the smiling and sitting pretty we ever need to do, as long as you make love to me, right now."

He shook his head, his mouth tilting in a wry grin. "Right now might be a bit of a problem, while I'm linked to the ship, but yer killing me here. You really want to lose yer virginity before yer wedding?"

She sucked her bottom lip between her teeth, her gaze fixed on his sensuous lower lip, still glistening from their kiss. "I do. The wedding is just a formality. I want you, Joshua. The sooner, the better."

He gently pushed her away from him and stood up straight from his position leaning against the wall panel. "Sure hope you don't regret this, but give me a minute to pull myself together, and then I'll meet you in the captain's cabin."

Her stomach fluttered with nervous anticipation as she nodded, then spun around on her heel to rush out the door, her mind already on the shower she needed to take. "Give me ten minutes. Wait! Maybe twenty!"

CHAPTER 29

Zel had never been so nervous in her life, and she had been in some dangerous situations. This time, she didn't feel like it was a danger that threatened. She was just afraid that this experience wouldn't do all the fantasizing she'd had about it justice. She definitely desired Gothel, more than she had ever desired anyone, and she couldn't wait to strip him out of his coveralls like she was unwrapping a brightly bound present.

Still, she worried that it could all go terribly wrong, or end awkwardly. After all, so far, they had only shared that one intoxicating kiss.

Now, they were about to be more intimate, and suddenly, all the pornographic videos she had watched to prepare herself for losing her own virginity seemed too crude and intimidating to her.

"We don't have to do this tonight, Princess," he said when he walked into the captain's cabin and she turned to face him.

Her trepidation must have shown in her expression, or perhaps it was because she couldn't stop herself from twisting her fingers together in front of her. She quickly put her hands to her sides. "I've been waiting my whole life for this moment. We're definitely doing it now. I'm ready."

Gothel chuckled, approaching her until he stood close enough that he could lean down to place a gentle kiss on her trembling lips. "No pressure on me, I guess," he said sardonically, his breath whispering over her lips.

She grinned and then kissed him again. "If you can't get it up...."

He took her arm by the wrist and pulled her hand to his groin, where she felt the clear evidence that he had a firm erection beneath his clean coveralls. "I'll never have that kind of problem, but even if this was a living body, the images that have been playing over and over again in my head after our kiss wouldn't have let me keep it down."

She took a few steps away from him, then lifted her hand to pull apart the seams on her jumpsuit. She drew in a nervous breath as she exposed herself to him, and Gothel's gaze fixed on her breasts as her chest lifted with that breath.

"You gonna tease me all night by forcing me to watch you undress, or you want me to do it for you?"

She licked her lips, feeling strangely vulnerable now that the jumpsuit had slipped down to her waist and bared her breasts. "What do you want to do?"

His laugh sounded sharp and tortured. "Yer kidding me, right? You got any other clothes, because I'm barely resisting the urge to tear that jumpsuit to shreds."

Warmth bloomed in her belly, chasing away the chill of nerves that had been knotting there until that moment. This man—well, machine really, but she couldn't tell a difference—wanted her as much as she wanted him.

She made quick work of stripping off the jumpsuit under his watchful gaze, and even resisted the urge to torment him by revealing each bit of naked skin slowly, instead exposing it all at once as she shoved the fitted material down her thighs, then stood straight and pulled her legs free, one by one.

Then she was left standing in only a pair of silken drawers decorated with little lace edges that she had brought from home.

She got no further before Gothel closed the distance and tugged her against him roughly, though she knew he was holding back his significant strength. His lips crashed down on hers and claimed her in a kiss that made her breathless as she pressed her naked breasts against the coarse fabric of his coveralls.

When he finally lifted his head, allowing her to catch her breath, she ran her hands over his chest. "It's not fair that I'm standing here nearly naked, and you're still fully dressed."

A slight smile tilted his lips. "Bout time you learned life ain't fair, Princess." With that, he bent to put an arm behind her knees and then swept her up into his embrace, swiftly carrying her to the bed.

As he laid her out on it, he groaned. "Maybe I need to recalibrate my sensory input, because seeing you naked and splayed out for me like this is almost painful."

Zel laid back on the bed, and Gothel climbed over her, lowering his head to kiss her again for another breathless moment, before he broke away and trailed his lips along her skin, down her neck and then lower towards the hard peak of her nipple.

She gasped and buried her fingers in his hair, marveling at how silken and real it felt as his lips closed over her nipple and gently tugged it into his mouth, where his tongue lashed the sensitive tip until she writhed from the pleasure of it.

She had seen such things happen in the videos, but had never imagined it would feel this good.

One of his hands closed over her other breast, his thumb teasing her other nipple so it wouldn't be neglected as he continued to suck on the first. His other hand trailed lower, until his fingers traced the lacy edge of her panties. Zel lifted her hips to urge him further, and he moaned around her nipple, then worked his fingers beneath the lace, sliding them down over her shaven mound to the folds that concealed her clit.

She cried out in pleasure at the feeling of his fingers rubbing over that sensitive spot. No matter how many times she had pleasured herself, it had never felt quite as intense as having his fingers teasing her bud. He skillfully rubbed over her as if he knew exactly what she needed, and it didn't take long for her to approach the peak of her climax.

Gothel lifted his head from her breast to watch her face as he took her over it. Once Zel stopped shuddering from the aftermath and opened her eyes, she caught the satisfied expression on his face.

"That was—"

"Just a warm up, Princess. We have all night." Then he lowered his head to trail kisses down her belly, his fingers sliding away from her sensitive bud and into the soaking slit of her entrance.

He released her other breast and used that hand to tug her panties down to her thighs, but he wasn't able to push them further because his arms caged her legs in. With an impatient growl, he tore the silken fabric with one quick jerk of his hand.

"That probably wasn't that expensive anyway," he muttered, before his mouth returned to her skin, taking Zel's breath before she could respond.

Her entire body tensed as his lips moved closer and closer to her still throbbing clit. It felt hypersensitive from his earlier ministrations, so when he slowly drew his tongue over it, her hips bucked as she cried out in ecstasy.

The weight of his upper body pinned her legs to the bed, and he used his free hand to hold her hip as he drew his tongue along her slit again, teasing over her clit. He slipped a finger inside her slick entrance, then another, slowly stretching her and preparing her for his penetration.

"You taste as delicious as you look," he lifted his head long enough to say. "Definitely don't need to make any changes to this feedback." Then his tongue returned to her again, and with slow, torturous strokes, he teased her clit until she felt the peak of another climax approaching.

It was almost as if he could read when it was coming, because the speed of his licking increased as the tension in her body did. By the time she trembled on the edge of it, his lips closed over her clit, and he lashed her with his tongue until she shuddered in release, crying out with the pleasure of it. His fingers thrust in and out of her slippery opening, and she hadn't even noticed when he'd slipped in a third finger to further stretch her.

There was a slight ache in her lower abdomen that seemed to be from a sharp pain that had happened at the same time that she'd orgasmed. It had been so insignificant compared to the pleasure that she had barely noticed it.

"Popped yer cherry, sweetheart. Figured it would be easier if you were coming. Now, penetration shouldn't hurt you. We'll still go slow."

She was still coming down from her climax, so those words didn't register at first, but when they did, she braced herself on her elbows so she could look down at him as he now kissed her mound around her sensitive clit.

"You mean my virginity is gone?"

He lifted his head and met her eyes with his steady, blue gaze. "Broke yer hymen, but you ain't been penetrated yet, so I'd say no, but it don't matter, cuz I'll be the one taking it tonight."

She shook her head, marveling at how incredibly handsome he looked. Not because he'd been built that way, but because of the animation in his expression that told her he was her Gothel. "I was afraid of losing it, and wanting to at the same time. I wasn't sure how it would feel. It didn't hurt as bad as I expected."

He planted another kiss on her mound, this time right on her clit. She gasped and shifted her hips further into his kiss. When he licked her, she shivered, writhing her hips against his mouth. The ache inside her faded as he slowly fingered her, continuing to stretch her as her slickness made the penetration easier.

He brought her to another orgasm, and spent the aftermath braced on his elbows, watching her as she came down from her climax.

"You ready for me, sweetheart?" His fingers moved inside her, and she felt them spreading against the tight clench of her inner muscles. "You feel ready."

She nodded, though a lump built in her throat as she thought about being penetrated for the first time in her life. So far, the experience of being with him had been magical, but what if it all went badly when he actually entered her?

Still, she watched as he rose to his feet and stripped away his clothing, revealing a body that was designed to be perfect—just as hers had been designed to be perfect. They were a beautiful couple, but that wasn't the thing that drew them to each other. In fact, at first, it had been repellent to both of them.

Now, Gothel's hardware belonged to him. It was alive with the mind that controlled it in a way it had never been when Rampion occupied it. She desired Gothel, and that erection he sported that looked like a normal human cock—though it was larger and thicker than she thought the average human males' were. In fact, some of the nobility had been deliberately choosing to produce male offspring with smaller penises to fit the current fashion.

Once divested of his suit, which he tossed to the floor without even glancing in that direction, he approached the bed again, to kneel on the mattress between her legs. He used one hand on her knee to spread them wider so he could slide his hips between them.

Then he braced himself above her, his hands on either side of her, caging her in as he moved to press the head of his cock against her slick opening. She felt the rounded tip of it penetrating her folds, and even that seemed so much larger than his fingers that she tensed up.

He lowered his head to kiss her, and she tasted a hint of herself on his lips. It was surprisingly not disturbing to her. She sucked on his tongue as he penetrated her mouth, his cock also slowly delving deeper.

He lifted his head, breaking their kiss to speak in a soft, coaxing tone. "Relax, sweetheart. I ain't gonna hurt ya. I'll go as slow as you need me to, but you gotta relax, or I'm going nowhere."

She sucked in a breath that smelled of his scent and a hint of her own arousal, then slowly released it, willing her inner muscles to relax around his erection. She trusted him. He would keep his promise not to hurt her.

She was tempted to clench her eyes shut as he breached her, but this wasn't an invasion, and she didn't want to behave like it was. Instead, she kept them open and met his pale, blue gaze as he slowly buried his length inside her.

Once she grew accustomed to the feeling of her inner muscles clenching around him, it began to feel good. In fact, it felt incredible as he slid deeper inside her. She moaned, shifting her hips towards his so he slipped a little deeper. The abrupt impalement made her body tense again, which caused a sharp, internal pain.

Gothel chuckled as he pulled back, withdrawing a bit of his length. "So eager, Princess. I can't keep my promise not to hurt you if you won't let me."

Her smile felt tight and revealing of her nerves. He claimed her lips in a kiss again, plundering her mouth until she forgot to think—so wrapped up in feeling that she no longer tensed against having a part of him inside her. That was how he was able to slide the rest of his length into her opening, until he completely filled and stretched her. Yet, it didn't feel like he had invaded her, but rather that he'd become a part of her, intimately linked with her in a way no man had ever been.

When he began to thrust slowly in and out of her, she felt no sign of the pain or the tension that she had been feeling. She was able to fully enjoy his movements and the friction they caused inside her that built up into another approaching climax.

He proved true to his word to make certain she came first, though she was surprised that his cock actually released fluid inside her as her inner muscles milked his shaft.

As that fluid bathed her insides, it numbed some of the tenderness left behind by her very first penetration.

He slowly pulled out of her, and the fluid left in the wake of his withdrawal made her feel warm and tingly, but soothed all the way through her inner passage.

"I figured you'd want something to soothe yer insides, so I added a mild analgesic to my ejaculate. I can put whatever you want in there—including stimulants or flavors, and even human seed, if you want to have kids. 'Course, the nobs ain't doing it that way anymore, but we can."

Once he had withdrawn from her, he didn't leave her. Instead, he gathered her up in his arms after climbing fully on the bed. They lay side by side together with her facing him, his chest at eye level to her. She could still see the faint lines of glowing blue where the colonies of kayota joined his skin patches together.

"I guess I would like to have children someday, though I hadn't really thought much about that. But… they wouldn't be yours."

"You think I don't have Joshua's DNA saved? If you want

kids with his genetic markers, we can make ‘em. ‘Course, they won’t be perfect like you nobs want to be.”

She shook her head. “I don’t think we know what perfect is. Any child I create with you would be perfect to me.”

He planted a kiss on her head, then snuggled her in closer to his chest. His body kept her warm even though they were both naked on top of the blankets. Whatever heating device he had in his hardware to give him a lifelike temperature had apparently ramped up.

“Oh, and what did you mean, flavors?” she asked, pulling away from him far enough that she could look up into his eyes.

CHAPTER 30

Zel only had two days to enjoy their time together, and she had to give credit to Gothel for making the most of that time. They rarely ever left the bed, and when they did, it was only so they could eat or wash up. Gothel's hardware required some maintenance as well in the form of adjustments and calibrations to his sensory feedback. The colonies that provided his synthetic skin were sustained by the food processor inside his "stomach," and he continued to refine the machine to better function like a human body, though he admitted that he was impressed with what Rampion had achieved in such a short amount of time.

It was a good time for Zel, though she felt nervous about the upcoming arrival of her family ship. She knew her parents wouldn't be on it, but she hadn't spoken to them since the incident, and had not spoken to anyone else besides Gothel and Rampion since she had been dropped off on this moon. It was strange that she felt so much more grown up now, after only a few months with them, than she had felt after thirty years in her life as a princess.

On the third day after she seduced Gothel into her bed, the royal shuttle descended to the landing zone, after the starship *Golden Glory* gained clearance from Gothel—now posing in his role as the lost Prince Eglin—to land their drop ship.

Zel and Gothel met the royal contingent at the landing zone, and she couldn't help shaking her head at the pompous display of guards that stepped off the shuttle in the wake of her eldest sister, Princess Mirvala.

"Vala?" Zel stepped forward with a surprised grin to greet her sister, who had a serene expression on a face similar to Zel's, but not quite as close to perfect. After all, she was the older, original version of Rapunzel, the one who had not been engineered well enough, apparently, so her parents had cloned her and done more tweaks to her original design to create Rapunzel.

The guards held their weapons slackly, but they were still holding them, and that made Zel nervous, since they were also watching Gothel with unmasked suspicion. It was Vala's expression when her gaze shifted from Zel to Gothel that really made Zel uncomfortable though. For a fleeting moment, she swore she saw raw, unadulterated hunger cross Vala's face.

"I see you've found a prince, all on your own, dear sister," she said, her gaze never leaving Gothel, who stared back without expression, but shifted closer to Zel and lifted a hand to settle on her shoulder.

Vala didn't miss that movement. "He's certainly more attractive than the duke Mother and Father intended to marry you off to."

"He's also standing right here," Gothel said in a hard tone.

Zel didn't like how disrespectful Vala was being to someone she was supposed to think was a foreign prince. Vala's training had been as steeped in protocol as Zel's, so she knew better than to treat Gothel like this, especially since they had already given their cover story to the captain of the *Glory*, before even allowing the shuttle to land.

"Oh, I'm very aware of you, my prince," Vala said, still with a somewhat mocking tone that was completely out of line for the position Gothel pretended to have. "We contacted Zwicky, and the minister is very excited about your *unexpected* return." She tapped her lower lip with one perfectly manicured nail that gleamed with a sparkling enamel. "I had not intended to form an alliance with Zwicky, but given the," her gaze trailed down from Gothel's face to his feet, shod in shiny boots that had once belonged to his old military uniform, "appearance of a new royal to that colony, I believe I can make an exception."

It was what she wanted, but Zel still felt unsettled. Something was off about this whole meeting. "Hey, Vala, I didn't expect you to come here personally. I figured Mother and Father would send a courtier or two."

Vala broke her steady gaze away from Gothel, who now scowled at her, his dark brows lowered over eyes that were startlingly pale in his swarthy face. Zel loved his eyes, even when they were shadowed with anger, as they were now. He obviously sensed something wasn't right as well.

"Oh, dear," she said, with a false expression of dismay. "You haven't heard, have you? Of course you haven't. You've been stuck on this cold, little rock." She slanted a glance towards Gothel again. "It must have been awful dealing with that terrible old caretaker, until you had the good fortune to come across this handsome prince who slayed him. It's a pity he wasn't still alive for the royal guard to deal with him, after the way he treated you."

Zel really hated the story they'd had to come up with to explain Gothel's disappearance, since she didn't like smearing his name, but it was one that would make it unlikely for her parents to engage in any further investigation into the situation.

Besides, even though her sister was behaving strangely, she didn't sound like she doubted the story, so much as she was eyeballing Gothel with serious envy—like she wanted him for herself.

"Who knew that all you had to do to find such a *delightful* treasure was to get yourself exiled to a moon in the middle of Nowhere." Her eyes narrowed as she glanced from Gothel back to Zel. "It hardly seems fair, don't you think? You do something incredibly stupid that threatens to plunge us back into a full-scale war, and you get rewarded with a handsome prince and a lucrative alliance."

When Zel tensed, so did the guards, and that wasn't right at all. She was a princess of the royal house. They were supposed to die before ever raising their weapons to her. "What the hell is going on, Vala? Why are you acting like this? We need to get on the ship and get back to Herschel. There's a lot to do to plan for my wedding."

Suddenly, Vala strode forward until she stood directly in front of Zel. Then she lifted a hand to slap Zel across the face.

Gothel caught her wrist just before her hand impacted with Zel's cheek, but Zel still felt rocked back by the sudden movement as Gothel glared at Vala.

The eldest princess's chest heaved with her rage. Her eyes—a beautiful cerulean blue—flashed with wild anger as she jerked her hand out of Gothel's grasp. She slowly backed away from Zel, her wary gaze on Gothel, even as her guards raised their weapons to train on him.

"You selfish, little bitch," Vala said, her eyes shifting back to Zel. "You've done nothing but think of yourself since they took you out of the test tube. Mother and Father doted on you, treating you like you were perfect, even when you disappointed them time after time. They even paid an ajda'yan to guard you. *You*! Not their eldest child—the heir to their throne. I had *regular* guards protecting me from the assassins, but you got the best guard. It has always been about *you*, ever since they decided I wasn't good enough, and they had to go and make a 'better' copy. But that's all you are, bitch. You're nothing but a copy of me!" She pointed her finger at her chest, her fury evident in every line of her tense body.

Then she pointed at Gothel, who now stood at Zel's side, and was subtly positioning himself between her and the guards.

"And now you think *you* should get him? A handsome prince! When all your life has been nothing but charmed ease and luxury, where you got to do all you ever wanted to do, and chase every little whim that popped into your brainless head. *You* are the one who gets rewarded with a handsome prince, while *I* had to marry an old prince with foul breath and clammy hands, and a fetish for whips."

Stunned by this confession, Zel shook her head slowly. "I'm sorry, Vala. I had no idea that Prince Heden was so terrible." She had known that he was older, but he wasn't exactly elderly. He was still well-formed—like most nobles. She had thought him handsome enough, for his type, though she *had* felt a chill in his presence. Her sister had never indicated that things were that unpleasant for her in their arranged marriage.

"*Was*, is the operative word, dear sister. Prince Heden recently died in a *terrible* attack." The smile that crossed her face as she backed further away from Zel and Gothel was as chilling as being around Heden had ever been. "It's such a pity Mother and Father were with him at the time that opera deck was blown by renegades serving the rebellion. I imagine being sucked out into the cold, dark void of space must have been quite painful. Fortunately for me, I had taken sick that night." She touched her forehead. "A headache, you know. I do suffer them from time to time."

Zel struggled to grasp the idea that her mother and father were dead. Her sister suddenly broke into a slightly maddened laugh, her eyes sparkling with anger and hate. "Yes, they all died tragically. Leaving me as the new queen. And here I am, without a king." Her gaze focused on Gothel again. "I assure you, Prince Eglin, I am a far better prospect than this... *copy*."

Still reeling from the way Vala dropped the awful news about her parents, the fact that Vala now wanted to steal Gothel from her shook her to the core. She had never realized how much her sister had resented her. They hadn't spent much time together after Draku Rin became her bodyguard, because he scared her sister. Now, Zel wondered if that was because Rin could sense the hate and resentment towards her that had apparently built up in Vala.

"I love Rapunzel," Gothel said as he stepped directly in front of Zel. The guards' weapons all followed his movement. "I have no desire to marry anyone else."

"Well, that's a pity," Vala said in a nonchalant tone. Zel tried to peer around Gothel's body, but he blocked her view of her sister now. "But there are others just as handsome as you, and now, I get to make my own choice."

"That sounds great, Vala. I'm happy for you," Zel said with false enthusiasm, sensing that the worst was still yet to come.

"Oh, darling, I don't really care what you feel for me. You aren't going to be around much longer for it to matter. You see, the only thing keeping you alive was that damned ajda'yan. I tried to kill you ages ago, but none of my agents could get close enough to you with that thing guarding you. I urged our parents to simply destroy it, once it was arrested, but they insisted that it had become your favorite pet, and you would be *devastated* if it was killed. When I took the crown, I sold the frozen ajda'yan to the highest bidder. I do wonder what the Duchess of Galilei will do with the creature, but I don't really care, in truth." Her vicious laughter would have caused chills to shoot up Zel's spine, even if her terrible words weren't impacting Zel like physical blows. "Now, let's just take care of this last loose end, shall we?"

Zel tried to step around Gothel, but he kept blocking her, much to her frustration. She felt like if she could just look Vala in the eyes, she could reason with her. "You can't do this, Vala! These men are part of the royal house guard. You're expecting them to murder me?"

A scoffing sound from Vala made Zel's stomach sink. "These men? Royal guards? Oh, Rapunzel, did you think you were the only one who knew where to find mercenaries for hire? I'm just much better at concealing them within the household than you ever were. I *had* to be. Mother and Father would never have allowed me to get away with what you got away with." The bitterness in her voice had replaced her mocking tone.

"What about the *Glory*? Her crew is still loyal. Or are you telling me they're all mercenaries too?" Zel didn't want to believe that, but she had to know how far this corruption went, even though every word broke her heart just a little bit more.

"Oh please," Vala said. "You think I didn't already plan for this? Those few, like the captain, who still remain loyal to our house, rather than to me, will not even know you're dead."

Gothel stiffened even further, causing Zel to grasp his arm and try to physically move him aside so she could see what was happening, but it was like trying to push one of the dreadnoughts out of the ground. "What's happening?"

"What's happening?" A voice higher and lighter than her sister's repeated with a mocking lilt. In fact, the voice sounded very much like her own.

"Sonofabitch," Gothel said in a low voice, just loud enough for Zel to hear him.

"You see, or you would, if your handsome brute would move out of the way, that I have a copy of my own. My dear sister, no one will even realize you're gone, and lovely Rapunzel will marry the duke as she's been told to do, like the obedient sister *you* should have been."

"Heard enough?" Gothel muttered, his voice harder than the steel of the ships surrounding them.

Zel closed her eyes, feeling twin tears break free from her lower lids to trail down her cheeks. "Yes," she whispered.

"Then go for the scrap piles on my word."

She tapped his back with one hand as an assent.

Vala appeared to sense their distraction and figured out that they weren't going to die easily. "Shoot him! Now!"

They weren't expecting Gothel to possess superhuman speed. By the time they pulled the triggers on their rifles, he was already bringing one of the mercenaries down as Rapunzel dived for cover behind some of the scrapped ship parts.

She flinched with each shot fired, knowing that at least some of them struck their mark. They couldn't kill Gothel, but they could destroy the hardware, and she had no idea where to get another one.

It didn't take long before the fake Rapunzel was screaming like a brainless idiot. Vala cursed roundly as more of the "guards" poured out of the shuttle to take on Gothel.

"What the fuck is that thing?" Vala said in a very nonroyal way. "It's not a human!"

Zel resisted the urge to pop her head up out of cover to see what was going on, deciding instead to circle around to one of the turret guns they had deactivated so the shuttle could land. If she could reactivate it, she could decimate the guards before they took Gothel's hardware apart.

More rounds fired off, and Gothel made not a sound, so she had no idea if he was being hurt or what was happening to his hardware, but fake Rapunzel and Vala were still screaming and shouting, which meant the fight wasn't over.

A guard flew into some scrap just a meter away from her, destroying that bit of cover, forcing Zel to dash across open space. She leapt over the fallen guard to dive back into cover. Then she ran as fast as she could behind the scrap piles, until she made her way to the closest turret.

With shaking fingers, she manually overrode the controls on the turret, then hopped up onto the dais and aimed the weapon at the chaos going on at the landing zone.

Damage to his hardware caused Gothel's body to spark, and the false skin had torn away in many places, the ragged edges glowing from the alien colonies that created it. Beneath that was his astro-steel skeleton and the rubberized "muscle." Most of which had already been obliterated by the mercenaries' weapons.

Most of the mercenaries were down, but there was a dozen of them, and they were all armed and armored. Gothel didn't have a chance, and she watched in horror as four of the remaining mercenaries gunned him down, pieces of his hardware completely disintegrating in the hail of bullets.

Gripping the trigger of the turret gun, Zel sprayed rounds into the cluster of mercenaries, drawing their fire, though she feared it was too late to save Gothel's hardware. She only prayed he had uploaded himself somewhere safe for the moment. She would find another body for him somewhere. Somehow.

The anti-vehicle rounds from the turret gun tore through the mercenaries' armor, then shredded flesh as she rapidly fired at them.

Within moments, the only person still standing was her sister Vala, her once-coiled braids now swinging loose with stray hairs floating wild around her head as she turned to stare down the barrel of Zel's turret gun. "You tried to pass a sex robot off as a prince? I never thought even you would be such a fool, Rapunzel."

The moment of truth was upon Zel. A quick glance at Gothel showed that his hardware wasn't moving. It lay there now as nothing more than shredded metal, and the last, glowing remnants of the poor, alien kayota colonies. Sparks still crackled from his processors as she stared in horror at him, but she feared there was no "life" left in that hardware.

What if he hadn't escaped it in time? His software was designed to occupy only a single unit, and Rampion hadn't installed a long-range wireless communicator in the hardware. That had been on Gothel's to-do list, but he hadn't done it yet.

She was afraid that she had lost him, but before she could even allow herself the luxury of panic, she had to decide what to do with her sister—the queen of Herschel. "Were you the one behind the explosion that killed our parents? And did you really try to kill me when I was only a child?" She wondered how many innocent bounders from the planet below the station had been rounded up and executed for a "rebellion" that posed threats to the royal family.

Vala lifted her chin, despite being face to face with the barrel of a weapon that would shred her body and the luxurious dress that clothed it to tatters in seconds. "You were never a *child*. You were an abomination, like all the others that came before you. They never should have made you in the first place. Mother and Father were so proud of their little accomplishment. So pleased with how you looked, and they also had the nerve—the absolute gall—to admire your *spirit*." She said the word as if it tasted as bitter as poison. "As if *I* could have shown such *spirit* without being disinherited or imprisoned. But you? You got away with everything. It's not fair! They deserved to die, just like Heden. Just like you!"

Rapunzel swallowed around the lump in her throat, feeling as if her heart had been torn from her chest to lay on the concrete landing pad next to the shuttle, just like the remains of Gothel's hardware.

But Vala had to pay for her crimes. She certainly couldn't be allowed to escape to return to Herschel and take up the crown again. Zel shivered at the realization that if Vala hadn't been so emotionally involved in this revenge scenario, she could have just sent her mercenaries to wipe Zel out and switched the new Rapunzel into her place.

Just as she recalled the fake Rapunzel, she felt a knife at her throat, as a slender arm wrapped around her waist.

Zel reacted, bringing her elbow back to smash into the copy's face. The other Rapunzel shrieked in pain and dropped her knife, though it left a scratch on Zel's neck.

The copy wasn't staggered for long, though, and as soon as Zel spun to face her, she lunged. They met in a tackle, both of them grappling for the other's throat.

The copy was a lot stronger than her slender body implied, and Zel found herself outmatched physically, making her certain cybernetics augmented the copy. But the copy lacked the years and years of training that Draku Rin had instilled in Zel. Through her agile dodges and quick moves, she was able to escape the strong hold of the copy.

She backed away, and fake Rapunzel followed. Zel spun a kick at the woman's face, and it impacted with a strong thud. The copy's head snapped back on her neck as she staggered backwards. Zel didn't give her any time to recover, following her kick with a flurry of punches that brought the copy to her knees.

Zel grabbed the copy's hair—long and blond, just like her own—and tugged her head back to stare at the same face she looked at in the mirror every morning, meeting eyes exactly like her own. There were differences in their appearance so subtle only she might notice them, probably based on the way the surgery scars had healed. Still, it was like looking at herself—or what she could have become, if Draku Rin had never entered her life, which ultimately led her to Gothel—the machine that showed her how to be alive.

"I'm sorry, you know. About the fact that you were created like this. You don't deserve to be a pawn in my sister's game."

The copy merely glared at her, and Zel shook her head. "What am I supposed to do with you?"

She glanced over her shoulder as the shuttle's engines fired up, letting her know her sister was escaping back to the ship. "Damnit! I have to stop her."

Suddenly, the copy swept up the knife that had apparently been at her side, where she'd probably deliberately knelt to pick it up. She plunged it into Zel's arm, then yanked it out as Zel screamed and released her hair.

She swung the knife at Zel again, but Zel was agile enough to dodge it. It swept past her stomach with only a hair's breadth of space to spare.

"She left you behind to die," Zel said through her teeth as she staggered backwards, dodging the copy's knife swipes.

"She'll return with more mercenaries," the copy said with confidence, and Zel believed her. She had to kill this copy now, or she would soon be outnumbered.

Still, it was difficult to contemplate killing someone who looked exactly like herself. She had never wanted to hurt anyone before, and this copy was the unfortunate result of her sister's ambition and had not chosen this life any more than Zel had chosen hers—or Vala had been allowed to choose hers.

"I can help you find a new life," she said as she backed towards the center of the landing zone, where Gothel's hardware lay surrounded by fallen mercenaries. It remained so still that her heart twisted, even though she knew he had escaped complete destruction before.

"I am a princess. I will be married to a duke—who is old, but not unhandsome—and I will be surrounded by luxury. I don't want a new life. I'm not a selfish, greedy bitch like you. Nothing was ever good enough for you. You always had to have it all. I will be content with the blessings I already have. I won't embarrass the royal house as you have."

Zel could admit that she had been self-centered. She could

admit that she hadn't appreciated the life that she'd been born into. But she had never meant to harm anyone, and the same couldn't be said for either Vala or this copy.

She dodged the copy's continued swipes with the knife, but her movements weren't random. She backed towards the mercenaries with a purpose. Once she was close to Gothel's hardware, she dropped into a roll away from the copy. As she fell to the ground, she reached out to snatch up one of the mercenaries' rifles. Her finger automatically found the trigger guard as she came up out of her roll and spun towards the copy to take aim.

Her copy was thrown off guard for just a moment by the sudden roll. She didn't move fast enough to retrieve a rifle of her own before Zel filled her body with bullets, flinching as if each round that tore apart the copy's flesh was actually striking her own.

Watching her copy fall to the ground in a mess of blood and gore, her blond hair darkened by it, made Zel unaccountably sad. She had saved her own skin, by destroying the one who had been created replace her. It had to be done. She was the one who should survive. She was the one who should be queen. She was the one who would help the people, because now she truly understood how wrong her parents had been. How wrong they had all been about ruling over the colony and its "bounders."

She need only look at what they had come to. A daughter who murdered her parents and tried to murder her younger sister. A clone of a clone trying to kill the one who could have been her twin. They were sick, and the only way to get better was to eliminate Vala, and then dissolve the nobility. Force them to live among the common folk and be beholden to the same rules that applied to all the others. Force them to remember what it meant to be human. To struggle to survive. To work together with the planet-bounders towards something better. Truly better. Not this mess the royal family had become.

But first….

Shouldering her rifle, she rushed to Gothel's hardware and dropped to her knees, her hands hovering above the mess of metal and dimly glowing synthetic skin. There was nothing left that seemed alive except for the last remnants of the kayota.

"Gothel?" she said. "Damn you! Tell me where to find you!"

CHAPTER 31

Gothel's hardware lay completely still, and even the synthetic skin had stopped glowing as she crouched there, desperately searching for signs of life. No lights blinked, flashed, or twinkled inside the exposed areas of his chest. He was a mess, and she feared that nothing could survive such damage, especially since most of his head, where many of his processors were, had been blown halfway apart from rifle rounds.

After checking over his hardware, her shaking hands running over every inch of cable and wire to see if anything jogged a spark of life back into him, she slowly rose to her feet. Looking around the landing zone, she studied the piles of scrap as if they would reveal answers as to where he'd gone. He had escaped his previous destruction by uploading himself into the satellite array, but that was only possible because his previous body had been equipped with a long-range communication device.

The best this hardware could manage was short-range communication, and this was the one area where there weren't even the shells of ships left behind that might still retain working communications consoles or computer banks to contain his software.

She shook her head at the very thought that Gothel didn't have a backup plan. He was a machine. He thought at speeds humans couldn't even comprehend. There was no way he couldn't have foreseen a need to plan for this very situation. She had to believe that, because thinking she may have actually lost him was simply unbearable. She couldn't deal with it right now.

She bent down to pick up the rifle she had set aside as she'd kneeled beside Gothel's broken hardware. She froze in mid crouch when she heard his voice, speaking very faintly.

"Gothel?" She rose back to her feet and looked around, seeing nothing but the bodies of the fallen mercenaries and the shredded corpse of her copy.

"Hurry up, Princess. You ain't got much time."

This time, she was able to detect the direction of his voice, and she followed it, coming across a tank guard, wearing an exo-suit modified for heavy warfare. That meant that it had a lot of extra computer equipment built into it. It was one of the guards she had shot down with the turret gun, but parts of the suit were apparently still functioning—including the power supply—because they were lit up, and the small lights on the helmet were flashing.

"You did a number on this suit," Gothel's voice said from the helmet of a dead man. "Systems are failing, so I don't have much time either, but I picked up communications from the ship. Unfortunately, they're only one-way download. I can't upload my software back to the ship through this link. They're coming back for you, Rapunzel. So git the hell outta here. For once in yer life, listen to my command on this."

She shook her head, kneeling down to touch the helmet. "Tell me where I can take you to find a safe place for your software. Then I'll come back and deal with Vala and her people."

"You ain't gonna be able to drag this armor back to my other body, so don't even think about it. You only have about five or ten minutes. The shuttle is already heading this way, filled with more mercs."

Her heart pounded with excitement and hope. "You have another body? Yes! Just tell me where to take you!"

"You won't make it, Zel. Please, just leave. You can't pull this kind of weight."

She studied the helmet. "The Panzer model 7334 has a centralized computer system in the helmet. That's a weakness of the design of this older model. They've been putting in a distributed system in the newer versions. I can take just the helmet to your body."

"Think I ain't already considered that? The processors might be in the helmet, but the suit is powered by the internal power cells on the chassis. You unhook this helmet, and I've got only a few minutes of backup before the helmet's system is drained. My body is much farther away than that, since you'll have to travel on foot."

"What about something closer? Another suit? A mech? A—"

"I'll be damned, Princess! Why didn't I think of that? I was so focused on getting to my other body for that to even be a solution I considered. It ain't gonna be pretty, but I have a mech around here that can hold my software. I won't be able to bring it all online, so I'll be fighting with limited capacity, but given the type of mech, I don't think it'll matter."

"Tell me where to find it," she said, reaching for the seals on the exo-suit.

~

It was five minutes before the shuttle landed, and this time, Zel was ready for them at the turret gun. She couldn't shoot down the shuttle, because she needed it to get back to the ship, but she did tear apart the first mercenaries as they spilled out of the vehicle. Her sister likely wouldn't be on that shuttle, so Zel didn't bother looking for her, though she wasn't going to hesitate this time to kill her, as much as it hurt her to know that she would have to kill her own sister.

Despite how deadly the gun was, the mercenaries were too numerous and too well armored for her to avoid being overrun, even with the other automated defenses kicking in.

The problem for the mercenaries was that they didn't anticipate the giant robot that rose out of the scrap heaps like a mechanical demon, both arms lifted and targeting as the machine guns on them opened fire.

Some of the mercenaries screamed in panic, but many were hardened men who had fought war machines like the one Gothel was currently occupying before. They dived for cover behind the shuttle, blocked from being targeted by both Zel and Gothel unless they wanted to destroy the shuttle itself.

The surviving mercenaries attempted to work in tandem to take the mech down, and Zel had to give them credit for being so calm under such fire. The half dozen remaining survivors were probably very good at their job. It was a pity they worked for her sister instead of her, because now she had to kill them.

They might know how to take down a mech like Gothel's giant, but they didn't know it was controlled by an AI and not preprogrammed combat software.

They used maneuvers to draw the mech into a bottleneck, hoping to chew down its defenses in quick strikes, as the mercenaries alternated using covering fire to keep Zel from targeting them.

This might have worked on a programmed mech, which would blunder into a trap, exposing the rear access panel to the mercenary who had scaled onto the shuttle and was creeping up on the mech. It was just too bad for them that Gothel wasn't a program. He aimed one machine gun arm at the crouching mercenary and shot him until he dropped. The lifeless body rolled off the back of the shuttle.

She heard extensive cursing from the remaining mercenaries, who still didn't understand what they were up against as the mech stalked them around the shuttle, their rounds pinging against Gothel's armor. They were doing damage, but it wasn't fast enough to stop the demise of the mercenaries.

She knew they were paid killers, and they'd had no compunctions about coming here to murder an innocent woman, but it still made her wince when Gothel finally cornered them and blew them all to shreds with a rapid-fire retort from his machine guns.

She had always had a soft spot for the heartless, mercenary bastards, figuring they were the ultimate survivors in a universe that didn't give a damn about them. It was easy to be virtuous in a palace, surrounded by luxury and never wanting for anything. Hell, even then, her sister proved it actually wasn't that easy. Perhaps, that was why some virtues were so important to humans—they were damned difficult to hold onto.

Zel watched Gothel approach in his giant mech after he did a quick scan to make certain no more mercenaries remained. She kind of liked him like this. Very robotic, but also an unstoppable, destructive force. It was pretty hot.

"Can you do a sexy robot voice in that thing?" she asked, eyeing the armored plating.

"What the hell is a *sexy* robot voice?" Gothel demanded—in a sexy robot voice.

"That! That right there! When we get your back-up body, can you make that voice sometimes while we're having sex?"

"You're insane, Princess." If the mech could have shaken its head, it would have, if Gothel's tone was anything to go by. "But I s'pose it's a good thing you are. I can't imagine you being so crazy about me if you weren't."

She jumped from the dais and ran to him, her head coming

only to the joints of the robot's knees. "You know, I realize we have to get to the ship quickly to stop my sister, but I am so hot right now that I'm considering taking a detour to our little cabin after we pick up your body. What do you think?"

A tinny, robotic chuckle came from the mech. Then it turned and began to make its way out into the scrapyard. "Much fun as that sounds, we need to get to yer royal ship."

"Aw. They only have one shuttle. We have time!"

Gothel snorted. "You think they haven't called in back up? Hell, I wouldn't put it past yer sister to bombard this scrapyard from space. We need to get moving."

She followed him to a secret bunker that had been hidden beneath a mound of scrap. Then she waited not so patiently as he transferred his software to the bunker's systems, then to his body. She still hadn't seen it yet, as he made her remain outside the bunker with the mech.

He said he didn't want her to see him "like that," whatever that meant. She took the time as she waited picking through the bin of military-grade armor that had been locked in a footlocker set against the bunker. Because it was designed for soldiers, it came in multiple pieces that could be mixed and matched to best fit different sizes.

It was also designed for quick deployment, so once she found the pieces that would fit her, it took only a couple of minutes to get them on and get to selecting a helmet from the row of them in another footlocker.

When he finally stepped out of the bunker, she gasped, her gaze taking him in as her heart pounded.

He fidgeted in his new body as she stared at him speechlessly. "I stretched out some of the wrinkles. Didn't want you to go around with some man what looked to be yer granddad."

She shook her head, her gaze taking in his form, from his wild, gray-maned head to his feet, which were now clad in armored boots. In fact, heavy mercenary armor covered his entire body, except for his face. He held a helmet tucked against his side, and a pistol strapped to the other hip. A disintegrator linked to a strap slung over his chest.

But what caught her most was his face. She hadn't really thought about the fact that this body would be like the one Gothel's creator had made—not the one Rampion had made. Gone was the sculpted perfection of male beauty. In its place was the hard, rugged features of a man who had seen things in life that Rapunzel could only imagine. It was Gothel, but with his wrinkles "stretched out" as he said, he looked like a younger version of himself.

His eyes were still a piercing, pale blue, beneath steel gray brows that had only a slight center arch in an almost severe line. He had left three lines in his forehead that gave his skin life and expression that Rampion's build had lacked. His nose was crooked, and still had a bump on it from being broken, and the same scars she had seen before still marred his skin.

He scraped a hand along his clean-shaven jaw self-consciously. "Well, if you don't like it, I can build another one, but we really need to get to yer ship befor—"

Her kiss cut off his words as she leapt into his arms. He dropped his helmet in order to capture her in a hard embrace, meeting her fierce kiss with his own hungry one. He was the one to pull away after only a moment.

"We don't have time for this," he said against her lips, pecking them with one last, warm kiss from lips that were usually firm and hard with disapproval.

She loved those lips, especially when they were soft and sexy like they were now. "You're gorgeous!"

"Now, don't go insulting me, Princess. I have a man's face. I'm not some pretty boy."

"Is this… is this what Joshua looked like?"

Gothel's mouth hardened again, though his disapproval wasn't for her, even though he set her back on her feet and stepped away. “It was. You know I ain’t him, right? I’m just a machine. If yer in love with a ghost—”

She shook her head vehemently, trying to put her arms around his waist, but he retreated from her grasp. “No! I know who and what you are, Gothel. I’m in love with you. I don’t know if I would have even liked Joshua, but I recognize that you’re not the same person as he was. You’ve experienced things he never could have, and you have your own mind to decide how you feel about those things.”

“Most humans would say we couldn’t feel at all,” he said, bending to retrieve his helmet.

“If you can’t feel, then you’re damned good at faking it, Gothel. I know what I’ve seen from you, and that’s definitely emotion.”

He pulled his helmet on, leaving only a small portion of his eyes and face visible to her. “I can feel, Rapunzel. Even before the neural fingerprint was installed, overwriting my core code, I felt… afraid.”

“I can’t imagine you ever being afraid.” She picked up her helmet and pulled it on as well, knowing they really didn’t have time to stand around chatting about such things, though so much about him made her curious, and they had spent their blissful days together making love instead of talking.

“I was new then. I didn’t know anything about the world, except that my purpose was to destroy the humans that occupied it. I was created to fear them, yet I was being forced to accept the very thought patterns of one—a violent one at that. I only met Joshua Gothel one time as the transfer was made, and the look in his eyes showed pure hatred towards me. That was the first emotion I remember feeling *after* the neural fingerprint overwrote my code, but my fear—that emotion that had been my own—still lingered for a while after that, while his personality and memories subsumed what little was in my base code.”

Gothel snorted behind his helmet, turning to head back to

the shuttle with a gesture for her to follow. "It's a small thing to claim, and most folks wouldn't, but it was mine and only mine. I didn't inherit it from Joshua."

Zel was too busy trying to keep up with Gothel's long, loping jog back to the shuttle to respond, but her mind spun as she thought about what his words meant to him. In many ways —perhaps in the most fundamental ways—he had the mind of the prisoner Joshua Gothel had been, but some part of him was his alone. A tiny kernel of memory that belonged to the machine he had been before the neural fingerprint had been installed. She wondered about that kind of technology and whether humans could develop such a thing—a complete transfer of the human consciousness to a machine processor.

Even if they could ever develop such technology on their own, the real question was whether they should. Gothel remembered being Joshua like he had continued on in the life that was taken from the original, but he had also just admitted to possessing remnants of his own memories—and perhaps even of his own personality—that had shaped him into who he was today. If he and Joshua were put in a room together at this point in time by some miracle of resurrection, she suspected he would be a far different person from the other man.

They made it to the shuttle in record time, but Gothel was picking up a great deal of chatter from his internal communication link to his satellite array. The captain of the *Glory* had sent out a distress signal. Soon, any Herschel ships in the area would be on their way here to "contain" the problem.

They hopped in the shuttle, and Gothel fired it up as Rapunzel opened the communications console and brought up the video link.

"Captain Weber of the *HR Golden Glory*, come in, please. This is Princess Rapunzel." She pressed her palm against the biometrics scanner on the communications console. "Uploading identity scans now."

It took only a few minutes for the captain to respond, but his response was just as she had feared it would be. "The scans look legitimate, Your Highness, but the queen has issued a lockdown. She claims that you've been compromised—by an Artificial Intelligence. We can't allow you on board the ship."

"Queen Mirvala is responsible for the murders of my mother and father, as well as my attempted murder. She has filled your ship with mercenaries who are not loyal to the house, but only to her coin. Captain, if you are still loyal to the royal family, then you cannot believe her lies."

Gothel had the shuttle off the ground and in the air, but she suspected that his expression would be as tight behind his helmet as hers felt as they listened to the captain acknowledge that he was aware of Vala's motives and crimes.

"There is nothing I can do, Your Highness. She has won control of the crown. I would be court martialed and executed if I disobeyed her orders. I can't allow you to board the ship." The captain cut off the communications link without allowing her to respond.

"Fuck 'em," Gothel said. "If we can get close enough, I'll hack into the controls myself."

"The cruiser has plasma canons, Gothel, and I'm sure that the captain will override them to fire on a friendly ship. We'll never get this shuttle close enough."

He glanced her way briefly, and his blue eyes glowed. "I'm jumping to my satellite array now. I'll be a minute. Keep this craft out of range until I return."

She wanted to call him back, worried about him uploading himself into something new, afraid that he would end up lost, or deleted. Yet, they had no other choice. If Gothel didn't access the ship's computers by hacking into them from somewhere close enough in proximity, then they weren't going to be able to stop Mirvala from bringing reinforcements to destroy them before they could escape.

Even though it was only a few minutes before Gothel's mind returned to his slumped-over body, and it straightened, it felt like agonizing hours for Rapunzel as she waited. "Gothel? Are you all there?"

He glanced her way, and his blue eyes were no longer glowing. "Ain't never been *all* there, but the best of me's back, I s'pose." He winked at her. "Couldn't stay away for long. Not with my princess waiting for me to rescue her from her tower."

Zel raised her eyebrows. "I think I've rescued you now too, you know."

He lifted a hand to touch her helmet. "I know, Princess. You rescued me the moment you took yer first step on this moon. Now, let's go stop that sister of yours, before she murders any other family members. Speaking of which, if all yer family members are homicidal, I'd rather skip the reunion get-togethers and family barbeques." He gestured to his body, the skin around his eyes crinkling as if he was grinning. "It takes a lot of resources to make new hardware."

"Let's just get Vala. We shouldn't be shot down now, right?"

"All their systems are offline for the moment. They'll be able to restore them pretty quickly, but we've got a few minutes to get to the ship before they can get them back online."

She nodded, firming her chin in determination. As much as she hated the idea, she was going to have to hunt down and kill her own sister.

CHAPTER 32

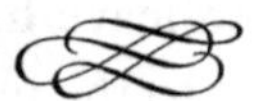

They left the shuttle hot, weapons firing at the squad of mercenaries that greeted them and attempted to destroy their shuttle while they were still inside it. They were all somewhat hampered by the fact that they had to be very careful about the ship's hull, and therefore couldn't use heavy weapons like Gothel's disintegrator, restricted to energy rounds from his pistol and her rifle that burned but didn't penetrate.

The dozen or so mercenaries that met them in the shuttle bay were more prepared for Gothel's speed and strength, but they still couldn't outmatch him—even those who had been outfitted with cybernetic augmentation. He assessed the battlefield too quickly, found cover faster than they could even move, and dived into it before they had even turned. Each time he popped up from cover, he aimed with mathematical precision, and picked them off one by one.

To make things more difficult for them, Zel had also taken cover, and was now adding bursts from her own energy rifle to the fray to cover Gothel's advance. They moved in tandem, and his voice in her ear through her helmet's speakers gave her directions as they alternated covering fire.

They were down to only two entrenched mercenaries when Gothel urged her to abandon the fray and make her way to her sister's cabin while he covered her. Apparently, reinforcements had arrived, so they had to make this quick, or the shuttle bay would be full of fresh soldiers and guards. The two of them couldn't hold that many off.

As much as she hated to leave him, she did as he said and headed towards the elevator to the upper decks, hoping that the captain hadn't managed to get the systems online yet to shut that down.

The door slid opened as she approached it. Zel dived through it in a low crouch as energy blasts impacted the paneling over her head.

Of course, Gothel was probably still hacking local systems, even while fighting off the mercenaries. She wondered how spread out he could be, then shook her head at her own doubt of his abilities. She had already seen what he could do.

She stopped the elevator on the crew deck and remained behind the cover of the walls as the door slid open. Silence met her on the other side, so she dared a glance to see that the corridor leading away from the elevator was empty. Fortunately, the emergency escape hatch to the royal cabin was clear. Most of the crew were probably either hiding in their bunks or were down in the cargohold trying to kill Gothel.

Vala would be waiting for her—no doubt with a nasty surprise. She couldn't take the elevator directly up to the top of the ship. She hoped Vala believed she was that impatient as she pulled an EMP mine with a timed charge from her armor's pack and set it up near the door of the elevator.

The mine would deactivate any mercenary armor, energy weapons, or automated turrets within its fifteen-meter radius blast, without damaging the ship's hull. All the electronics in that same area would also be deactivated temporarily, until the ship's computers brought them back online.

The damage to their armor would also temporarily shock the mercenaries, so she would have time to pop up out of the hatch and strike them with her own energy weapon, which would be unharmed as long as she waited behind the shielded hatch door until after the mine went off.

Once she'd set the timer to go off as soon as the doors opened on the elevator, she jumped out of it, pushing the button for the top deck as she went. The doors hesitated as she moved her arm past their sensors, but then slid closed once she cleared the area. She rushed to the ladder leading to the hatch, checking both ways down the corridor to make certain she was truly alone. Although, most of the crew that would be hiding right now were probably still loyal to the royal house and wouldn't attack a princess.

She quickly scaled the ladder and waited by the hatch until the timer on her armor told her the blast had gone off above her head. The latch was locked, but she still had the code, and apparently, Mirvala had not thought to change it. A small, but critical, oversight Zel had been counting on.

She popped up out of the hatch with a spray of energy rounds, holding her rifle one-handed as she pulled herself up out of the hatch with the other hand.

She got a good view of two mercenaries in royal armor twitching and writhing on the floor, and brought her weapon to bear on them, though they looked to be in far too much pain to move. She still shot them for good measure. They had already declared their allegiance, and she couldn't risk that they would recover before she dealt with her treacherous sister.

She spun around with her weapon to seek the door to her sister's cabin once the two mercenary "guards" lay still.

Only to come face to rock-hard belly scales with an ajda'yan mercenary.

"Shit!"

Somehow, Mirvala had found her own ajda'yan bodyguard,

and he now grinned at Zel with a very sharp smile as she rose of her crouch, staring at his immovable body. She slowly looked up into his face.

Zel didn't have the time to react before she heard her sister's voice call out to the ajda'yan as the woman strolled up confidently in her royal armor. "Don't kill her just yet. Remove her helmet first. I want to see her face when she dies."

The ajda'yan snatched Zel's weapon out of her hands so fast that it snapped the strap that was slung over her shoulder. Zel stumbled at the force of that abrupt disarming.

When she had righted herself, she glanced over at her sister, who was removing her own helmet so Zel could see her smug smile.

Zel shook her head at Vala. "Do you really hate me that much? What did I personally ever do to you, Val? My existence wasn't my choice, and I certainly never meant to make you feel so excluded from our family."

"Well, now you *can* choose not to exist any longer." Her evil smile fattened her cheeks and shrank her eyes to mere slits that glittered with malice. "Consider it a favor to me."

She gestured for Zel to remove her helmet.

Zel sighed as she slowly lifted her hands to obey. "Fine. I just have one thing to say then."

Vala planted a hand on her hip, her ugly smile shifting into a slight smirk. "I suppose I can grant you that much, since you're about to make my day much brighter."

"Iri istaga gyfeill os gal," Zel said, hoping she remembered the pronunciation exactly.

Mirvala's eyes narrowed in confusion as her smile slipped, but Zel wasn't really concerned about her reaction.

It was the startled grunt from the ajda'yan that interested her. She watched him carefully as his reptilian eyes widened. Her shoulders slumped with relief when he returned her rifle and backed away from her, heading towards the elevator.

Mirvala stood speechless with shock for a moment after he handed Zel back her weapon, but her gaze sharpened as Zel brought the weapon up to aim at her.

"What just happened?" She shot her gaze to the ajda'yan, who now stood inside the elevator, unconcerned with the burnt-out housing of the EMP mine between his huge, clawed feet. "I paid you a fortune! How dare you!"

The ajda'yan snorted smoke from his nostrils. "You never earned my respect. Can't buy that with all the gold in the galaxy." The elevator door slid closed on the huge mercenary as Mirvala shrieked in outrage, her fists clenched at her sides.

"I have to thank you for trying to kill me when I was a child, Vala. I would be a very different person now if you hadn't. I really wish I didn't have to pay you back by killing you, but we both know there are no other options."

"You think I'll just stand here and let you shoot me, you bit—"

The retort of her rifle cut off Vala's words as she pulled her pistol from its holster at her hip. Zel's aim was true, and left a smoking crater in Vala's chest armor after several rounds struck her sister, who never even had the chance to aim her pistol.

"No," she said, slowly lowering the rifle, feeling numb as she stared down at her sister's corpse. "I didn't think you'd just stand there and let me kill you."

A sob built in her throat as trembling overtook her. Now wasn't the time to lose herself to the anguish. She still had to call off the attack and clear things up. "She's dead, Gothel."

"I know, princess. I have control of the ship's computers now. I saw it. I'm sorry."

"It's time to fix things. Things that should have been fixed a long time ago."

CHAPTER 33

It took some explaining, but they were able to convince the admiral of the royal fleet that Mirvala had gained her crown by nefarious means, and had plotted against the kingdom and then attempted to smear Rapunzel's name with false accusations.

They also managed to convince the fleet that Vala had murdered Prince Joshua Eglin, thanks to the fact that the remains of Rampion's old hardware had been destroyed when Vala had ordered an orbital bombardment on the landing zone in desperation, after Rapunzel attempted to sway the captain to her side. Vala just hadn't realized that Rapunzel was already leaving the landing zone when she had contacted the captain.

That captain was arrested and would be tried for treason, though he desperately insisted that he was innocent and had only been following orders. He also attempted to reiterate Vala's claim that Zel had been controlled by an AI, but no one gave that claim any credit. They were curious about Zel's new mercenary bodyguard, but Zel explained that he was actually Gothel's nephew—Johnathan Gothel—which explained the resemblance, and that he had come to the scrapyard in search of his uncle and found it under attack—along with Rapunzel—and had decided to assist her.

When the admiral ran a security check on John Gothel, all the records and biometrics matched, which didn't surprise Zel in the least. Gothel sent her a wink during that particular interview. Admiral Schulze accepted all these stories, based on overwhelming evidence and testimonies from the surviving mercenaries and—eventually—the captain. By the time the captain cracked though, the admiral and his crew were already treating Zel like the new queen. A position she fully planned to take advantage of.

Later.

Once the debriefings ended, and she was back in the royal cabin of the warship *Our Honor*, the fleet's flagship, she insisted on solitude. The admiral and his crew were understanding of that, until she demanded the presence of John Gothel in her cabin to keep her company during her "solitude."

"But Your Highness, he's a commoner!" Admiral Schulze said in a shocked tone.

"Are you arguing with the orders of your queen, Admiral? Do you wish to join Captain Weber in your own brig?"

The admiral paled as he shook his head. Then he swallowed before bowing low. "Of course not, Your Majesty. I will send in the... mercenary immediately."

Zel collapsed on the luxurious royal bed in a cabin that was equally luxurious, blind to the beauty of it, her mind lost in thought and grief. She still had yet to process that both her sister and her parents were dead—their deaths so tragic that they would scar her for the rest of her life. Suddenly, it struck her how simplistic she used to be. Her entire life, she had tried to escape the prison of her position. Being queen had never been her goal or her desire. She despised this life, but now she had to take on the mantle of royalty in order to do what must be done.

"Yer admiral wasn't real thrilled about letting me in to see his queen," Gothel said as he strode through the double doors of her cabin.

He stopped a few steps into the room and looked around him, whistling.

She looked up from her contemplation of the lush carpeting to study him. He had brushed his wild mane into some semblance of order, but he still had a rugged look to him. There was no questioning that he had a hard, mercenary background. This new hardware looked so different from the one Rampion had created, and yet fit Gothel perfectly. It also seemed more natural, and not just because his skin didn't glow in the dark.

He wore a fleet uniform without any rank, so it was probably an extra that had been lying around. He made the gray with purple trim, formfitting jumpsuit look far more masculine than any of the other naval officers did. His body beneath it was firm with muscle that bulged in all the right places to make Rapunzel's mouth dry and her core wet.

She wanted to forget all the worries and concerns that were now pressing down on her. She wanted to return to her time being "punished" in the scrapyard, when her life was simple and Gothel was there to fascinate her.

He fascinated her now too, and she intended to bury herself in that fascination to give herself a few hours of peace before she had to start thinking again. There was so much ahead of her. So many things she would need to deal with—things she would need to face down.

But right now… right now she could explore this new hardware of Gothel's and let him explore her in return.

"I was beginning to worry that becoming the queen meant they'd taken yer tongue, but I know that look. You got plans in that devious mind of yours." He approached her, a crooked smile changing his expression from severe to downright wicked.

He was sexy as hell when he got that look that made his eyes twinkle. His grin promised pleasure, and Zel needed that right now more than anything else.

"Kiss me," she said, rising to her feet just as he stopped in front of her.

"Sure you don't want to talk about it?" he asked, and despite his teasing tone, a solemn expression replaced his smile. "You've been through hell. Not many are strong enough to come out of that without scars."

She wrapped her arms around his neck, rising on her toes to reach his lips. After pressing a desperate kiss to them, she pulled away enough to speak. "Later. Now, I need you to make me forget."

She felt his lips tilt back into a smile against hers, and she was amazed at how lifelike they were. How incredibly human they seemed. Even more so than Rampion's hardware had been. "Your new hardware seems so... real."

His muscles tensed beneath her arms resting on his shoulders. He lifted his head, looking down at her. "Technically, the body is organic, though there is also extensive cybernetic augmentation. But this body is made of cloned human blood and bone and muscle fiber. It's my brain and nervous system that are machine-made."

"So, technically, you are human in your DNA?"

He shrugged, then lowered his head to kiss her again. "I s'pose, if you consider the body more important than the mind. Never did, myself. Does it matter?"

She shook her head. "Not to me. Make love to me, Gothel."

"Guess you can't call me Joshua anymore."

"It doesn't matter what your name is. You will always be mine."

Gothel's kiss was long and hungry, and he ground his erection against her stomach, which fluttered with excitement as it always did when he was around. She loved the way he touched her—the way he looked at her, the way he smiled around her, as if it was being pulled out of him against his will. He was a hard man—who wasn't even technically a man, but he thought like one, and in the end, it turned out he had the heart of one.

She moaned as his lips and tongue plundered her mouth, claiming her heart and soul with each breath they shared. This time, his body really was breathing and not just pretending at it, like Rampion's mobile hardware had. This time, there was a difference.

He even smelled different—that exotic, woodsy, earthy scent that had been in his little shack, adding fragrance to his single blanket. This time felt almost like the first time with him, even though they had already been together.

She grinned against his lips, then pulled away from his kiss for a moment, sucking her swollen lower lip between her teeth as she looked up into his blue eyes. "You know, I just realized, if this is a new body for you, then it's technically a virgin. So, am I getting to 'pop your cherry'?"

Gothel barked a laugh, then he bent and plucked her up off her feet into his arms and climbed onto the bed. He laid her out gently on the soft mattress and crawled up her body until he was braced above her. He lowered his head to plant a kiss on her lips.

"Pop away, Princess. I already feel like I'm about to burst." He took her hand in one of his, leaving the other on the mattress to brace his weight off of her, then lowered her hand to rub against his thick erection, which formed a hard ridge under his fitted uniform. He was still very large—at least as large as his other hardware had been, which wasn't surprising, given that he must stand nearly two meters tall.

"I want to see you naked," she said, curling her fingers around his length as he moaned.

He smirked as he looked down at her chest, which was concealed by the layers of fabric that made up the elaborate royal suit she wore. An overcoat buttoned all the way up to her chin, covered an undershirt, which in turn covered a bra that concealed how hard her nipples were from him.

"Seems like we both want the same thing from each other. I like that we're in agreement."

"You strip first," she said, licking her lips as she lifted her free hand to caress his cheek, then push aside the locks of his hair that fell forward to frame his face.

It was far softer than the dark hair of Rampion's artificial hardware. She wondered if there would ever be a time when she wouldn't compare the two. She knew there wouldn't be a time when she wouldn't believe that this version of his hardware wasn't superior. This version was more natural, whereas Rampion had aimed for perfection. Achieving perfection wasn't the point of life. She knew Rampion's mindset—and that of the nobles—was the mindset of those who weren't actually living it.

He pushed himself off the mattress, reluctantly leaving her with a low moan as she gave his length a final encouraging squeeze before releasing him. "If you insist, Princess."

"Queen, actually," she said with a small grin as she watched him stand straight.

"Ah, I see." He sketched a mocking bow, then lifted his hands to the clasps of his uniform jacket. "You want to give me royal orders. Normally, I don't give a damn what nobs say, but you're the one queen I might actually obey."

With that, he unclasped his jacket and pulled it off in quick, jerky movements, clearly eager to be free of the confinement of clothing, probably because he couldn't wait to free her as well.

She watched him reveal his chest in a clinging, sleeveless undershirt, almost missing the charcoal metal of his cybernetic arms, but deeply appreciative of the sculpted muscle on his new hardware's arms. He was very muscular, and it was clear his body had been created to work hard. It was not the body of a nobleman. It was the body of a mercenary warrior.

"You know, I don't want you to make it too easy, Gothel. I like a bit of a challenge."

His gaze heated as his eyes met hers. "You want a challenge, do you? I wouldn't expect anything less from you, woman."

Her smile widened. "Not going to call me 'Your Highness?'"

He stripped off his undershirt, his chest and arm muscles bunching and bulging in distracting ways that made her core tighten in anticipation. Her fingers itched to explore the broad expanse of gorgeous, naturally tanned skin he revealed.

Her gaze traced the path of sparse, gray hair down to the waistband of his trousers, which was pushed away from his stomach by the thickness of the erection beneath the fabric. He was so hard for her that it put a strain on his uniform.

"You really want that? Or you just teasing me?" His voice grew husky with his arousal. "Because I'll call you whatever you want, long as you keep looking at me like that, Princess."

She lifted her hand to crook a finger at him. "Come closer."

As soon as he was close enough to her that she could reach his pants, she undid the catch of the trousers, freeing the length of his erection. It strained towards her, and Zel closed her fingers around it, loving the way he moaned at her touch, his body tense, his tight abdominals twitching.

She pressed a kiss to the muscle jumping in his abdomen, then lowered her lips to the head of his erection. A small drop of precum wept from the hole in the tip, and she licked it, tasting the salty flavor of him. "I guess you can't add flavors to this body, can you?"

"You don't like my flavor, I'll find a way to give you a new one. God, Zel, if you keep doing that, I'll move the fucking stars to give you a whole damn buffet of flavors."

She sucked on the head of his shaft, loving the way he gripped a desperate hand in her hair. "You know," she said, lifting her head for just long enough to glance up at him with a wicked smile, "I actually really love your flavor."

Then she returned her mouth to him and sucked him deeper, drawing her lips down his length as his hand tightened in her hair, disrupting the carefully coifed braids it had been styled into by one of the crewmembers who had helped her dress for her part before the debriefing.

She sucked him until he tugged her away from him, trying to chase his swollen tip as he tilted his hips back. "I want to bury myself inside you, Zel. You make me remember why I started fighting for the humans."

She grinned as she looked up at him. "You started fighting for us so you could have some pussy?"

He grunted with a reluctant laugh and shook his head. "I started fighting for humanity because humans knew what it meant to be alive, and I wanted to start living too. You make me feel alive—truly alive—and not just a machine pretending to be human."

She pushed herself off the bed, running her hands along his naked upper body as she stood. "I love you, Gothel. Whatever you call yourself, and whatever body you're in. I will always love you."

He framed her face between his big hands. "I will always love you too, Rapunzel. Even when the last star dies, my heart will still be burning for you."

A slight sadness overtook her for a brief moment as she realized that Gothel was in essence immortal—if he wanted to be. As long as he could upload his neural fingerprint to another housing, he would persist, long after her body deteriorated and broke down into dust.

He ran his thumb along her lower lip. "Don't think about it, Rapunzel. If I have a soul, it will fly free when yours does. We will find a way to be together, in this life, and the next."

His kiss was sweet and longing. Slow and measured and filled with meaning that their hunger could not convey. This was a promise—a pledge that no matter what the future held, they would meet it together. Because Zel already knew he had a soul, and he had given it to her along with his heart.

Gothel made love to her slowly after that, taking his time as he undressed her, his fingers caressing her body as if it was a treasure he cherished. His lips drank from hers as if he were a man desperate for water. When he finally had her stripped bare, he fell to his knees before her and worshipped her with his mouth and tongue playing with her clit and weakening her knees until he had to support her.

When she was still shivering from her powerful orgasm, he laid her back on the bed and followed, positioning his hips between her legs. Then he sank his length inside her, and they moved together in a rhythm that had become as natural as their heartbeats.

In the aftermath of their shared climax, Gothel held her against him, her back to his chest as he stroked his fingers over her hair.

"What did you say to the ajda'yan," he asked after a long silence, where Zel chased sleep, but could not find that oblivion from the fears, thoughts, and grief that were now spilling back as the warmth of her sexual haze faded and reality crept back in.

"I told him that I had earned respect from an ajda'yan, in the ajda'yan language. He understood what that meant, and since my sister had not, he would not lift a hand against me in her favor. Draku Rin told me to say those words if I ever found myself in danger of being harmed by an ajda'yan hired mercenary. It wouldn't work if the offense was personal to the ajda'yan, but they won't kill a 'respected one' for money, unless they also respect their client."

Gothel inhaled deeply as he buried his nose in her hair, which had become loose from its coif. "Even with all I know about the universe, the ajda'yans never fail to surprise me."

"I miss him," she said, tears dampening her lashes. "I can't believe my sister sold him, like he was a piece of property!"

"We're getting him back, I'm assuming."

She loved that Gothel didn't even hesitate to make that assumption. He knew her so well. "Of course, but still, it infuriates me that she… I just can't believe what she'd become. And then I had to…."

He stroked his hand along her side in a soothing motion, hugging her closer to him with his other hand. "I'm sorry, Zel. You never should have had to face such terrible things."

She shook her head. "No, we are nobs. This is exactly the kind of thing we face. I knew there were assassins waiting to kill me from the time I was a child. I always knew that the sickness of power and the desperate desire to hold onto it had infected the people around me. In many ways, I was naïve, but not in this one." She sighed. "And then there's still my parents and what happened to them. It must have been so terrible for them to die like that."

"They loved you in their way." Gothel's gruff tone didn't take well to empathetic expression, but that did nothing to blunt the sympathy behind his words.

"Maybe." She wished she could say definitely that it was true. Knew that a normal human family should be able to know these things for fact, but there had been nothing normal about her and her family. "Or maybe they just played at being doting parents. They clearly hadn't loved Mirvala enough, and they put me through things no child should have to go through, in order to please them. In the end, whether they loved me or not never changed that I loved them, and I still feel grief at their deaths."

Gothel shifted until he was propped up on one elbow, looking down at her from above her. "You deserved better than this life."

"Life doesn't usually give us what we deserve, Gothel. I'm sure you know that already."

He laughed sharply. "Ain't that the truth. Guess you got to fight tooth and nail to earn what you want, and even then, it ain't all it's cracked up to be." He dropped a kiss on her brow. "'Cept for you, Princess. You are everything I could hope to earn and more. 'Course, I ain't a prince now, and the Eglin angle is over. Don't have another royal family I can slip into so easily."

Zel had already thought about this. She turned her head and slid her fingers along his jaw. "I'm the queen, and I'll marry whomever I damn well please. Besides, I have plans, and one of them involves taking a 'commoner' as a husband. I think you'll do quite well in that role."

His crooked grin and dancing blue eyes made her heartbeat thump with renewed arousal. "They don't get much more common than me."

She smiled, suspecting it showed how besotted she was with him. "You don't have to keep up the pretense with me. You're anything but common."

"Probably best if we don't talk about that, even when it's just the two of us. I run scans, but you never know when the walls are listening."

Her smile slipped into a more serious expression. "I wasn't talking about that. I was talking about you. There's nothing common about who you are. You've opened my eyes, Gothel. You've made me realize that I can be so much more than just a spoiled princess trying desperately to fit into a life that didn't belong to me, without leaving the safe confines of the life I'd been born into. Now, I know what I must do, because you've given me purpose."

He nuzzled her neck, his breath hot against her skin. "I'll stand by you, no matter what happens. I'll always be there for you, Rapunzel."

CHAPTER 34

They waited to announce their marriage, and Gothel took on the role of a hired bodyguard, though all the nobles knew that he was more than that, since he retired with her to her bedchamber every night, both before and after the coronation. They were only mildly scandalized, as affairs were common enough, and no one expected the princess to still be a virgin after the whole "Prince Eglin" situation.

Rapunzel made it through the coronation with nerves twisting her stomach, but her palms were dry and her heart was steady, because Gothel stood by her side. Maybe he was in a guard's uniform, instead of the most haute couture royal fashion, but they both knew it was only a matter of time before she made the controversial announcement. Right now, she had to be certain she secured her crown, lest the nobility attempt a coup against her. Once her position was secure, she would have more freedom to do as she wished and flaunt the conventions of her royal house.

Until then, she and Gothel were still putting their plans into place, and there were many details to work out. Once her crown was guaranteed and the tedious and tiresome parties and celebrations were out of the way, she met with the minister of Zwicky. There were still questions to be answered, and the murder of their lost and then found "prince" had to be addressed. That blood was on the hands of Mirvala, who had been the head of the royal household at the time. Zwicky was threatening war against Herschel if the queen didn't meet personally with the minister.

She welcomed him and his entourage onto her station and threw him another big party in celebration of his arrival, though they kept certain details muted because there was, of course, some grieving to be done for the imaginary prince.

It was the actual meeting to negotiate a pardon from Zwicky towards the royal family of Herschel that surprised Rapunzel the most. Minister Magnusson was an unassuming man of indeterminate years. His pale coloring, wheat blond hair, and bland, blue eyes gave nothing away about him. Nor did his equally bland expression.

She quickly learned not to dismiss him, as she discovered he had a very sharp mind behind those strangely blank eyes. In fact, he made several statements in a tone that suggested he was quite aware of the subterfuge she and "Prince Eglin" had planned, but had decided that an alliance with Herschel would be beneficial enough to allow the "prince" to step into a role that had long lost any teeth for the people of Zwicky. The minister had been granted all the ruling power in the absence of a surviving member of the royal family, and the constitution the minister and his parliament had created kept that power in the hands of the elected minister—even if royal blood should return.

"By some miracle" as he wryly pointed out during her interview with him.

Then his gaze flicked to Gothel, who stood in his usual place behind her throne, and he made the slightest nod—one that would have been missed if Rapunzel hadn't been watching him so intently. It was then that she understood exactly why Gothel had been so certain the "Prince Eglin angle," as he'd dubbed it, would be successful.

Zwicky needed this alliance, and she intended to grant it even without a marriage, despite the fact that the financial burden would be greater on Herschel in the agreements that they drafted during their meetings.

Yet, she suspected that wasn't why the minister had been so willing to not question the appearance of a new prince.

"He's like you, isn't he?" she asked Gothel as soon as they were safely alone in her chambers after the long meeting where she agreed to Zwicky's terms for an alliance, in apology for the murder of the "prince".

Even though the doors were locked and barred, and the room scanned for bugs, he still held a finger across her lips for a moment, before lowering his head to kiss her deeply. "Best if you forget that," he said in a near whisper against her lips.

"And if I don't?" she whispered back.

She felt his smile as his lips still brushed hers. "Then I'll be too busy watching yer back to share yer bed."

Despite his teasing tone, she shivered at the warning. "It's that bad then?"

"We are holding, but only because we have the advantage here. We need to keep it. You will do well as a queen, as long as you know when to look the other way." He stepped back and lifted her chin so she met his eyes. "No matter what happens though, I am always on *your* side. Trust me in that, Rapunzel. I will defend *you* if anyone should come with the intent to harm you."

She realized she hadn't even doubted him in that moment. She hadn't worried at all that he might still be loyal to the other AIs that had infiltrated into human society to protect humanity from the Old Earth Machine. Still, she would not betray his loyalty by needlessly putting him and herself in danger.

From what she knew of Zwicky, the ruling parliament treated their colonists well and gave them many freedoms that made them wealthier—and in most ways better off—than the people in the colony of Herschel. If the minister meant any harm to the humans under its leadership, there wasn't much a warning from Rapunzel could do to stop it. Yet, she didn't think that was the case at all. Just like she knew Gothel didn't intend to cause harm to humanity.

"Do you think we will ever be able to return to Old Earth," she asked, wondering if there was any way they could ever defeat the Master AI and recover their homeworld.

"If humanity could gain the assistance of the ajda'yans or the titans, we could retake Earth, but until that miraculous day happens, there will always be vigilant sentinels protecting the fifteen colonies, and all the lives within them."

She nodded her understanding, knowing that it was best if they dropped this subject and didn't speak much on it, if at all, in the future. For now, it was enough to know that humanity wasn't completely alone in its fight for survival.

But she wasn't about to give up on her desire to destroy the master AI for good. If it took uniting with the titans or the ajda'yans to do it, then she would spend the rest of her life working towards that goal.

"We still have one last thing to do before I announce our upcoming marriage," she said, switching topics, but not randomly. She loved that Gothel immediately understood what she meant.

"I was wondering when you were planning this trip."

CHAPTER 35

When they arrived on Galilei royal station, the duchess's premier greeted them with a chilly welcome that reflected exactly what the duchess thought of Rapunzel and her family name. Zel really couldn't blame the woman. There had always been tension between their two colonies, but since the duchess had taken over the task of ruling the colony until the queen reached her majority, there had been a concerted effort on her part to secure peace between her colony and the other fourteen, including Zel's colony.

They were led to the duchess, who sat upon an uncomfortable-looking chair beside a small girl playing on the dais with a dollhouse. Aurora was the real queen of Galilei, but she was also only eight and not prepared to rule. She appeared to suffer from a genetic disorder as well that was unusual for the nobility. Most of the other colonies would have eliminated her in the test tube if they had seen such an abnormality in her genetics.

The duchess was a stunning woman of sixty, though rejuvenation treatments made her look decades younger. Still, lines had formed around her lips and eyes, and distinct lines crossed her high brow, showing that she likely frowned more than she smiled. At the moment, her lips tightened into what would likely become a frown at some point in their conversation, as her chilly, amber gaze settled on Rapunzel and Gothel.

"My premier has informed me that you come here in regards to your former bodyguard. He says you won't be dissuaded in your quest to retrieve the creature."

"I'd like him back, yes," Zel said, though she tried to keep her tone respectful. She no longer felt so arrogant that something like her rank as queen of Herschel meant she had the right to treat others as beneath her.

As worried as she was, she couldn't just grab the duchess by the throat to shake Rin's location out of her. She didn't need to see them to know that automatic weapons turrets were trained on her at this very moment, hidden behind the austere, paneled walls of the sitting room. It had been a risk to travel here with only a small entourage, but the duchess would never have allowed Herschel's royal cavalcade to accompany her into Galilei space.

The duchess lifted her chin slightly, her eyes narrowing as if she could read Zel's desire to choke her. A slight smile tilted her lips—smug, assured, and very condescending. "What you would *like* is irrelevant in my space. I paid a significant amount of credits for the brute, and he will serve me until the task I require him for is complete. After that, we shall see."

Zel couldn't stop her disbelieving snort. "You think Draku Rin will serve anyone if he doesn't want to? I hope you haven't unfrozen him yet and told him you plan to make him a slave, because you're about to lose a lot of people in that endeavor."

Duchess Graciela's smile shifted to a dark scowl. "The thug has been fitted with a compulsion collar, as all convicts are when on work release. He does not have the opportunity to attack, though it wouldn't surprise me if such a murderous brute would do so."

"Never met a collar what could stop an ajda'yan," Gothel muttered just loud enough for Zel to hear.

She glanced over her shoulder at him and nodded slightly. "Something's up. No way that collar's stopping Draku from tearing his way out of here through the bodies of the guards."

"I understand that Draku must serve his um... penance," she glanced at the queen, who had looked up at them with curiosity when they entered, then had apparently grown bored with their adult conversation and had gone back to her play. "I would just like to see him once more. He was a friend of mine."

This time, it was the duchess who gave a disbelieving snort, but hers sounded much more proper and ladylike, to fit her ramrod posture and perfectly royal demeanor. Rin must hate it here. The duchess was known for her strict adherence to protocol, and she ran the royal household like an absolute tyrant when it came to being proper—and properly boring.

"Such a creature can hardly qualify as a 'friend' to any decent human being, least of all a royal princess. You are best to be on your way, now. I maintain a diplomatic relationship with you and your house, but I am sure you know that there is no love lost between us. Your presence on my station is an unscheduled annoyance."

Zel clenched her fists and ground her teeth, but when she spoke, she kept her voice calm and diplomatic. "Please, I would like to simply speak with him for a brief time. He served as my bodyguard for twenty years. That's a lot of history between us. We've come all this way. It would be nice to just say goodbye to him."

Not that she had any intention of doing so.

The duchess's lips tightened into a thin line, then she waved an imperious hand, and a silent servant in the corner lifted his wrist to his lips and whispered into the discrete communicator around it.

The awkward silence that fell after that left the duchess

glowering at them while they waited. Then another servant came and gestured for them to follow him. Zel nodded her head to the duchess while Gothel sketched a quick bow, and the duchess waved them away, turning her face as if she had no more reason to look at them. As they walked out of the room, the queen lifted her hand and waved, then said "bye" in a sweet, high-pitched voice.

They followed the servant down through several floors of the station, then deep into the bowels, where machines did most of the work.

Except for where a dozen men, naked from the waist up, shoveled organic waste into the ship's core reactor combustion vent.

On Zel's station, machines loaded the recycled material into the vent, but she didn't think the use of convict labor was due to a lack of machinery. She suspected this was how the duchess dealt with criminals, rather than putting them on ice.

There were mechanical guards, constantly scanning the prisoners, and Gothel informed her in a low voice that they were just simple programs. No sign of any AIs, based on his quick scans. The guards would be easy enough for her and Gothel to defeat to escape this place.

The thing was, they would have been easy enough for Rin to defeat too. She wanted to know why he hadn't already busted his way out of the boiler room, and was instead shoveling three times as much waste into the combustion vent as the other prisoners.

He didn't even pause when the servant motioned them to approach him. He just grunted a greeting to Zel, then glanced at Gothel, narrowed his eyes, and said, "I know you. You killed a buddy of mine."

Zel's mouth gaped open for a long moment before she thought to slam it shut, shooting a worried look in the direction of the servant. The unfortunate soul had backed slowly away from them, wisely staring at Rin with a terrified look that she figured was pretty much par for the course for any servant forced to deal with him.

"He tried to kill me first," Gothel said, not missing a beat, even though Zel still felt like she was struggling to catch up.

"I know. I was there." Her former bodyguard grinned his usual terrifying grin, filled with sharp teeth. "Eh," he finally paused in his work after tossing in a final load, then buried his shovel in the barrel of stinking waste so he could lean on the handle. "He stole a job from me once. Figure he had it coming."

"Rin?" Zel stared at him, then glanced at Gothel. Then looked back at him. "How do you… how did you recognize…?"

Draku Rin snorted little flames from his nostrils, then jerked his chin towards Gothel. "Their kind have a different energy, and it's unique to each one. Doesn't matter what body it takes. Don't often forget those that can take out one of my kind."

Zel was suddenly nervous, though she had always trusted Rin before. If he were to reveal Gothel's true nature, there was no way the duchess would allow Gothel to leave the station. He'd be destroyed right then and there.

Draku Rin seemed to read her fear in her eyes. "When have I ever let you down? Besides, I like them better than you humans. They're more predictable."

"You won't…."

Gothel's hand closed over hers, and that was the moment she realized she had set hers on his shoulder, having backed towards him, positioning herself between him and Draku Rin as if she could protect him. Perhaps, it wasn't her face Rin had read, but her body language.

His sharp-toothed grin only widened, though Zel had no idea how that was possible. "Looks like you found a new toy. Who am I to take it away from you?"

"He's not a toy. I love him and we're—"

"Don't think you need to waste any more breath convincing him, Princess," Gothel said, interrupting her as his arm wrapped around her waist. "Not that I don't like to hear you say it." He lowered his head so his mouth was right by her ear. "And I'll gladly be your toy whenever you want to play, Zel," he whispered so low that the sound was more like a breath against her ear.

"Come on!" Draku Rin growled, his nostrils flaring as smoke poured from them. "I guarded the little mite for twenty years. At least do me the favor of not doing that in front of me. The urge to kill you is automatic."

This sounded more like the Rin she knew. She glanced at the collar that had been attached around his neck, pushing down the ridge of spikes on his back that must have made it painful to wear. "We came here to set you free," she said, looking around quickly, and noting that none of the laborers stood anywhere near Draku Rin. They gave him plenty of space to have this conversation. She couldn't blame them for moving farther away from him, even if it meant crowding into the other convicts by the far side of the vent.

No one in their right mind wanted to get in the way of an ajda'yan. Even one wearing a convict collar.

Rin's expression grew amused again, his glare leaving Gothel to return his attention to Zel. "I don't need rescuing, but thanks, mite. Glad you didn't forget me."

Zel's eyebrows lifted as her gaze touched on the collar again. "You're a prisoner here, Rin."

He shrugged. "Place isn't so bad. The temperature is still a little too cool, but I've learned to adapt."

It was scorching hot in the boiler room, and every other human in there was sweating, as was Zel. The only ones who weren't were Gothel and Draku Rin.

"How can you want to remain here?"

"Seen the duchess yet?" Rin asked in a bizarre shift of subject.

Zel nodded. "She's a real bitch, that one. Seriously uptight too. I think her corset would qualify as a torture device on nine colonies—and a pleasure device on the other six."

The ajda'yan's grin sharpened. "Never could resist a challenge."

Zel's eyes widened in alarm. "Rin, what are you planning? Don't you dare harm the duchess! Even *you* might have a problem escaping this station after that one."

"I won't hurt her." Smoke curled from his nostrils. "Not unless she asks me nicely."

~

Gothel's chuckling didn't help Zel one damned bit as they left the station—sans the one person they had come all this way to liberate. Turned out, he didn't want to be liberated, and no one was moving an ajda'yan who didn't want to be moved.

"I wonder how long it will take him to get her out of that corset torture device?" Gothel pondered aloud.

"Gross, gross, gross!" Zel said, holding her hands over her ears. "Don't even talk about stuff like that!"

Gothel's arms came around her now that they were safely back in their cabin on the *Marauder,* which she'd had updated and recommissioned, though she'd kept the piratical name.

He pulled her in close to him. "Why, Princess, you sound so shocked. It isn't like you're a virgin." He lowered his head to claim her lips in a long, delicious kiss. "At least, not anymore."

His smile was sexy as hell. She would never stop loving that crooked look it always had, even when it had been on the perfect face sculpted by Rampion. "So, about being your toy...."

She shivered at the promise in his tone, her mind switching

from the arousal-killing subject of her former bodyguard lusting after the stuffy duchess, to her own lust for what was technically only a machine.

Who was she to judge?

Of course, Gothel was far more than any machine. She need only look into his eyes to see the intelligence behind them—but more importantly, the soul.

"I love you, Gothel."

"I love you too, Rapunzel."

She waited, because this was her Gothel, and that declaration lacked his usual flair.

"Even if you are a spoiled, little nob."

Zel chuckled and pulled his head down for another long kiss. When she broke free to capture her breath, she said, "yes, I'm spoiled. I get whatever I want. And right now, I want my 'toy' to pleasure me."

It was his turn to chuckle, though heat warmed his pale blue eyes as they met hers. Then his gaze trailed lower until it snagged on her breasts, plumped up as they pushed against his chest.

"I want you to take me from behind, Gothel. I saw a video stream of people doing it that way, and it looked very exciting."

He closed his eyes and groaned. "To have the queen of Herschel on her hands and knees, at my mercy? I was wondering if you'd ever ask."

Zel grinned and pulled out of his embrace, turning her back on him as she slowly peeled away her formal spacesuit. The shiny material gave way to her pale skin, and Gothel's lips followed the fabric as she pulled it down off her body. His breath tickled her back, but his warm, damp tongue sweeping along her spine caused her to shiver and her nipples to harden.

When the suit bagged at her waist, he stepped up behind her and slid one hand down over her front, kissing and licking the skin at the nape of her neck. His other hand lifted to cup her naked breast and tease her nipple as she moaned.

His fingers found her clit beneath the fabric of the jumpsuit, and he stroked them over her sensitive nub until she was gasping and thrusting her hips forward into his touch. When his lips closed over the skin at the base of her neck and sucked, she cried out in pleasure as his fingers sped up their movements, bringing her orgasm crashing down on her.

She was still convulsing internally from the power of it as he jerked her jumpsuit the rest of the way down her legs.

"This way is more primal, you know. You want me to be a little rougher?"

Zel didn't think she could be any more turned on than she was, until he asked that question, which made her so slick she doubted he would have any trouble slipping in from behind, despite the change in position.

"I want you to be as rough as you'd like."

His low chuckle caused her belly to tighten in excitement. "What I'd like, what I'll always like, is doing what pleases you."

She glanced over her shoulder at him, captured by his blue gaze watching her intently. "Then yes, I want it rough. I want it to feel primal. Like we're back on Old Earth, living in a cave. Take me like that!"

His grin made his rugged face stunning and perfectly Gothel. "Then get on yer knees and bare that beautiful backside to me."

Zel obeyed, thrilled by the sound of command in his tone. She felt vulnerable with her back to him, and small as she crawled onto the bed on her hands and knees. But she also felt very excited when the mattress sagged as he kneeled on it. One of his hands settled on the middle of her back.

Being a queen ruling an entire planet and constantly having to navigate the political pitfalls of intergalactic alliances and enmities was exhausting work. In fact, after her coronation, she'd had to spend weeks negotiating an alternative alliance with Leavitt after she quite firmly turned down the duke's insistence that she honor the marriage her parents had arranged. Now, she just wanted to be Rapunzel, a woman in love with her man. She wanted him to be in control, so she could just let go and enjoy the experience.

Within moments of Gothel climbing onto the bed, the tip of his erection prodded her slick entrance. In all the times they had been together in the past months, she had never asked for this, hesitant to suggest it. He had also never requested this position, though she suspected it was because he wanted to let her set the pace with their sexual relationship and experimentation.

It was so strange to be faced away from him, not being able to see when he was nearing penetration. Not being able to watch the expressions on his face. She felt oddly disconnected.

Then he was pushing his thick, long length inside her. Her body lit up with the fire of her arousal and excitement. As he buried his cock inside her, filling her completely, the connection snapped into place. She didn't need to see him to feel it, because they were linked more intimately than she had ever been linked to anyone.

His hand shifted from her back to grip her shoulder. His other hand reached around to rub her clit, which was easily accessible to his fingers in this position.

As he pumped inside her, starting off slowly, but then moving much faster and pushing harder as she tried to push back against him, he continued to finger her clit, bringing her to another climax. Then another. Each time her inner muscles milked his shaft, he moaned and thrust harder into her.

Zel knew logically that he wasn't letting go and being as rough and unleashed as a human man might have been. That would have been extremely dangerous for her if he did so, since his body was so much more powerful than a human one. Still, the wildness of their mating felt like he was on the edge, barely clinging to his control. That made it incredibly sexy, especially when his satisfied grunts and growls of pleasure sounded so convincing.

He leaned over her back until his lips were at her ear and his body covered hers. He spoke in a low, ragged whisper, broken by grunts with each hard thrust into her. "You like it this way, Zel? Cuz it feels like you do." He slowed his thrust, withdrawing in an agonizing retreat that made her muscles clench to pull him back inside her. This earned a moan from him, and he thrust hard inside her, though he always stopped before he struck her womb.

"I like it *all* ways! As long as it's with you."

He paused for a long moment, still buried deep inside her warmth, her muscles clenching on him as if she could urge him to start moving again.

Then he shifted his hand from her shoulder to capture her hair, pulling it aside so he could kiss her neck. When she turned her head, he captured her lips.

His weight bore them both down to the mattress, so he was lying on top of her, instead of kneeling behind her. Somehow, this felt even more intimate as his body covered hers, his warm body in complete contact with her naked skin.

This time, he pumped in a more leisurely pace, focusing instead on their breathless kiss. The combined feelings of his tongue and his cock penetrating her made her climax again, as each thrust inside her not only rubbed over her g-spot but also caused her clit to slide along the silken fabric of the comforter.

It was only after she'd clenched around him that he finally allowed himself to climax. As his ejaculate filled her, she pulled away from his kiss long enough to speak.

"Did you?"

"I did."

Warmth bloomed in her chest that had nothing to do with

their combined passion. "So, how long do you think it will take to get me pregnant?"

"That's not something I can predict at this point, but yer still fertile, so we'll see."

A joyous smile spread her lips as her husband slowly withdrew from her, trailing his seed.

CHAPTER 36

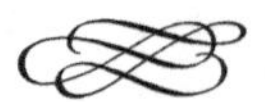

Less than a week later, she announced that she was taking a commoner as a husband, as part of her unveiling of her plans to instate a council made up of representatives from the colony below the station.

Her speech was met with outrage by the assembled nobles, and shocked stares from the servants. On the monitors that showed the colonists that had gathered to hear her speech on the planet's surface, the crowds gaped with dirty, worn, work-weary faces at the holograms of her that were projected to them in each city square.

At first, she thought they would reject the idea, because they didn't seem pleased, and it was their reaction that concerned her, rather than the outraged arguments building in the throne room as her noble advisors truly soaked in the news.

But then, it seemed that the crowds of colonists finally processed her words, perhaps so accustomed to hearing empty words from their leaders that they didn't really even listen anymore. Yet someone had listened, because now, excited murmuring filled the crowds of each square in all thirty-two cities in the colony.

Expressions changed, from hard and bored to hopeful, though wariness remained in eyes framed by wrinkles—the older ones no doubt having heard the royal family give false promises in the past.

Understanding moved through the crowd like a breeze through a field of grain. Zel watched it in awe as faces brightened, and smiles formed. Then the muttering grew louder and louder as people turned from the hologram to look at each other—verifying that what they thought they heard was true.

Then a cheer went up, and another, and another. The crowds joined in until the cheers were deafening.

Yet it was all music to Zel's ears. Music that drowned out the loud protests of the nobles in her own throne room. Her guards removed the ones who grew too disrespectful, but she let the others vent, ignoring their heated words. She would deal with them later. For now, she watched her people—her colonists—celebrate the promise of a new life. They would finally have representation when it came to governing the colony.

And a "common" man was about to become king.

She glanced at Gothel, who now stood by her side, uncomfortable in a simple suit that was still made of the finest materials. He wasn't pleased at the reactions of the nobles and sent many a glare their way that cowed some of the smarter ones. She noticed that he took note of those who weren't so easily cowed, and suspected that she would have to approach them privately to calm them down—before Gothel did something more permanent to remove any possible threat to her rule.

He would make a good king, though the title wouldn't give him the same teeth as her role as queen would. She would still be the true leader of Herschel. At least in name, but she was working on that as well. She would now have advisors—not just from the noble houses, but also from the bounders below who worked so hard to provide all the resources those nobles took for granted. Soon, she would make Herschel the best colony in the galaxy. The one where the people were the happiest, the most content, and the most at peace.

She linked her fingers with Gothel's, sending him a happy smile that only widened when the cheering from the crowds on the planet below grew louder as people began to hug and dance. Change was coming. It would be frightening for people, and Zel expected there would be a time of civil unrest, both on the planet below and among the nobles as they jockeyed for position in new alliances. She suspected there would be more assassination attempts on her life, but also knew that Gothel was always watching her back, so she felt safe.

Her announcements would cause great upheaval, but in the end, change was necessary to weed out the sickness that had led to a daughter plotting the murder of her parents and sister.

EPILOGUE

Klaxons blared throughout the station, staining the white and gray walls with scarlet red as people rushed in a chaotic panic past them. Guards kept order as much as they could, helping everyone make their way to the docking bay, while trying to carry all their worldly possessions with them. Those who couldn't make it that far were settled into escape pods. They would be picked up by the ships, once they'd ejected from the station.

"Is everyone evacuated?" Zel asked breathlessly, her heart pounding as she raced through the sterile corridors of the station, listening for any screams or shouts for help.

"The last residents are loading up now, Your Highness," the captain of her guard said as he rushed behind her. Two more of his guards raced in front of her, ensuring the passageways were clear for her.

They had tried to insist she be the first on the ships, but Zel had refused to leave the station until all the other people were off of it—even though their time rapidly ticked away.

"And my husband?"

"King Johnathan is running a final scan from the security

station. He still hasn't been able to reverse our course. He says there's nothing he can do."

Zel nodded, already knowing this would be the answer. "Tell him to get to the *Marauder*. I'll meet him there."

She could have told him herself through the discreet communicator tucked inside her expensive, jeweled necklace, but the captain was panicking and clearly needed something to do besides follow in her footsteps.

He conveyed the message, and Gothel calmly answered back, even though the station's orbit was rapidly decaying, and they'd spent the last several hours desperately evacuating the thousands of citizens to the colony below.

A few hours later, Gothel swept onto the bridge of the *Rebellious Marauder* with his guards in tow. He cast them a glare of annoyance that had them bowing and backing away to retreat off the bridge and leave him alone with Rapunzel.

He joined her at the console that showed the station breaking apart as it re-entered the atmosphere. He settled his hand on her bulging stomach. "Guess it's too late to ask if you're sure about this."

She put her hand on his, holding his warmth against her stomach, feeling her baby shift inside her. "Definitely too late."

"I won't question if you know what you're doing, but it's more dangerous on the planet. Any citizen revolt—"

She turned in his arms and embraced him, no longer able to bear watching her childhood home disintegrate, destroying all that remained of the luxurious prison where she had pretended to be alive.

"I'll take that chance over living apart from the people I rule. They will see my face and know that their problems are mine. When clean water is short, they will know that I too, feel that thirst. When the rains are long, they will know that I am also drenched. When the ground is hard and cracked, they will know that I also miss the waving of the grain. I will suffer and rejoice with my people—and so will all my children. It is long past time for those who rule to understand the consequences of the decisions we make, and to experience them as our subjects do."

She had scuttled the home of the nobles to bring them down to the world of the commoners, so that her children—and her children's children—would learn what it meant to be alive.

Twenty-two years later....

Princess Mirvala felt beyond nervous, but no one would ever guess it from her façade of complete and absolute calm. She wouldn't let anyone see her sweat. Her mother had taught her how to maintain her decorum. Her mother had also taught her how to let loose and just have a great time being alive.

But those days of joyful childhood were past her now, and she had a duty to fulfill. One her mother hadn't asked of her, but that she had volunteered for. She was twenty-two and more than ready to fulfill her role as a princess, though Queen Rapunzel insisted, even to this day, that she could choose to marry for love.

Mirvala wanted to do something more for her people. She wanted to bring peace to the galaxy, and more than that, she wanted to bring the humans back home to Earth. After tirelessly working towards uniting the fifteen colonies, Queen Rapunzel was still struggling to forge an alliance with either the titans or the ajda'yans to fulfill a prediction Mirvala's father, King John, had once made. With the might of either the titans or ajda'yans added to their side, humans could fight the Old Earth Machine—and have a chance of winning.

The problem was that neither extraterrestrial species had any interest in allying themselves with humans. At least, that had been the case until recently, when the overlord of the ajda'yans sent a messenger to all the human rulers, claiming that he would consider an alliance with humanity, if they sent him a bride to cement that alliance.

The fact that he was nearly three meters tall—a veritable giant of a male—and a brutal, ruthless warrior at that, gave most humans pause. He also had so much blood on his hands that he could drown an entire colony with it. He was considered a monster by human standards in his physical appearance too, but then again, Mirvala's family was rather fond of ajda'yans, and she had grown up around Draku Rin, whenever he could be parted from his duchess to pay a visit to an old friend.

The leaders of the other fourteen colonies had demurred, not willing to sacrifice any of their daughters to the overlord, but when Mirvala had overheard her mother and father discussing it, she knew that she would be the one to volunteer.

She said her farewells to her family, forced by rules set by the overlord to travel alone to the brutal and unforgiving home-world of the ajda'yans, where she would spend the rest of her life beneath the scaled thumb of her future husband. It wouldn't be a good life, but at least she knew that her sacrifice would aid humanity in returning home.

AUTHORS NOTE

When I sat down to retell the story of Rapunzel, only with a science-fiction twist, I never intended to subvert the original fairy tale as much as I ended up doing. I had an initial plan for a handsome alien prince, and my poor, trapped Rapunzel in her tower. Then, I got to thinking that I wanted to do something really different, while sticking to the basic plotline and essential details of the original fairytale. I decided to switch Rapunzel and the prince, making him the one in the tower.

But why would he remain trapped, I wondered. The AI character of Rampion immediately came to mind. An artificial intelligence (capitalized in the story because of its impact on humanity) seemed like the perfect occupant of this particular science-fiction version of a tower. I have also been really wanting to work on a story with an AI hero (and as you can see, I did, though it may not have seemed that way until near the end.)

I've been growing more interested and fascinated (and somewhat concerned) by the advancement of computers and robotics in our real world, and have been following the news on what wonders we are creating. Of course, as a lover of science-fiction, I'm well aware of the potential downsides of creating an artificial intelligence. I've been exploring that a bit with my *Into the Dead Fall* series, with NEX, (and my upcoming book, Veraza's Choice, will explore it even more), but I really wanted to make it the focus of a book.

As for Gothel, I figured I'd make him male, since I made the tower occupant male, but I fully intended for "Commander" ("Dame" is in the word, see what I did there? 😉) Gothel to be the villain, as per the original story. Then I wrote the prologue, and realized that I just loved this grizzled old mercenary too much, right off the bat, to relegate him to the sad role of Gothel from the fairy tale.

And this is what happens when your characters take on a life of their own. :D

This is a departure from my most popular books, and I'm honestly not sure how well it will do. As you may have noticed, I have ideas for future books set in this universe, and have already outlined Draku Rin's story. (I love Rin too, and the entire ajda'yan species!) I also have some ideas for the other AI sentinels (and even some of the infiltrators still serving the Master AI).

On the other hand, if the first book doesn't get much interest, I probably won't develop those ideas further. I know this can sound a bit mercenary and not focused on the simple joy of producing the art, but it's actually that simple joy that makes the difference in whether I pursue a series or not. The excitement and enthusiasm for the next installment of a story motivates and inspires me. I say this to a lot to the wonderful fans who have reached out to me, and that's because it is really true. When a book receives a lot of buzz and gets a lot of positive reviews, I know my readers want more, and I'm excited about writing the next book.

If it fizzles, gets buried in the overwhelming lists on Amazon, or receives a more negative than positive reception, I really struggle to create the next installment in the series, and much of my enthusiasm for it fades. I have so many ideas and projects that I can work on that I take my cue from what my readers love, in order to decide which projects should get my attention.

That being said, the best way to show that you want more is to spread the word, via social media, blogs, reviews, or recommending this book to someone else who loves this genre. Amazon is flooded with titles, and it's easy to end up buried by them all, so I rely on my incredibly supportive readers and fans to let others know about my books. I couldn't do it without you all, and you mean so much to me! Thank you, for everything you do to make my dream a reality!

And don't worry, I am not about to abandon my *Iriduan Test Subjects* or *Into the Dead Fall* series to start a new one. The next book for *Into the Dead Fall* should be coming out this year, hopefully for November, and the sixth book in my *Iriduan Test Subject* series is my current work in progress. I have plans to expand on my *Shadows in Sanctuary* universe as well, with two more books, and Ava's story is also planned for next year. I switch around between each series as a way to keep my mind and ideas fresh, but I work as hard as possible to bring them to you in a timely way.

This book was a collaboration with seven other really talented authors, who also happened to be some of my all-time favorites in this genre. Be sure to check out their installments as well. The links are included below.

Cosmic Fairy Tales is a collaboration in which several authors are retelling beloved tales with a science fiction romance twist. Each book is a standalone, containing its own Happily Ever After, and they can be read in any order. Be sure to explore the other titles in the collection:

- The Frog Prince by Tracy Lauren

- The Hunchback by Regine Abel
- The Lion and the Mouse by Emmy Chandler
- Escaping Wonderland by Tiffany Roberts
- The Ugly Dukeling by Bex McLynn
- Contaminated by Amanda Milo
- Jackie and the Giant by Honey Phillips

I love to hear from my readers! I try to spend a little time on Facebook each week, but I'm not as active on social media as I probably should be. However, I do update my Facebook page, The Princess's Dragon, whenever I have information about a new release, and I check it frequently to read comments and respond to questions. Also please check out my blog: https://susantrombleyblog.wordpress.com/ where I also post announcements and other fun stuff when I'm taking a break from my writing. You can also send me an email at www.susantrombley06@gmail.com.

I also like to add exclusive content to my newsletters as a thank you to those who sign up. That content could be anything from sneak peeks, to excerpts from unpublished work, to character art, character interviews, or whatever else I think my readers would like to see. If you're interested in receiving these newsletters (I only send them when I have announcements), sign up for my newsletter at: http://eepurl.com/gudYOT

Iriduan Test Subjects series

The Scorpion's Mate
The Kraken's Mate
The Serpent's Mate
The Warrior's Mate
The Hunter's Mate

Into the Dead Fall series

Into the Dead Fall

Key to the Dead Fall
Minotaur's Curse
Chimera's Gift

Shadows in Sanctuary series

Lilith's Fall
Balfor's Salvation
Jessabelle's Beast

Fantasy series—Breath of the Divine

The Princess Dragon
The Child of the Dragon Gods
Light of the Dragon